Dack 4

THE WHEATLEY SCHC

P9-CBE-520

XAN01002434   FIC VAL
              Unraveled

THE WHEATLEY SCHOOL
INFORMATION MEDIA CENTER
11 BACON RD.
OLD WESTBURY, N.Y. 11568

The Official shrugged. "It's up to you," he said. "If you want to keep running, I'll keep chasing, but you won't ever be out of my sights. Don't think there are things I will do and things I won't do. Your parents can't help you. By involving yourselves in all of this, you've already put your brothers and sisters in danger. Surely, you don't want to put them at any greater risk."

. . . I felt the electricity intensify as all of us considered the risk we'd exposed our families to—I was thinking of Iris and Pen, how both my parents had sacrificed so much to keep us safe, and how I'd thrown it all away.

"Though frankly," the Official went on, speaking almost to himself now, "the closer you get to Amanda, the closer I get to Amanda, so I'd almost just as soon have you on the run as have you in my control."

. . . I felt the fear too, creeping into my body like some sort of fast-moving frost. I was trying not to panic, not to beg. But I didn't know how long I could hold out.

the AMANDA project

Unraveled

BOOK FOUR
BY AMANDA VALENTINO
AND CATHLEEN DAVITT BELL

DISCARDED

HARPER TEEN

An Imprint of HarperCollinsPublishers

FOURTH STORY MEDIA
NEW YORK

HarperTeen is an imprint of HarperCollins Publishers.
Unraveled
Text copyright © 2012 by Fourth Story Media
Illustrations copyright © 2012 by Fourth Story Media

Fourth Story Media, 115 South Street, 4F, New York, NY 10038

All rights reserved. Printed in the United States of America.
No part of this book may be used or reproduced in any manner whatsoever without
written permission except in the case of brief quotations embodied in critical
articles and reviews. For information address HarperCollins Children's Books, a
division of HarperCollins Publishers, 10 East 53rd Street, New York, NY 10022.

www.epicreads.com

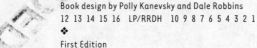

Library of Congress Cataloging-in-Publication Data is available.
ISBN 978-0-06-174219-4

Book design by Polly Kanevsky and Dale Robbins
12 13 14 15 16   LP/RRDH   10 9 8 7 6 5 4 3 2 1
❖
First Edition

For Max and Eliza,
my very own guides

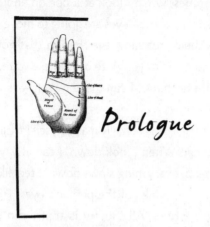

Prologue

Zoe here. The secret guide. The one who's been shadowing everyone else. Keeping information to myself, watching from a distance, hiding clues. Not fun, I know—I didn't like it, either. But I didn't have a choice, as crazy as that sounds.

The craziest part, though?

I've started to be able to do this thing. I can barely say it out loud—because first of all, I'm not sure it's true. And second, no one would ever believe me.

I wouldn't believe me.

Except it's just what happens.

I've always been good at reading people—listening to them, knowing what they are thinking even when they don't say it out loud. I think because of this, I've always been good at hiding, too. Hiding in plain sight—when Amanda and I were little that was a game for us.

But now, sometimes, when I look at a person and really focus, I can tell exactly how their eyes are going to move. I can sense the music of their breathing, the rhythm that governs when they blink, when their eyes glaze over into a stare. And because I can see these things, I can make myself—as far as that person can tell—invisible.

Don't get me wrong. I can't actually make myself invisible— I don't really disappear. When I look down, I can always see myself. But in my head, everything slows down. I feel like my breath lines up with the blinks of the person's eyes. I'm not actually sure how it works. All I know is that I can make it nearly impossible for that person to see me in that moment.

It's easy to hide when you know where someone isn't going to look. And since Amanda left Orion, I've been hiding all the time.

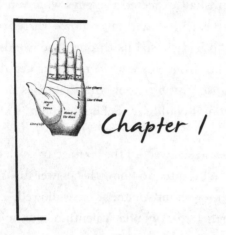

Chapter 1

For a minute, I thought Nia was going to pass out.

We were sitting on a bench outside school. I'd dragged her there when she'd started to slump over in the lobby of the auditorium just after the school talent show. She was leaning forward, her dark hair flopped over and exposing the back of her long neck. I wasn't sure if she needed air, or if I should be calling an ambulance. I was trying not to panic. In the chaos at the end of the show, we'd lost track of Callie and Hal, the only other people who had a chance of understanding what was going on.

"Keep your head between your knees," I told Nia, m̶ ̶wn head swimming with bad ideas. Should I get a ̶ ̶My mom? My instinct was to hide.

̶ath," Nia whispered again, looking up, her dark ̶ouded with fear. "I can't stop seeing it."

I glanced over my shoulder to make sure no one else could hear. I half expected the guys who were after Amanda to be bearing down on us now—there were a few of them who had chased us through the woods earlier in the day. But from where we were sitting I could see the main entrance to the school, and there was no one. Or at least no one I could see. School at night is always a little eerie.

I bit my lip and screwed up the courage to ask a question I wasn't sure I wanted to know the answer to. "You're *definitely* not talking about Amanda?" I swallowed.

I was referring to Amanda Valentino, our missing friend. About a month ago, she'd disappeared, and we'd been looking for her, following a series of cryptic clues she kept leaving in our path. Now we didn't know if she was still in Orion, or hiding out somewhere else. We'd met the man we believed to be her father—but only after he'd been captured by the people who were after Amanda.

While Nia, Callie, and Hal had been working as a trio, I'd been looking for Amanda on my own—though Amanda hadn't wanted it that way. When she'd left me clues that clearly indicated we four were supposed to band together as her guides, I'd revealed myself . . . hard to believe it had only been this afternoon. It felt like forever.

Nia rubbed her eyes and sat up. She was dressed in a white boatneck shirt, black skinny jeans, and black-and-white-striped ballerina flats, an appropriate color scheme

4

considering Nia tends to see the world in black and white. You're her friend or you're not. You speak the truth every time you open your mouth—or you're a liar. If she had bad news for you, she wouldn't sugarcoat it.

"I told you," Nia said. "I can only see into the past. The death wasn't Amanda's."

"Here." I lifted a vintage pink purse off Nia's lap and she sighed in relief, as if it were a heavy suitcase I was offering to help her carry.

Nia, Hal, and Callie had first seen the purse a little over a week before, in the hands of a woman named Waverly Valentino, who claimed to be Amanda's aunt. Then, half an hour ago, we'd seen it again. This time, with a woman with dark skin, dozens of little braids, and blue eyes. She let us buy the purse from her for less than she'd paid, and then disappeared into the night. Nia had opened the purse to find it lined with a scrap of old baby blanket that had been embroidered with the name Ariel—which we'd come to learn was the name Amanda was born with. Touching the bit of blanket—that's what had set off Nia's vision.

Since we started looking for Amanda, the four of us have been able to do things that should be impossible. Hal knows things he shouldn't, all psychic-style. He gets premonitions and hunches that are always—as in, 100 percent—right. Callie has gotten really strong—she can tear a door off its hinges. And Nia can often touch an object and feel something or know something about its history. She knows who used it or touched it last and what it witnessed. I haven't even told the others about what I can do—how do you explain making yourself virtually invisible? Weirder still, the first time the four of us gathered, we'd noticed that when we were all touching, we felt an electric charge run through us.

Now, as I was opening the purse to take another look at the blanket, Callie and Hal ran out to join us. When Callie was one of the über-popular I-Girls, I'd seen a lot of her. I blend into lots of groups, so we ended up at the same parties and club meetings. Sometimes we ended up at different ends of the same table at lunch. I could always tell she didn't think she was as pretty as Kelli, Traci, and Heidi—the other I-Girls. She didn't seem to realize that there was something about her beauty that goes beyond theirs. Her smile could make the difference between an overcast sky and a sunshiny day.

Hal, who was jogging along at Callie's side, is also a sunshiny kind of guy—he's had a thing for Callie for years and it's pretty obvious it's mutual. He was gazing at her, kind of dumbstruck, until Nia stood up and positioned herself between them.

"Wasn't Hal amazing?" Callie said, her freckled skin glowing. His band's performance in the talent show had been awesome.

"Aren't you glad Heidi and her I-Girl lip-sync routine didn't win?" Nia added.

None of us are really fans of the I-Girls. Granted, we all have our biases, and it's hard to see things objectively some times. My friend Kenzi, who is popular but isn't part of the I-Girl clique, tells me that a lot of them can be sweet. I'll believe it when I see it.

"I'm so glad Bea won—she totally deserved it," Hal said diplomatically. Bea Rossiter had survived a hit-and-run car accident earlier in the year. Only the four of us knew that the Queen Bee I-Girl, Heidi Bragg, had been behind the wheel, gunning for Bea because she'd mistaken her for Amanda. We'd all known Heidi was evil, but we hadn't realized how far she'd go. We still didn't know why she'd done it. Now Bea was back from surgeries and rehabilitation, looking better than ever and surprising everyone with her beautiful singing voice.

"Yeah, Bea was great," I agreed. I gave Hal a little wake-up punch on the shoulder. "But hey, something came up."

"Right . . . ," said Hal. Callie shook her long hair out behind her. Nia straightened her glasses.

"The purse that woman sold us," I went on. "It's lined with part of Amanda's baby blanket. Nia got a sudden wave, touching it."

"I felt death," Nia said, then quickly added, "but not Amanda's."

Hal picked up the purse and passed it back and forth between his hands like it was a basketball. He opened it and peered inside, poking at the lining.

"Look," he said, pulling out a postcard. "This was

7

tucked inside the lining."

"What's on it?" Callie said, taking it out of his hands. "It's some kind of monument." She flipped it over and read the caption. "The World War Two Memorial. In Washington, D.C."

"Okay," said Nia. "That's kind of random."

"Do you think it's a clue?" Callie asked.

"Maybe we're supposed to go on the History Club trip to Washington," I said. The man we believed to be Amanda's father? He was actually the vice principal of our school. Mr. Thornhill. When we'd discovered him in an abandoned airplane hangar after he'd been abducted, he'd told us to go to Washington to look for Amanda's sister, Robin.

"That reminds me," Nia said now. "I pulled a few strings with the president of the History Club, and guess who are all now members in good standing, and eligible for participation in the field trip to Washington that leaves Monday?"

Callie laughed, and Hal smiled too. Nia does not mess around.

I took the postcard and held it up to the streetlight. I'm really into photography and I was hoping that with all the time I'd spent looking at photos for newspaper and yearbook I'd see something the others had missed. And I did. I think.

"Look at that," I said, passing the card to Hal, and pointing to where a little mark had been pressed into the cardstock. The mark could have been made by a fingernail.

"You think this dent is supposed to tell us something?" Hal asked.

Callie took the card. "This could have been made by accident," she said.

"I don't know," Nia sniffed. "Nothing with Amanda ever seems to be an accident."

Hal was staring at the front of the purse now—it was adorned with a leather sunflower. "Wait a second . . . this is brilliant. Do you see?"

"Um, no?" I said.

"Callie?" he prompted, like she should be the one more likely to. Callie has a genius math brain inherited from her astronomer mother—who is also missing, by the way. Callie doesn't know where she is, only that her mom felt she had to leave in an effort to protect Callie. "Don't think of it as a flower," Hal said. "Don't think of the petals. Think of something else."

"Of what?" she said, squinting, focusing. And then suddenly, she got it. "It's a clock!"

"Exactly," Hal said. And then I got it too. Because surrounding the yellow petals of the flower were green leaves—twelve of them to be exact, spaced evenly around the flower like the numbers on a clock. Except when you looked closely, there weren't twelve. The leaf in the nine o'clock position was missing.

I got this weird chill down my spine that I always get when Amanda's clues start to make sense. It's like,

9

suddenly, she's with you. She's here. She's speaking to you again, but in a language only you can understand.

"And do you see how she's done the minutes?" Nia was saying. Most of the petals on the sunflower were yellow, but a lot of them—forty? fifty?—were tinged with brown. Except one of the tinted petals wasn't brown. It was a shocking, stand-alone pink. And now I didn't have to count the brown petals. I knew there would be sixty of them, as in sixty minutes to an hour. The pink petal was at the thirty-minute mark.

"Nine thirty," I said. "Which might mean—"

"We're supposed to meet Amanda at the World War Two Memorial at nine thirty on the day of that field trip to Washington," Nia finished.

Hal and Callie nodded.

"Are we assuming the chick with the cornrows stole the purse from Amanda's so-called aunt?" I wondered aloud.

"There's still so much we don't know," Nia said. "For instance . . . what are we supposed to be doing in the fifty or so hours between now and nine thirty on Monday?"

No one had an answer for her. We looked out at the deserted school parking lot. I had a feeling Amanda would let us know.

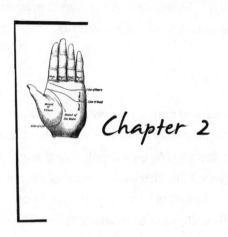

Chapter 2

I remember the day I first saw Amanda at Endeavor High. It was in the cafeteria, on Halloween. There were stuffed paper bags painted orange that were supposed to look like pumpkins hanging from the ceiling on fishing line.

I was sitting at the band table, thinking about those pumpkins, sort of listening to Dwayne Wright from band go on and on about his girlfriend from camp.

I've always been good at reading people. When someone's talking, most people only hear their words, but I hear more. I hear throat clearing, I register hesitation, I note stutters. I take in the way they shift their feet, grab their own arms, look away. Which is how I knew that Dwayne's girlfriend was not for real. I couldn't blame him for making one up. I would have, too, if I were constantly bullied for being the shortest kid in the class.

I took a bite from my bologna sandwich—I hate bologna but my mom buys it because it's cheap—and I happened to look toward the lunch line and saw something that made me freeze.

I saw her.

My friend.

My best friend, and maybe my only real friend ever.

Ever since Arabella Bruyere had moved without so much as calling me to say good-bye—I'd only found out she was gone when I saw the FOR RENT sign in front of her house—I hadn't had anyone I could call a real friend. Sure, I was a member of about fifteen different clubs and activities. There were a ton of people I said hi to, in the halls at Endeavor and out and about in Orion. But Arabella had been the last person who made me laugh so hard I blew soda through my nose. Whom I told every secret I had. Who was as comfortable getting herself a snack in my house as I was.

I literally had to blink to convince myself I was really seeing her. I hadn't laid eyes on Arabella in three years, and that was when we both lived clear across the country.

Arabella's family were the only people I'd ever met from my dad's past. I was about eight when they moved to our town and right away, we'd started hanging out together. My mom would cook dinner or play music, and Dad and Arabella's mom, Amy, would rehash old stories about when they were younger. Arabella and I thought they were talking about summer camp, or boarding school, or college, maybe. Sometimes they referred to "the lab," but it was never clear what that meant—a science lab? When we first started getting together, my dad and Amy had done a lot of laughing, but in the months before the Bruyeres left, there was a new tone in my dad's and Amy's voices. They were scared. Apparently, we'd all been in danger—my dad and Amy must have known at the end. And then the Bruyeres were gone.

And now here Arabella was again, slipping into the dwindling end of the food line, looking exactly the same in spite of being dressed in an Asian-inspired high-necked gray dress with two sticks holding back her severe bun. The last time I'd seen her she'd been in braids.

Seeing her—just that glimpse of her gray-green eyes, her full lips set in a determined expression of calm—everything about her, about my old life, came flooding back. I remembered all I'd been working so hard to forget—how it had felt when my dad was alive, and my mom didn't seem scared all the time, before Arabella had moved and my emails to her had started to bounce back, before my mom took us on a colossal "you're being homeschooled in an RV moving all over the country" road trip, before we'd come here, to Orion.

Before.

When I'd thought my life was normal.

Seeing Arabella, I felt this amazing light turn on somewhere deep inside me. I felt the way I do when I'm alone, playing the sax—like I can finally turn off the part of myself that was figuring everyone else out and listen for a second to what was inside me.

She was stepping out of the lunch line, walking past our

table. I could see that she'd snagged a slice of cheddar cheese off a sandwich and put it on her piece of apple pie. Along with the carton of milk on her tray, she'd re-created my dad's favorite late-night snack. He used to fix it for Arabella and me when she had sleepovers at my house.

"Arabella," I said out loud. I was already half out of my seat to run after her when Justin, who plays tenor sax in the jazz band, spoke up. "The new girl?" he said. "Her name's Amanda actually. Not Arabella. She's in my math class." I sat back down.

Why would Arabella have used a different name?

My eyes trained on Arabella's, I waited for her to see me, and when she did, she looked at me hard. But there was no smile, no sign even that she recognized me. Without seeming to move a muscle, she mouthed the words, *"L'observateur est un prince qui jouit partout de son incognito."*

Arabella knew I was quick with music and languages, and of course, we'd had a lot of fun teaching ourselves to read lips in fifth grade while practicing to be spies. But how had she guessed I'd picked up French while Mom dragged us through Quebec on the RV trip of the century?

And what the heck did "The observer is a prince who enjoys hiding his identity wherever he goes" mean? Knowing Arabella, it was probably some random quote. She used to collect quote dictionaries for fun.

But I didn't get it. Arabella had been my best friend. Since she'd moved, I'd been imagining running into her in every mall and every movie theater I'd set foot in. Why wasn't she dropping the tray and running over to me instead of mouthing the words to some arcane French quotation?

I decided to approach this logically. The observer—that describes me perfectly, but "the observer enjoys hiding his identity"—that had to be her. She was the one who had changed her name. And you don't want someone to blow your incognito status if it is something that you're enjoying. So I got the message—I'm Amanda now, not Arabella, and I don't know anyone here. Including you.

With a shiver I made a connection to the stories I used to hear my dad and Amy telling. That camp place or school—sometimes it sounded almost like a prison—Arabella had heard those stories too. Arabella had disappeared only a few weeks before my dad had died. Was it possible those two events were connected?

For the briefest second, I just didn't care. About the stories, or the danger I'd sensed was lurking in them. Why did this have to be my problem? Why couldn't I just be a kid and have my best friend back?

I wanted to run up to her and squeal like other girls my age. I wanted to jump up and down and look ridiculous. But I didn't. I couldn't. I knew what was at stake. "Amanda, is it?" I said to Justin now. I had to feel how the word Amanda sounded on my lips. If this was her new name, I'd learn to use it. If this was what she wanted, I'd give it to her. In honor of what once was. Of who I had once been. Of the danger my dad had tried so hard to protect my family from.

"You know her?" Justin asked.

"For a second, I thought she looked like someone I used to know," I answered. "But it's not her."

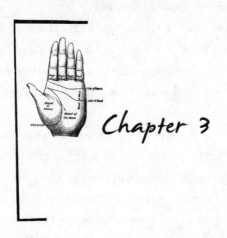

Chapter 3

The morning after the talent show I had a text waiting for me from Hal when I woke up. That's weird, I thought, rubbing my eyes as I checked my phone. After all the excitement of rocking the talent show and figuring out the latest Amanda clue, I assumed we'd all be sleeping in—Nia's death vision or no, we needed sleep.

HAL   07:53:41
CORNELIA FOUND SOMETHING. GET OVER
TO MY HOUSE AS SOON AS YOU CAN.

Cornelia was Hal's sister—she's a technology whiz and good at keeping secrets. Cornelia helped Hal hack into Thornhill's computer and set up the Amanda Project website to track Amanda. Though I hadn't been part of all that, I already knew Cornelia because my twin sisters, Pen and Iris, were in her grade at school.

Cornelia was one of those rare kids who was really rocking middle school. She was good at school and sports, she was a computer genius, and when she had something to say, she just said it. I was always glad to see my sisters hanging out with her.

Since I'm a "ten seconds to throw on some clothes and brush my teeth" person, I took a really quick shower and slid a note under my mom's door: *Quiz bowl team practice—all day.* Which technically was true. One of the secrets to hiding in plain sight is knowing that the more clubs and activities you're a part of, the better. When you don't show up for things, people just assume you have somewhere else to be.

I hopped on my bike and took off. It was weird how used to my mom sleeping in I was getting. Sure, it must be exhausting singing gigs at jazz clubs and the occasional wedding, in addition to teaching music at Endeavor, but she'd never seemed to be *this* tired before. She'd also never seemed to have this many gigs.

The fact that she might be lying to me, that the gigs might not really be gigs—this was something I hated to think about. I didn't want to acknowledge that Mom was never, ever home, even on Mondays when most jazz clubs are closed.

But I was thinking about it. And I had a suspicion.

Given all the crazy stuff that's happened to my family,

I knew my suspicion wasn't the only explanation, but still, I felt it in my gut. Mom had met someone. A guy. A man.

Ugh. I pedaled harder.

I know my dad is dead. I know he has been gone four years, but still, I wasn't ready for my mom to be seeing someone new.

And honestly? Neither was she. We were told he'd had a heart attack during a late-night sales event at the car dealership where he worked. That wasn't the whole story, though. My mom knew there was more, and I found out later what she knew. At the time, all I understood was that we were leaving our home in Pinkerton, California, without even arranging for my dad's ashes to be scattered—there wasn't even time for a funeral. We'd left a house full of furniture, milk in the fridge, all the artwork we'd made as kids in frames in the hall. We hadn't even packed our answering machine. Just because "closure" is a word you mostly hear on daytime talk shows doesn't mean it isn't real, or not something people need after a death. And—unlike the smile my mom pastes on her face whenever a new acquaintance asks what happened to Dad and she gives some vague line about his passing—it isn't something you can fake.

In my mind my dad was still tinkering with cars in the driveway, still standing in front of the coffee maker watching the drips fill the pot on school mornings. He was still there, waiting for us to come home.

Last winter Amanda and I were watching an old

movie called *An Affair to Remember* on late-night TV, and I was complaining about how unbelievable the movie was. She got a melodramatic, mock-dreamy look in her eyes and said, "Maybe, but you don't have to understand something to believe that it can be true." We laughed, because it could have been a line from the movie. But still, she looked at me kind of intensely, like she was hoping what she was staying would stick. I wondered if she'd been talking about the way I make myself disappear. But later, I realized Amanda might not have been talking about that. Maybe her question had been her way of letting me know that she understood I still believed my dad might still be alive somewhere.

I left my bike in the back of Hal's house, next to the garage, and since I heard voices in the kitchen, I knocked on the back door. Hal opened it and I could see that he'd been eating breakfast with his whole family.

Uh-oh, I thought. I was going to have to talk to them.

"Who's that?" I heard Hal's mom call.

"A friend," Hal called back. To me, he said, "We're just finishing breakfast. Want to join us?"

I shrugged, moving into the room.

I felt kind of stupid for interrupting them. Since we left Pinkerton I've tried to avoid friendships with people who might ask questions like, "Where's your dad?" or "How come there isn't any stuff in your house from when you were little?" Sitting down to breakfast with

Hal's family felt dangerously close to the kind of friendship encounter I'd been trying to avoid.

But Hal's mom pulled out an extra place setting so quickly it was as if she'd had it waiting for me. She poured me a glass of orange juice, and Hal's dad said, "One pancake or two?"

"Don't worry," Hal's mom added. "I didn't make them." From the way everyone laughed, I gathered Hal's mom is not that much of a cook.

But if there was a picture in Wikipedia next to the entry for "beautiful family," Hal's would be it. Mr. Bennett is really quiet, but Mrs. Bennett is the kind of person who, when she's focused on you, you kind of feel like no one else is in the room. While I inhaled my pancakes—I'd forgotten to eat anything at home—she asked me a litany of questions. Wasn't I on the newspaper and how does the layout work and isn't that amazing and what a great thing to be photo editor.

Cornelia admired the antique pendant I always wear. It's a lachrymatory—a fancy little Victorian silver box with a glass vial inside, originally meant to hold your tears after someone dies. Amanda gave it to me after I admired it on her and I always wear it now, tucked under my shirt. When she'd first left it under my pillow, she'd put a note inside: *May you fill this, and heal your heart.* "Thanks," I said to Cornelia now, tucking the pendant back inside my shirt.

When the doorbell rang, Cornelia ran to get it. Even

though she was dressed for soccer in a baggy T-shirt, silky shorts and shin guards, you could tell she was going to be gorgeous—she has huge, beautiful blue eyes, and moves like someone who has never doubted her place in the world.

Cornelia led Callie and Nia into the kitchen, and Hal stood up anxiously. He looked at Nia quickly, but when he looked at Callie, his gaze lingered. She blushed, looked down, then quickly looked up again, meeting his gaze. Neither one of them noticed Mrs. Bennett's sharp glance, but I did. She saw exactly what was going on.

Cornelia started peppering Callie with questions about the talent show, and pretty soon all of us were discussing it. After going over the details, Cornelia said, "Hey Callie, let me show you some videos of the talent show I found online." I could tell she was making an effort to keep her voice from sounding rehearsed.

"Meet me in the office," Cornelia said. "I'm going to grab something from my room." We'd barely had a chance to sit down in the office when Cornelia was back, carrying a CD.

"Is that Girl Like Me's new single?" Nia asked, one eyebrow raised. Girl Like Me was Hal's band.

"It's better than that, if you can believe it," Cornelia said. "This, people—" She was so excited her face looked like it was about to explode. "This is Thornhill's hard drive."

"What?" said Hal.

"How did you—?" said Callie.

"I worked some very special magic," Cornelia said, twirling the disc on her index finger and clearly enjoying our looks of surprise.

"I was working in the computer lab after school yesterday, wiping the hard drives of faculty machines that were going to be reassigned. It's usually pretty boring. After we wipe the data we optimize the drives and beef up the memory and make sure peripherals are mounting, install new system software. You know."

When Cornelia said, "You know," the sad fact was we didn't. Whatever the reasons Amanda picked us to be her guides, our collective computer savvy was not one of them.

"When I opened up Thornhill's machine," Cornelia went on, "I recognized the IP address right away. I couldn't believe they'd sent it down to us already. I mean, wouldn't he need this stuff if he was coming back?"

I exchanged a glance with Nia. "I suppose no one really believes he's coming back," she said.

"Or maybe someone figured that his machine was fried," Cornelia said. "Which it was." Cornelia looked toward Hal. "The data was completely scrambled, and at first I thought that the drive had been ruined by a virus. I had to put the drive into two different machines before I could get it to mount."

"So you're saying the data is gone?" Hal said.

"Nothing in the world of digital information is ever truly gone," Cornelia said. "You just need to know where—and how—to get to it. I attached the drive to a functioning system—offline of course."

"You're losing me," said Hal.

Cornelia ignored him. "I used recovery software better than what they have at school and it managed to retrieve some data. Then I ran some other programs that go a little deeper."

We were waiting for her to start speaking English again.

"The long and the short of it is, if you put this disc into Mom and Dad's computer, you'll be able to see whatever you were trying to access before."

"You mean, I'll be able to see what I was looking at when his machine shut down before?" Hal said. "Like that random list of people who live in Orion?"

Cornelia nodded.

"So what are we waiting for?" Callie said.

Cornelia shrugged, amused. "Just me to stop explaining how I saved the day, as usual." She slid the CD into the computer and clicked an icon. A list of documents opened.

Hal leaned forward, excited. "This is exactly what I saw before," he said, flashing a smile at his little sister. "This is everything that was on Thornhill's machine. Wait, scroll down. That one." Hal pointed. "That's the file."

The file was labeled *Cast List—Much Ado About Nothing*. "Remember—the play this year was *As You Like It*?" he said. I could hear the pride in Hal's voice. Back when he'd first broken into Thornhill's computer, he'd cracked the code. What he didn't know is that I'd been peering in the window of Thornhill's office that afternoon, watching him. I didn't mention that now.

Cornelia opened the file, passed Hal the mouse, and we all gathered around the screen. There was total silence. We didn't even breathe.

Spread before us in a grid was a series of columns, symbols, numbers—coding so confusing it was overwhelming just to imagine figuring it all out. But we could see many names that were familiar.

Some meant nothing to me. *DeLonghi, Habbinson; Cole, Samara*—but more of them I recognized.

"Isn't that that artist friend of Amanda's you saw in Baltimore?" Callie said to Hal, pointing to the name *Starfield, Frieda*.

"Louise Potts." Nia had her index finger on *Potts, Louise*, the woman who ran Amanda's favorite vintage clothing store Play It Again Sam.

"When I was looking at this before, I realized that many of the names here"—Hal pointed to the column of names—"correspond to a number there." He pointed to a second column buried between a slew of dates and figures. All the numbers started with C33.

"The whole Bragg family is on there," I said, pointing to *Bragg, Heidi*; her brother *Bragg, Evan*; *Bragg, John*, who is Heidi's police chief dad; and *Bragg, Brittney*, Heidi's local TV news celebrity mom.

"And that must be Amanda and her family," Hal said, pointing to *Beckendorf, Max*; *Beckendorf, Annie*; *Beckendorf,*

Robin; and *Beckendorf, Ariel*, which we'd recently learned were Amanda's family's real names. "I'd thought it was strange before that so many names caught up in all of this were there, but not Amanda's."

"Robin," whispered Callie. "That's the sister Thornhill asked us to try to find in Washington. She might be able to lead us to Amanda."

"And here's Zoe Costas," Hal said, turning to me with an ironic "You're famous!" smile.

I smiled back, but I also squinted at the screen. I saw it too. My name: *Costas, Zoe*. Right below *Costas, Iris*, and *Costas, Penelope*. Above *Costas, Constantina*.

And then there was *Costas, George*.

George Costas. My dad.

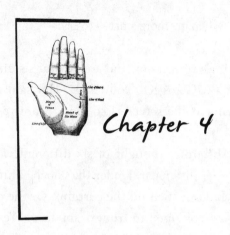

Chapter 4

I still can remember the phone call that changed everything. I was watching TV with my mom—a Food Network show about a chef who travels the world trying to find the most disgusting-sounding foods. Bugs, worms, animal intestines, sausages made from blood that are called puddings. The show was almost over and I was annoyed that my mom was going to miss the end. So I was only half listening to her.

"Yes, this is she," and then silence, and then the word, "No," and then her voice starting to shake, "No."

I remember she sat down on the floor. Right on the linoleum.

I remember that the show was still going, but I wasn't watching anymore.

I remember that Pen was sitting at the kitchen table doing her homework. She was really little then, but she knew something was wrong too. I could see her moon face through the door.

I remember when my mom started to cry.

"Constantina's your mom, and aren't your sisters Iris and Penelope? So George is your dad." Hal said now. I was still staring at the screen. I so didn't want to talk about this.

I swallowed hard. I thought of six different ways I could make myself disappear. Under the couch. Through the open French doors. Behind the curtains. Or the desk. Or by holding a book open in front of my face. "Yes . . . George Costas is my dad," I said.

"Oh," said Callie.

"I wonder why his name is highlighted in yellow like that?" Nia asked.

I was doing a really good job hiding my emotions, but I know my voice shook when I said, "Maybe because my dad's dead."

I could tell from the silence that no one knew what to say. I guess they were all thinking about whether to say "Sorry," but they couldn't tell if that would just make me feel worse.

I was glad I'd told them. Sort of. I also felt my brain traveling to the hall closet. I could pretend I needed to go to the bathroom and hang in the dark silence for a while, and then slip out the front door.

But instead I forced myself to look at the computer.

Hal scrolled down the list again. "Here's my family," he said, tight and grim. He looked up at Cornelia. "See, Corn? There's you." For the first time, Cornelia didn't look like she was one step ahead of all of this. Her eyes opened wide. I thought for a second about Iris and Pen. They didn't know what I did about how my dad had really died.

Nia crossed her arms in front of her chest. "Am I on that list?" she asked. Hal scrolled through. "There," he pointed for her.

Nia leaned forward then shot right back up again. Her eyes narrowed. "My parents are on there too. And Cisco."

"Are mine?" Callie asked. Hal scrolled down some more and found hers. "My mom—" Callie said. "Is her name the regular color?"

"Yes," Hal confirmed. "It is."

Hal scrolled down from her name, and clicked on one of the other names on the list. A new window opened.

"So let me show you how this whole thing works," Hal said. "Ever heard of Marguerite Blaine?"

We all shook our heads.

"Me neither," said Hal. He clicked on the paper clip next to her name. "But here's her driver's license." And there it was. A scan of a Indiana license, showing a woman with tight curly hair, big blue eyes and a goofy smile. Hal scrolled down. "She lives in a town called South Whitley. She's forty-three. Five foot six." He scrolled down and we saw another license, this time from Maryland.

"Look, she's younger here," Callie said. Marguerite

Blaine's hair was long in this picture, her cheeks fuller. "She was living in Orion when this license was made."

Hal clicked again. We saw a document that at first seemed like gibberish. Lots and lots of words. Nia squinted. "I think this is the deed to her house," she said.

Hal clicked again. We were looking at a form I recognized because we'd just talked about them in Civics. "That's a census form," I said. "Look, it shows where you live, how much you make, your job."

"How did Thornhill get all this stuff?" Callie said.

Hal shrugged. He clicked past a diploma and a copy of an email Marguerite had sent to the Dannon Corporation complaining about a bad yogurt.

"Click on Louise," Callie said, a little breathless. "I want to know where she lives."

But when Hal got back to the list, Nia said, "No, wait. Click on Mrs. Bragg."

Hal clicked. We were looking at Mrs. Bragg's latest health history—something her doctor would have filled out at a physical. "She's allergic to honey?" Cornelia said.

Then Hal clicked onto what almost looked like a Facebook photo album, except these weren't the kind of pictures you'd see on Facebook. A lot of them were blurry and it took a second to even tell what they were. There was one of Mrs. Bragg picking up a box of cereal in the grocery store, but taken from a weird angle—she was only in one corner of the photo and she wasn't smiling. Clearly she had no idea the camera was there. "Do you think it was taken by a surveillance camera?" said Callie.

"That sounds right," said Hal.

"And creepy," I said.

Hal kept paging through and found some pictures of Heidi. School pictures mixed with shots of her at playgrounds when she was little, and then winning a junior beauty pageant in sixth grade. Pictures of her now. Some that looked like they were scanned from a yearbook, and some with her face half-obscured, like the surveillance images of her mom. In one, you could see Heidi's face and most of her arm. She was talking on a cell phone while her dad pumped gas.

"I didn't even know there were cameras at the gas pumps," Callie breathed.

"Apparently," said Hal, flipping through image after image of Heidi's mom, "they're everywhere."

"Try Max Beckendorf," Nia said.

Hal went back to the master list, and suddenly there was Mr. Thornhill, but much younger—the picture was a group shot from the newspaper—people who'd raised money for an animal shelter before Amanda, or any of us, were born. "Look at his hair!" Callie said.

"Look for Annie Beckendorf," I asked.

Hal went back to the list, but before he could click on Annie's name, we heard footsteps coming our way. Cornelia moved like lightning, clicking on a video of the talent show.

Mrs. Bennett was now standing in the room. "Having

31

fun?" she said, flashing a smile that was as warm as it was clear. She looked at her watch. "Cornelia, it's time for your game. And then, I'm sorry, but you're going to have to come with me to the open house after." Mrs. Bennett worked in the admissions office of the local community college. "Hal, can you rake while we're gone? Say, in about half an hour? The lawn looks like it could use a little help."

"Sure," Hal said. You could almost see the wheels turning in his brain, thinking of the hours ahead to pore over the files on the Thornhill disc. Maybe Mrs. Bennett felt like she could see them too.

"Dad's going to be home all day, so he'll check in with you about the yard," she added.

"Sure, Mom," Had said, swallowing hard. Half an hour wasn't nearly enough time.

As soon as we were sure Mrs. Bennett was out of earshot, Nia rolled up her sleeves. "If we only have half an hour to work together," she said, "we're going to need to be quick."

"No kidding," Callie said, sucking in a breath, her eyebrows raised.

"Furthermore," Nia continued, "as fun as it is paging through this information randomly, we need to be more systematic."

"Agreed," Callie replied. With her math brain, Callie liked nothing better than data organized into a chart.

Better even would be something she could graph.

We dove into the project of trying to figure out what all these people had in common. We took notes. We made charts. We opened files and closed them, paging through the people, trying to cross-reference them, figure out family relationships, who lived in Orion when.

What connected them?

We realized we were going on longer than a half hour, but we figured Hal's dad would come get him. We wanted to go as long as we could.

"Fact one," Callie said.

"Everyone in Thornhill's files seems to be placed into two age groups," said Hal.

"People our parents' age, approximately," said Nia, speaking slowly so her note taking could keep up. "And people our age, approximately."

"Fact two," I said. "The people on the list who are in our age group are the children of people in the older range."

Nia was biting her lip as she wrote, repeating slowly: ". . . in the older range. Got it."

"Three," said Hal. "Most of the people in the files live in Orion."

"And a lot of the ones who don't live here *now* used to," Callie said.

"Four," I said, holding up four fingers, "there's at least one older member of every family who has a Social Security number starting with 090-56-24. The last two digits are the only ones that change from individual to individual."

"I'd have to go in and look at them all systematically," said Callie. "But I can't remember seeing any of the last two digits that was a number less than twenty or higher than sixty or so."

"Iris's and Pen's Social Security numbers are only one digit apart," I said. "Because they were assigned at the same time."

"So you're saying something like forty of the people in this group," Nia said, "these people who come from all over the place and don't even know each other and are all different ages—you think they all got their numbers at the same time?"

"That's impossible," Hal said.

"I know."

"And fact five," Callie said. "People with these closely sequential Social Security numbers are also the ones who have those long numbers that start with C33 after their names. And they are missing information about their youth."

Callie was right. All the young people like us on the list had tons of information about their childhood. Report cards, school schedules, bus passes, sports achievements, pictures playing in backyards that looked like they'd been taken by a satellite. Every time Nia had made honor roll it had been printed in the newspaper. Programs from my early piano recitals were in there. School pictures.

And for some of the older people, that stuff was there too. I saw pictures of my mom, the farm she grew up on in Oregon. An article in the newspaper about her family manning a Greek culture booth at the grange fair—that was so them. My grandmother, who we called Yiayia, probably brought her homemade yogurt and pastries and wore her embroidered skirt and headscarf from Limnos. My mother had always celebrated our Greek heritage. She had joked that my dad was just barely Greek enough for her parents, but he squeaked by.

Hal recognized his mother's pictures too. She was a majorette—funny—and then he laughed so hard I thought would die when he found out she'd failed Home Ec. Callie's dad was a basketball star in high school. There were lots of team pictures for him, write-ups in the paper.

But my dad—it was like he hadn't even existed until suddenly he had a driver's license at nineteen and a high school diploma in the form of a GED. He'd worked in a factory for about six months when he was twenty. He'd taken a couple of classes at a community college. He'd always told us stories about hitchhiking across the country the year he turned twenty-one. There was a picture of him standing with a frame pack outside a truck stop— he was in the background of a picture of a motorcycle. Then there was a picture of him at a bank when he must have been about twenty-two. A record of a hospital visit six months after that—apparently he'd burned himself cooking.

There was nothing about Callie's mom until she started a graduate program in astronomy. At age sixteen. "Wait," Hal had said. "Didn't she even go to high school? College? Wouldn't that be on here?" There had been nothing.

And nothing about Hal's dad until he was eighteen years old and suddenly, there he was, in a picture of the summer intern program at some accounting firm in Philadelphia. We had transcripts of his college classes, his business major, his straight As.

Lots of the C33 adults were like that. At least one in each married couple, and when an adult wasn't married, you could count on his or her childhood, or large parts of it, being missing. Louise Potts was like that. So was Frieda Starfield.

"Except my parents," Nia said. But she didn't write this down on her list of facts. Instead, she took the mouse and reopened her mother's file. There Mrs. Rivera was, age ten, looking very much like Nia, in braids and a school uniform, standing with her classmates in rows. The caption on the photo was in Spanish, but Nia translated.

"That's her fifth-grade class picture," she said. "My mother grew up in Colombia." Hal flipped through some pictures. "That's my *abuela*'s house." She pointed.

"So how come everyone has a parent with a blank childhood but you?"

"Maybe they don't follow your life until you marry

the person they're following," said Callie.

"That makes sense," Hal mused.

"But it doesn't," said Callie. "Because my mom is the one that disappeared, not my dad. She's the one that's part of all of this."

"But look at this," Hal said. "We've seen this before." There was a small card scanned in, topped with a number that began with C33 and then the word *discharge*. Then a signature at the bottom we could hardly make out, and in very tiny script below that, *Facilitator, Orion Pharmaceutical College*. We kept skipping over them because we didn't understand them. "Everyone without a documented childhood has one of these. Both Amanda's parents have them. They both have C33 numbers and no childhood documentation." He turned to Nia. "Your mom has one as well."

"What *are* those?" Nia said, as much to herself as to us. "Why do they all have them?" She thought another minute, biting on a nail. "And why are there no other pictures of my mom before she was ten? I mean, my dad's got stuff in here from birth."

"Hold on," said Callie, her eyes closed like if she looked at us, the idea she was holding on to so very gently in her head would float away. "Nia, how old is your mom?"

"She's young," Nia said. "She married my dad when she was still in college. He was in grad school. So she was only twenty-two when Cisco was born. She's thirty-nine now."

"Zoe, how old would your dad be if he were still alive?"

"He'd be forty-eight," I said.

"That makes him nine years older than my mom," Nia said. "And three years older than Callie's. Hal, how old is your dad?"

"Umm . . ." Hal said. "Hold on." He did some quick thinking, and then answered, "Forty-seven?"

"Wow," said Callie. Her green eyes lit up with the knowledge that she'd just solved a complicated math problem.

"Uh, Callie?" said Hal. "I think you forgot to show your work."

"What?" Callie said, as if she couldn't understand why we hadn't followed her. "So the ages our parents are in the first picture or record or whatever we have of them are all from the same year."

"What do you mean?" I asked.

"Your dad, Zoe, he would have been nineteen when my mom was sixteen, Hal's dad was eighteen and Nia's mom was ten. They all started to have a record of their existence at the same exact time."

"Wow," said Nia. "So something must have happened in that year. Something that started all the information about them being collected."

"Nineteen eighty-four," Callie said. "What the heck happened to everybody in nineteen eighty-four?"

Before we had any time to think about that, we heard the garage door open. "Shoot, that's my mom," Hal said. He was closing the file and ejecting the disc. "How long have we been here?"

Nia looked at her watch. "It's been four hours!"

"I never raked the lawn."

"Your dad never came in to get you," I pointed out.

"That's weird," said Hal. "He's usually totally on my case about that kind of thing."

We all rushed into the backyard through the French doors in the office. The yard was already raked.

And there was Hal's dad, drinking a cup of coffee, reading the paper, his raking gloves on the table as if he'd just taken them off.

Hal gave his dad a look, and Mr. Bennett flexed his arms comically.

"Sometimes raking is just what a body needs after spending a whole week crammed like a sardine into a plane," Mr. Bennett said.

Hal laughed. Sort of. He kind of choked. This was not how the Bennett family normally worked, I surmised.

Then Mr. Bennett winked. "No need to tell Mom, though, okay?" He lifted the paper back up in front of his face before Hal had a chance to answer.

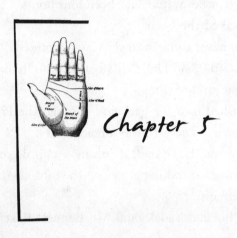

Chapter 5

Two days after my dad died, my mom pulled into our driveway in a used RV she'd bought without a word of warning. She's so tiny she could barely reach the steering wheel from the enormous "captain's chair" that is the driver's seat. Still, she loaded Iris, Pen, and me into the RV and pulled out of the driveway without looking back. That was the last we saw of the house we'd all been born in.

We'd said good-bye to no one. Not our friends. Not our teachers. Not the neighbors we had known all our lives, whose casseroles we left to rot in the fridge. We ran like people being chased. I found out later that we probably were.

When we asked my mom why—which, trust me, we did many, many times over the course of the year we spent on the road—she would close her eyes and say, "I'm sorry. It was just something I had to do." Once, when we were lost in Arizona, and it was hot out, we had to drive with no A/C because we were about to run out of gas in the middle of the desert. Pen, who is not one to keep her opinions to herself, said, "Why are we even doing this? Answer us for real this time, okay?" Pen had sounded like she was about to cry, and so my mom said, "I don't know. I'm following instructions, okay?" And her voice was so desperate we didn't follow up with any more questions, even though what she'd said made absolutely no sense.

At the time I thought, basically, she'd lost her mind. Sometimes I noticed when she registered us at campsites, she would even go so far as to use different, random names— Dolly Nabokov, Mrs. Reginald V. Quilty, Arianna Adore. Weird stuff. When we finally landed here in Orion, and my mom enrolled us in school, she went back to using our real names, though she made up this story about losing all our files in a fire to explain why we weren't forwarding our transcripts from our old life and wasn't able to produce Social Security numbers. In a way, it was as if our entire existence—my dad, California, all of it—had never been real.

The day after we'd gone through Thornhill's computer files at Hal's house was a Sunday. Nia had church and a family lunch, Hal texted that he was going for a long run, and Callie was helping her dad haul and stack wood for his new furniture building business. I made toaster waffles for Iris and Pen while my mom slept in, recovering from whatever she'd been doing until four in the morning—I heard her car roll into the driveway.

At noon, my mom emerged, ate a leftover waffle, and took the girls to a birthday party. I practiced the sax for awhile, though it was hard to focus. I couldn't stop thinking about the pictures and documents that were on Thornhill's computer. If my mom was at the grocery store, was someone taking pictures of her right now? Did whoever was collecting all these pictures and information know what she was doing at night? I wanted to warn her that her private life was not as private as she thought it might be. I didn't want to talk to her about the obvious fact that she had a boyfriend, but was it irresponsible not to let her know that someone, somewhere was watching?

At two I left the house on my bike to meet up with Nia, Hal, and Callie at the gazebo in the center of town. We'd told our parents we were meeting to study at the library.

"I did some research last night," Callie said, when we were gathered—Nia was last, rushing from the Rivera four-course Sunday meal. "Orion College of Pharmaceuticals was founded in the 1950s. It got some kind of government grant and was able to build a campus outside town—as well as purchase buildings in town—all in its first year. That's pretty fast for a college, apparently. Most start small and build up over time, but OCP hit the ground running. Which means it had money from the beginning, and lots of it."

"Okay," said Nia. "Why did they close?"

"Try a different question," Callie said. "Not *why* did

they close. But *when*. Remember 1984, that magic year when half our parents suddenly start to have lives? The year when your mom is ten, my mom is sixteen, Zoe's dad is nineteen and Mr. Bennett is eighteen?"

"Yeah," I said. I felt a kind of shiver of dread. After twenty-four hours and hardly any sleep, Thornhill's computer file made no more sense to me than it had the day before. And I wasn't exactly filled with optimism that some innocuous explanation for what we'd found was waiting around the next corner. There was just no way this much surveillance could lead to good news.

"That would be the year." Callie pursed her lips in grim resignation.

From the gazebo, we rode our bikes to the library, locked them there as a decoy in case any of our parents came looking for us, and then took the city bus to the OCP campus. It was a short, easy ride out there, and for a second I wondered why Orion would still bother to maintain a bus line going out to the campus of a school that had been closed for more than twenty-five years.

We found seats in the back and, since the bus was empty, we were able to talk in low voices about the Thornhill files and strategies we might employ to find Robin in Washington, D.C.

"So has anyone had any more thoughts about the files?" Nia asked.

"It seems so weird," Hal said. "That he'd be compiling

43

all that information. It's creepy."

"I know we've been assuming he's a good guy and all," Callie said. "But what if *he's* a criminal? What if he's stealing all those people's identities or something?"

"Frankly," said Callie. "It's a just a little hard to take in. I mean, a couple of weeks ago I would have sworn Mr. Thornhill's one goal in life was to punish students, and now I have to reconcile that with him as . . . a human being. Someone's dad."

"And Amanda's dad no less," Nia added.

"He wasn't awful," Callie mused. "He was strict, but now that I think about it, he was always fair, too."

"And outside of school, he was actually nice," I volunteered, immediately regretting that I'd shared this information.

"What?" said Nia. Three pairs of eyes turned to stare at me.

"You knew him outside of school?" Callie's voice echoed Nia's tone.

"Sort of," I answered. "He was a family friend." I didn't add that, in Orion, he was our only family friend.

Nia put her fingers on her temples as if a headache had just exploded.

"When we moved to Orion, he took care of everything for us," I reluctantly went on. "He got my mom the job at the school. He helped us find our house. He was—he was the only person we knew in the world. My mom told me my dad trusted him. Now that I know he's

44

Amanda's dad, I can see why."

Suddenly the three of them were staring at me like I'd done something wrong. "What?" I said.

"Nothing," Callie answered, looking away, like if I didn't get it, maybe I didn't deserve to.

Hal was the one to explain. "It's just that it kind of blows our minds that you know all this stuff about Amanda's life that we don't. That you knew Amanda when she was—" It was clear he didn't know how to finish that sentence.

"The *real* her," said Nia.

"I don't know how much of the person I knew was real," I offered.

"Yeah, but you knew so much more than the rest of us," Callie said. "Sometimes I feel like everything Amanda ever told me was a lie. I know she had to, but still. I wonder."

"I still can't believe her name isn't even Amanda," Nia said.

"It isn't Arabella either," I pointed out.

"But you *knew* her," Callie said. "Before she was starting to figure all this stuff out. Before she was prepping us to be her guides. There's something about all these secrets . . . I don't know. It's just wrong, somehow."

"Yeah," I said. "But it isn't her fault. All of this— those sneaky pictures, all that collected information. That's what's really wrong."

Callie nodded, reassured.

* * *

45

With squeaking brakes and a grinding engine, the bus came to a stop across the street from a decaying sign hanging crooked from a single post: ORION PHARMACEUTI-CAL COLLEGE: WHERE FUTURE PHARMACISTS COME TO LEARN.

"Maybe that tagline was what did the college in," Nia suggested. We all laughed.

It took us about two seconds to see that the campus was heavily guarded, and when I say heavily, I mean guards pacing the perimeter. The whole campus was basically half a dozen brick rectangular buildings with flat roofs and dirty glass windows. It was surrounded by a chain-link fence that looked like it had been there since the place was closed.

"Whoa," said Hal.

"Double whoa," said Callie.

We were standing in the bus stop shelter. One of the guards was already watching us. "Let's move," I said.

"Where?" Callie said, though she was already jogging along at my side, Nia and Hal not far behind. And, *ugh*, Hal was swinging his arms as he ran. I guess because he's a runner he was used to doing this to go faster, but the movement called a lot of attention to him.

"Anywhere, just as long as it looks like we have to be somewhere that isn't here."

"But where are we going?" Nia said. With the exception of the chain-link-encircled OCP campus, this was pretty much Nowheresville. There was a barely unfrozen cornfield across the street from the college and woods on either side of it.

"Where we're going isn't the point," I said. Would they believe me? I took a deep breath. "The point is just to disappear."

"Disappear?" Nia scoffed.

I pointed to a thick-trunked maple tree that must have been standing in this spot for more than a hundred years. "Stand here. Make sure to stand in the shade. The sun is coming from right over the college, which means anything shaded is blocked from view by the tree."

"Okay," Callie said. She had her hands on her hips. She was looking at me like her eyes were going to bug out of her head. "Now what?" she said.

"Stay still," I said. "Until the guards forget they ever saw you."

"How do you know they will ever forget?"

"Because this is what I do," I said. "I disappear."

"You what?" This was Nia.

"It's not like I actually turn invisible or something," I said. "Just sort of invisible."

I remembered English class: give an example.

"When I cut class," I said. "I can walk down a hallway past a teacher and never get asked for a pass."

"Seriously?" said Hal. Before Amanda, Hal had cut class, like, maybe twice in his life.

I rolled up my sleeve. The henna tattoo of a chameleon

47

was almost gone, but I'd kept it alive by tracing over the lines in pen from time to time.

"See that?" I said.

"Yeah," said Nia in a tone that let me know she was still waiting for me to explain.

"Remember," I said. "That is me."

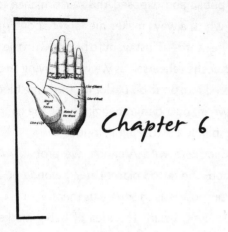

Chapter 6

About two weeks before Amanda chalked Thornhill's car, I found a flyer taped to the outside of my sax case advertising a piano-sax duo playing a set at Arcadia, the club in Orion that has a jazz night once a week. I'd thought the group looked mildly interesting until I read at the bottom who they were—The Brubella Duella, the group was called, with Zoe Costas on sax and Amanda Valentino on piano. Um, Zoe Costas? That's me.

Amanda had scrawled a note on the bottom of the flyer: *Rehearsal Tomorrow @ 5.*

I showed up at the rehearsal nervous and early and full of questions but there was something about the way that the room was set up (no privacy from the club staff) and the way Amanda kept interrupting me—I was never able to ask a single one. Once the sound check was completed, the list of songs set, and we'd started to play, I forgot all about questions and how public and exposed this performance felt. It was just music, which always makes me forget about what it means to see or be heard—I just want to be one with the thing I am making. After the rehearsal, as we were leaving Arcadia, Amanda wandered into a tattoo parlor on the same block, as if she were drawn in, by a design hanging over the counter. I followed, nearly blinded by the lights inside.

Like everything else with Amanda, we probably didn't just "happen upon" the tattoo place. Later, I wondered if the club date's sole purpose was to situate us there.

"Who gets these?" I said. The idea of being marked by something, permanently, of never being able to change that . . . I'd never understood the appeal.

But then Amanda, who changes everything about herself from day to day, lifted the sleeve of her biker jacket to show me her henna tattoo, a coyote design on her inner arm. "Want to pick something too?" she asked. "For the show?"

"Okay," I said, reminding myself that these tattoos wash off. I pointed to a canary. "How about that? You know, a music maker?"

Amanda shook her head. She was wearing a platinum blond wig that hung down past her shoulders, red velvet leggings, and sneakers with platform heels. With the biker jacket, she looked, frankly, like the lead singer from some kind of screamer band.

That afternoon, through her music, I'd kept feeling her almost tell me something and then hold back. She would start phrases with a lot of weight to them and then she'd end them softly. Chords got complicated, and never quite resolved. I liked what she was doing musically, but it made me feel worried.

But now, in the tattoo parlor, she was smiling widely, like something was funny, and I followed her finger with my eyes to a crescent-moon of an animal with short legs and a long tail that always made me think of the southwest.

I laughed.

The chameleon. Master of camouflage. A lizard who can go anywhere without being seen, and pass as anything—a leaf, a dried stick, a pile of sand. They fit into their surroundings so well, they seem to disappear.

"I guess that's perfect," I said.

"It is," she answered back. "But not for the reason you're thinking."

"Huh?" I said.

"People used to think the chameleon changed for camouflage, but we know now there's a lot more to them than just hiding."

"Then what's the hiding all about?" I asked. "They do it just for fun?"

"Scientists now think it's all about communication," Amanda said. "Chameleons change color to send messages to each other."

"Really?" I said. "But how could that even work?"

"You tell me," she said, staring with her large gray-green eyes at the animal etching on the wall.

* * *

"Hiding in plain sight is something Amanda taught me," I explained to Callie, Hal, and Nia now. We were still hiding in the shade of the maple tree across the street from the heavily guarded Orion College of Pharmaceuticals. "Or sort of taught me. When we were little, we used to practice." They were staring. "Together." Still: stares. "For fun?" Hopelessly not getting this. "We'd pick a stranger at the library and follow them around town as they did their errands."

"Wow," said Hal. "That certainly is an *unusual* form of entertainment."

"It was," I insisted. "You see, there were tricks we started to learn and I've kind of gone on to perfect them on my own. Like I was telling you: lockers. In school you can do a lot with lockers."

"You hide inside lockers?" Callie asked.

"No," I said. "I can't fit inside a locker. Plus I don't know the combinations. Plus other people's lockers probably have old food and nasty gym socks in them. But all I need is one open locker to keep a teacher from seeing me when I'm in the hallway and not supposed to be."

"Wait," said Nia. "You can be walking down an empty hallway and pass a teacher and they seriously will not *see* you?"

"It's not so much that he hasn't seen me," I said. "It's more like he doesn't know that he's seen me. Or he doesn't remember that he cares."

Nia, naturally, needed evidence. "So . . . how? How exactly do you do it?"

"I slow my pace," I began, "but almost imperceptibly. Then I kind of—I don't know—I hold my breath in a certain way. I sing silently inside my head. Or sometimes I hum out loud if I don't think it will be distracting. I pick a song I think is going to help me. Sometimes it's something that distracts the person, sometimes it's something that is so the opposite of them . . . it puts me in a rhythm that basically they cannot respond to. Like a modern and dissonant harmony for someone who only can hear pop melodies. They'll tune the song—and me—out."

"I would definitely think the singing would draw attention to you," Callie said.

"If you do it right, they don't notice. Think about music you hear in a store. You don't think twice about it, right? If the store were quiet, *then* you'd feel weird."

"Um . . . okay?" Nia said. Obviously, this was going to take a little more explaining.

"The trick with the locker," I went on. "The other day I used that when Mrs. Mukoski caught me out of class during History without a pass. I saw her coming and I started to hum 'Strangers in the Night.' Do you know it?"

"As a classic example of schmaltz, yes," Nia said.

"But not to Mrs. Mukoski," I said. "She was probably in college when that song was popular. To her, it might be all about falling in love. So I looked not exactly at the

53

teacher, not exactly away, more like at the open locker, so Mrs. Mukoski started looking at that locker also. She's wondering, Why am I looking at this locker? Why is it open? Has something been taken from inside it? And then she's hearing the music, and it's triggering a memory for her. She's suddenly remembering some 1960s sorority dance or something. She wasn't thinking about me, that's for sure. And two seconds after I was gone, she wouldn't remember that I was even there."

"That works?" Hal asked.

"Of course it works."

"You know," said Nia, "what you're doing has a name."

"It does?"

"It's called misdirection," she said. "I read about it in this book about Harry Houdini. It's how magic tricks work. Misdirection means you flick your wrist as you pull a quarter out of a kid's ear so the kid thinks you're maybe flicking a quarter out of your sleeve instead of guessing that you're hiding it inside a closed fist. Misdirection is how pickpockets make it so you don't feel their hand in your purse—they're stepping on your toe, apologizing, directing your attention to something else. Psychologists have done studies—if someone wearing a red handkerchief in their jacket pocket tries to sell you the Brooklyn Bridge, you're less likely to question them than if they pitch the bridge with no hanky. It's like your brain gets distracted by the color. It breaks up your concentration, your ability to think logically."

"Wow," I said. "What was that word?"

"Misdirection," Nia repeated.

I felt a little stupid for not knowing that word, but when I looked at Callie she shrugged, and then Hal said, "Nice SAT word, Nia."

"Misdirection," I repeated, trying out how the word sounded on my lips. I didn't say that what I was doing was misdirection times ten, that even Harry Houdini couldn't disappear the way I had been disappearing lately.

"So what do we do now?" Hal said. "How do we walk out from behind this tree and get into the campus without being seen?"

"It's just like I said," I explained. "We walk in the opposite direction of the campus, and we walk like we're late. We split up. They're probably looking for a group of kids. If we each seem to be alone, the guards see us but they dismiss us right away. The most important thing is that we're not threatening to them, and as guards, their brains are trained to focus only on what might possibly be a threat."

"Okay," Callie said.

"And Hal?" I added. "Don't swing your arms. It doesn't make you look purposeful. It looks too much like a wave. And the last thing we want to be doing is waving at these guards."

"Whatever," Hal said, but he kept his arms down from

then on. We walked out of the guards' direct line of sight before crossing the road, and cutting back toward the campus through the woods.

"Now what?" Nia said.

"Now I don't know. We'll get as close as we can from here and hope we can find another way in."

"I know one," Hal said. "There's an unguarded back entrance near an old jogging trail."

"Did you just have another premonition?" Nia asked, sounding excited.

"No," he answered, a grin sneaking onto his face. "I just run here sometimes."

"Oh," she said, sounding deflated.

He added, "I don't think I've seen these guards before though."

We walked down toward the woods, then slipped through them around the corner of the chain-link fence. Hal was right. There was an old garage right on the fence's edge. Next to the garage was a gate in the chain-link fence—unfortunately securely closed and locked with an intimidating iron chain. Between the cover of the woods and the large garage, the guards patrolling the front and the back of the facility couldn't see us.

"You sure we want to go in here?" Nia said. "Not even the airplane hangar was this heavily guarded and we almost got caught there."

Hal looked at Callie. Callie looked at me. I looked at Nia. "Okay, okay." She sighed. "We need to break in here precisely because this place is guarded so heavily."

"Precisely," Hal said.

And then, as if it were no big deal, Callie broke the lock on the chain. The gate swung open and we slipped silently inside.

There were enough big trees on the campus that we were able to dart from one to another without the guards spotting us. We had to just pray there weren't any cameras installed—I didn't see any. We hid behind some overgrown bushes on the side of the first building we reached. Nia stood up and looked through a window.

"It's an old classroom," she said.

"Anything remarkable about it?" I asked.

"No," she said.

Still keeping ourselves hidden along the walls and behind trees, we made our way over to another building. From the outside, this one seemed very large—about the same size as our high school. Once we got to the windows, we could see that it seemed so big because it enclosed a large courtyard. The interior windows looked through to the classroom we were peering into now.

As we leaned against the building wall to see better, Nia suddenly jumped back, pulling her hands off the wall and rubbing them together as if to erase the feel of the bricks. "Whoa," she said.

"Did you feel something?" I asked.

"More like heard," she said. "Kids' voices. It sounded

like recess at an elementary school, like kids were playing outside. I think the courtyard in this building was used as a playground."

"A playground at a pharmaceutical college?" Callie said. "That would be some pretty young pharmacists-in-training."

Nia nodded, grimly. "I don't think they were training to be pharmacists."

The windows were locked, but by pushing hard enough, Callie managed to snap the lock and lift the sash. Hal hoisted himself up and over the windowsill and the rest of us followed.

"Do you think it's strange," he said, "that we aren't hearing alarms go off?"

"Yes," Callie said. "If they took the trouble to encircle an abandoned campus with a chain-link fence and patrol it with guards, you'd think the least they would do was install an alarm system."

"Maybe they did," Nia said. "It could be a silent alarm."

"Do you have a sense of anybody coming?" I asked Hal.

Hal paused for a moment, as though concentrating. He got a sort of faraway look on his face. Then he shook his head. "Not right now," he said. "But still, we'd better hurry."

Walking down the empty hall, we poked our heads into one unremarkable classroom after another, but once we rounded the corner, we noticed a change. When we tried to open doors to peek into classrooms, we found these doors were locked.

When Nia put her hand on a doorknob, a strange look came over her face. Was she mad? Scared? Upset?

"I can feel some little kids," she said. "This was the door to their quarters. They touched it hundreds of times, from the inside only. They used to stare at it all the time. They used to wonder what was on the other side of it. They wondered if the normal world, the world they read about in books and saw in educational videos—they wondered if it was just outside this door. They weren't allowed to leave."

Hal looked at Callie significantly.

"You want me to—?" she said.

He nodded. Callie stepped forward and put her hand on the door handle. There was a lever on top that you depressed with your thumb to disengage the lock. When Hal had tried it, the lever wouldn't move. But when Callie tried, her face twisted for a second and suddenly, the door was open. And the door handle was hanging from a single screw.

"Nice," Hal said, high-fiving her. She blushed.

"Guys?" Nia said, half-joking. "Focus here?"

We were standing inside a long room lined with small iron beds that were rusting where their white paint had chipped away. Most of the mattresses were gone, but a few beds still had them, thin and forlorn, striped and stained.

Nia looked around, her eyes huge. "Those kids . . . they must have slept here."

Callie drummed her fingers lightly on a bedstead. "What *was* this place?"

I decided to check out the set of double doors at the end of the room. They had the same kind of locking handle as the one Callie had broken open, but this time, they weren't locked. I noticed a plastic panel with a speaker and a button mounted on the wall next to the door below a sign that read BUZZ FOR ENTRY.

Hal stepped through the doors with me. "This was a school," he said. In one corner of the large space there was a blackboard and some desks scattered in front of it. A very dusty-looking and long-faded rug was half rolled up in a corner. Low tables and child-size chairs were grouped together in the middle of the room, the chairs turned upside down on the table as if the janitor were coming in to mop. Roll-down maps were bolted to a wall—the map of Europe was dated from the time when the Soviet Union still covered most of Eastern Europe.

My dad loved history. When we were driving in the car or waiting in lines, he liked to tell me stories about how people used to live, or stories of great figures from times past. One of his favorite things to tell me about was the Cold War, which was going on in his youth— he was born in 1965. Back then, he said, everyone in the U.S. was terrified of being attacked by the Soviet Union.

"The U.S. and the Soviet Union were the biggest powers in the world," my dad had explained. "They wanted to fight, but the two countries couldn't go head to head because they both had so many nuclear weapons that even the smallest scuffle had the potential to turn into a nuclear catastrophe." When he was in his twenties, the Soviet Union dissolved. All the countries they had colonized in Eastern Europe went back to being independent and the Cold War came to an end.

There were shelves off to one side of the room lined with cardboard file boxes. Some were labeled with subject names I recognized: Math, Language Arts, Chemical Science. Others seemed more unusual. What kind of studies were involved in something called "Metric Planning"? "Diplomatic Realities"? Or "Intelligence Maximization"?

I pulled the lid off a box marked SLEEP STUDIES. Inside were four fat accordion files. I lifted one up and read on the front, SLEEP STUDY 17: SIREN STUDY. I pulled out a sheet at random. It read across the top: MARCH 12: DAY 7, SIREN DECIBEL 35. Below I read what looked like a lab report for a very bizarre experiment.

Test Subjects: C33-4867, C33-2990, C33-1109, C33-9821

Objective: To measure voluntary and involuntary fight or flight response in test subjects

enhanced with extra-genetic sensitivity hormone 5K.

Methodology: Subjects exposed to gene therapy
and varying levels of extra-genetic sensitivity
hormone 5K during a nine-month experimental
testing program were informed that due to the
presence of a (fictional) contagious virus in
the dormitory, they were being assigned sleeping quarters in Experimentation Chamber 16,
which had been converted to a bedroom laboratory for the purpose of this experiment and
equipped with soundproofing, two-way audio
channeling, and video monitoring to allow for
clinical observation.

At 20:28, all four subjects were injected
with a mixture of sleep-inducing narcotics
and, after some initial protest from C33-2990*,
subjects entered REM cycle at 20:35, 20:42,
20:51, and 21:07 respectively. Siren effect C
(British Air Raid) was broadcast into hidden
speakers in room at 21:12:00 at 35 decibels
(rough equivalent of a foghorn held three
feet from the ear).

At 21:12:12, 21:12:16, 21:12:16, and 21:12:21
subjects' eyes had opened, and heart rates

were increased by a uniform 45%. Later blood work demonstrated increased levels of adrenaline as well as a surprising increase in cortisol. All subjects attempted to remove themselves from leg and arm restraints, with C33-2990* in fact freeing his left hand and partially removing IV tubing such that technicians were required to enter the laboratory, subdue subject, and reinsert the IV needle before trials #2-#14 could be attempted in the same testing period.

*C33-2990 continues to display a troubling tendency to sabotage experiments. In this case, subject was effectively sedated.

PRESSURE RESISTANCE, I read on another box. In this experiment subjects were pitted against one another—all of them were told that the first to complete a series of intelligence tests would be given a prize. At first they completed the tasks unhindered, but then were required to undergo different testing while encumbered in some way: either wearing a lead jacket, or glasses that obscured their eyesight. At one point they turned the heat up so high that one of the subjects fainted and at another time researchers made the room so cold the report read, "subjects struggled valiantly despite bruising later detected on spots where numb fingers had been clutching pencils."

And what was the prize so amazing that these test

subjects were willing to work against the odds to complete the intelligence exams? The prize was a week off of "going to the nurse."

"What do you suppose 'going to the nurse' even means?" Callie asked. We were all reading the reports together now.

"I'm not sure I want to know," I said.

All of the write-ups had a line at the bottom for Lead Researcher. And time and again, the person listed in that capacity was a man whose job title read DIRECTOR, CLASSIFIED C33 HUMAN DEVELOPMENT RESEARCH PROGRAM. But it wasn't his job title that stuck out. It was his name. Familiar from Thornhill's discharge papers from the hospital in Orion. Familiar from all the stories I'd heard my dad revisiting with Amanda's mom. The man running all of this research was none other than Dr. John Joy.

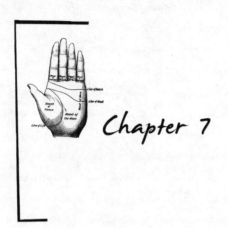

Chapter 7

On our cross-country trip, my mom kept the cash in a coffee can tucked under the driver's seat of the RV. Once, at the very end of the trip, she'd taken my sisters out somewhere. I pulled the can out to count the money, and I found a piece of paper, worn and folded many times. We'd been living on the road for a long time then, and were just about ready to move to Orion. I'd been lost and confused the whole time we were on the trip, but this note offered some glimmer of understanding.

My darling Tina:

If you are reading this, I must be dead. I pray that you are safe, that whatever has happened to me has left you alone. In the last few months, I have thought of nothing but how to keep you and the girls safe. I've given this letter to a friend, someone I trust, who will be watching us—and you.

If I'm gone, I beg you to do what I am about to tell you, and to do it fast. Believe me when I swear that it's the only way. First, sell your piano. There is a man I have worked a deal with downtown—I'm writing his address on the back of this note. He'll pay cash, which you should bring down to Sam at the lot. He'll set you up with an RV cheap. The day you buy it, load up the girls and leave town. For a week, keep moving. Don't stop in campgrounds. Don't register anywhere. Sleep when you can but mostly just go. Always pay cash. Steal if you have to. Remember—you are saving our children's lives.

Until you hear otherwise, change your name every time you are required to write it down. Never use names of people or places on the phone. If you've been one place a week, it's time to go. If you think someone's following you, hit the road. Do this for a year, and if you feel you are safe, make a new email account at a public terminal and send the words "missing you" to rot1956@gmail.com. Travel two hundred miles, switching directions before you check for a reply. You'll get instructions from there.

All I can do is hope and pray you'll never see this note, that you will never need to read this, that the stuff I'm worried will happen is too terrible to be real.

And please know that if there is any way for me to watch over you all from beyond, I will be with you.

Always,
George

The day after I found and read this letter, the coffee can was gone. I must have folded the letter funny or made some other kind of slip-up that let my mom know I'd read it. Still, she said nothing to me. Two months later, when we were living in Orion, I found the coffee can again—it was hidden inside a canister marked FLOUR (no one uses flour in our house), but the letter was gone.

Callie hiccupped. Or at least I thought she hiccupped. When I looked up from the research files I saw her standing by a shelf of puzzles, holding one in her hands as if it were a bomb that might explode any second. Her eyes were wide, and a tear had slipped out of one of them.

"What is it?" Nia asked.

"This puzzle," Callie whispered. "It's got five thousand pieces and none of them are the same shape. There's only one company in Germany that makes puzzles this way."

"How do you know that?" asked Hal.

"Because my mom special-ordered this exact one. Two Christmases ago. She said it reminded her of one of her favorite things she had as a kid."

"Oh, man," Hal said.

She drew a deep breath as if she could inhale her feelings. "I can't think about this now. Not now. The guards."

"She's absolutely right," said Nia sharply, giving Hal a warning glance.

"What do you think is through there?" said Hal, as if to distract Callie. He pointed to a set of double doors also equipped with a buzzer entry panel—was this some kind of suite?

This door was unlocked too. Hal opened it and we all stepped into a room that looked like a hospital. Or a doctor's office. Or something in between. There were examination bays separated from one another by curtains. There were exam tables, a few hospital beds, old metal cabinets with doors hanging off their hinges, ancient machines with leather seats and small screens that looked like they came from the dawn of the computer age.

In one corner, I saw about a dozen lights on stands, like you'd have in an operating room. Most of the glass on the lamps was cracked and they were super dusty, but they probably had been pretty powerful. "It's a set-up for surgery? Were they doing operations in here?" Hal wondered aloud.

"I wonder if this is where they went when they had to visit the nurse?" Callie said.

"Did they do electroshock therapy here too?" Nia asked, pointing to a bed with electrodes hanging off the side, an ancient-looking machine next to it with a big scary dial.

"Or was it straight-up torture," Hal said. "I mean, you look at this stuff, I can see why it would be worth it to take an IQ test over and over in the freezing cold to avoid having to come here."

Nia rested her hand on an exam table. "Wait," she said. "I'm getting something here but it's faint. Maybe I'd have a better sense of it if we held hands?" It only took me a second to realize she was talking about the charge that seemed to flow among us when we held hands. I guess she thought this might make us stronger.

Callie and Hal understood this right away too, and we all grabbed for each other's hands.

I immediately felt the charge. "Is this helping you?" I'd started to ask Nia, when suddenly, I saw something that pretty much blew my mind.

I was expecting our contact to enhance Nia's vision. What I wasn't expecting was to be able to see Nia's vision myself.

As soon as the four of us were holding hands, I felt an incredible urge to close my eyes, and when I did, I saw something that looked like I was watching TV on the insides of my eyelids.

I snapped my eyes open. "Did you guys—" I started to ask, but Nia cut me off.

"Don't distract me," she hissed. I squeezed my eyes shut again.

I saw a kid sitting on the table. He was little—seven,

maybe? Definitely in elementary school. "Criss-cross applesauce, Morton," said a nurse in a brisk, business-like voice. I couldn't get a fix on the woman's face—her whole body was a blur of white nurse's uniform—but I could see the boy clearly. He had a pointy chin and ears that stuck out beyond his short hair, and his cheeks were sunken in a way that told me he was afraid. "I'm extra scared of those things," he said, lip trembling. "I'm more scarded-er than the other kids. I'm the most scarded-er."

"You're all scared," the nurse grumbled.

The nurse peeled a foil top off a glass vial. I saw an extra-long needle and an empty glass vial on a tray.

"I want my mommy," the boy breathed. His eyes were wide, his breath was coming fast. I could see that he was about to cry. Or maybe pee in his pants.

"You don't have a mommy," the nurse growled. "Your mommy didn't want you. That's why you're here."

Suddenly, Nia let go of our hands. "I can't look any-more," she said. I saw that Callie had tears in her eyes.

"I hate this," Hal said.

"Can you imagine—?" Nia asked. She shivered.

I couldn't even talk about it. How could anyone do that to little kids? To keep the others from seeing the tears that were forming in my own eyes, I looked away.

I was going to bring up the subject of how we'd man-aged to see the vision that Nia was having, but just then, I saw the file cabinet labeled "Subject Profiles." These must have been the nurse's, to look up the treatment protocol for each of the kids who'd come to see her.

"Guys," Hal said. "Look."

He slid open the drawer, and it was full.

Jammed, actually, from front to back with folders, each labeled not with a child's name, but with a number. Each number began with C33.

"Look up C33-2990," I said. "That's the kid who was fighting off the experiments."

Hal pulled it out of the file and passed it to Nia. She opened it up and gasped. "2990 is Max Beckendorf."

"Thornhill?" Callie breathed.

"Look," said Nia, turning so we could all read the file.

At the front of the file was a summary paper, stapled to the folder's inside left-hand cover. It read: C33-2990, indicated that the "Subject's Name" was Max Beckendorf. There was a space for "Original Name," but whatever name was written there had been covered over in thick black marker. There was a line for "Genetic Therapies," another for "Surgical Enhancements," and another for "Immuno-Tech." We didn't know what any of these things meant, which made them all the more grisly. And this kid had endured a lot of them, too. I thought about that poor little guy in Nia's vision.

Following the list of therapies was something called "Talents." Max Beckendorf, C33-2990, apparently had many, including: Leadership, Self-Discipline, Self-Sacrifice, Strength, Endurance, Ideological Commitment to Concepts such as "Honor" and "Service." At the bottom of the summary sheet there was a write-up, which read like the most messed-up report card in history:

C33-2990 is an early and fine example of an enhanced warrior prototype. While possessing a keen intelligence and ability to think strategically, 2990 is capable of great personal sacrifice, endurance, and long-standing suffering in the pursuit of ideological concepts. As a prisoner of war, the subject will tirelessly conceive of, test, and execute well-planned escape attempts, always drawing in other, weaker members of any "team" of which he feels himself to be part. Kind to animals, younger children, and anyone he deems weaker than himself, 2990 is a fierce combatant when paired with equally matched opponents—such as C33-1780—in boxing, martial arts, or other pre-combat activities. Recently, 2990 has been conducting a romantic relationship with C33-3496, which he is taking great pains to keep secret from research staff (and believes he has been successful).

The rest of the file consisted mostly of updates, of records of experiments conducted and treatments received, weekly physicals, regulation of vital signs. Never did it once list a birthday, though the last physical put 2990 at nineteen years of age.

All of these files and entries, including the write-up in the front of the file were signed and dated by Dr. John Joy.

With shaking hands, Hal immediately pulled the file for C33-3496. It was Annie McLean. "That must be Amanda's mom," Callie said. "So they were high school sweethearts. That's adorable."

Nia looked at her with one eyebrow raised. "This wasn't high school."

Callie tucked her hair behind her ear. "Oh, right."

Annie McLean's file followed the same format as Max's. She'd undergone approximately the same number of treatments as Max, but different ones. Under "Talents," her file listed: Language Acquisition, Grammatical Logic and Understanding, Empathic Communication, Analytical Listening, and Disguise. Her report card read:

C33-3496 continues to use her keen understanding of languages and communication to build a
feeling of community among study subjects and
to develop her sense of mission. Pursuant to
3496's mastery of Swahili, she was introduced
to Urdu and several forms of Maori dia-
lects which she has mastered in a time frame
shorter than anticipated. During the last

73

three months, after sessions with an acting coach, she was brought off-site and was able to penetrate receptions at the Thai, Iranian, and Swedish embassies, where she was able to extract dummy codes hidden by friendly operatives before the party had ended. As always during these off-site visits, subject was informed that all other humans she encountered were project employees or actors hired for this exercise. See note on file C33-2990 as to continued development of personal relationship.

"Look up Brittney Bragg," Nia suggested. "What special skills did she have that led her to become an anchorwoman?"

"Do you know her number?" Hal asked. "They're organized by number."

"C33-4750," Callie said.

"You just happen to have memorized it?" Hal asked.

"I kind of do that with numbers," she said.

"Okay, here she is." Hal had the file in front of him. "Whoa, she had a lot of surgeries and enhancements."

"That would explain some things." Nia was reading over Hal's shoulder. "What's this Genome Reconstruction thing, do you think?"

Hal flipped through the file, paging through the summaries of all the different procedures, tests, and monitoring. "There," Nia said when he passed it. He paged back and read out loud.

Genome Reconstruction Therapy

On November 6, 1978; January 23, 1979; May 14, 1979; July 8, 1979; and June 7, 1980; Dr. John Joy pioneered the technique of Genome Reconstruction Therapy. Juvenile subject C33-4750 was injected with genetic material from human adult subjects while simultaneously undergoing plastic surgery. Genetic material was extracted from human adults with 90% recognition rates for "beautiful," "lovely," "fun," "attractive," "charming" in studies conducted in Nielsen-ratings households between October 1976 and July 1977. Nose, chin, cheek, mouth, and eye shape as well as other nonfacial physical features were targeted, with genetic material as well as images of presentation in childhood pictures of models used as sources. 4750 was physically modified and genetically enhanced at ages seven, eight, and nine over the period of time the surgeries and gene therapies were completed.

"Is that saying what I think it's saying?" said Hal. "That they took photographs of models when they were kids, and cut up Brittney to look like those models as kids, then injected her with the models' genetic materials so she'd grow up to look like them too?"

"That's horrible," Callie breathed.

"Read her talents," I said, wondering how all that plastic surgery would have affected someone that young.

Hal flipped to the front of Brittney's file. Under talents, it listed: N/A.

"N/A," Nia read out loud. "Non-applicable."

"Look at her write-up," Callie said, and all of our eyes scanned down the summary page of her file.

```
C33-4570 continues to struggle with issues of
inferiority, low self-esteem, and self-hatred.
With others, 4570 is aggressive, quick to anger.
As her treatments have been restricted to
alteration of her exterior features, her brain
development lags greatly behind the others.
Dr. Ellen Schwartzman, a psychiatrist spe-
cializing in anorexia nervosa, was consulted
after 4570 stopped eating between penultimate
and ultimate treatments. After eight weeks
treating 4750, Dr. Schwartzman violated her
confidentiality agreement and attempted to
abduct 4750 (see file #25-B). Dr. Schwartzman
was removed and Dr. Joy attempted to address
subject's depression and anorexia through
behavioral modification therapy, based on a
```

```
demerit discipline system and days of solitary
confinement. Subject has responded.
```

"Plastic surgery on a little kid—that's so creepy," Callie said. "I wonder what happened to Dr. Schwartzman?"

We collectively shuddered. But we had to keep going.

"There was another kid listed in Max's file," Nia said. "The one they said he was well matched with. What kid is that?"

Again, Callie remembered the number. "C33-1780," she said.

Hal found the file, opened it, closed it, and then handed it straight to me. "You might want to read this one yourself," he said. The name in the file was "George."

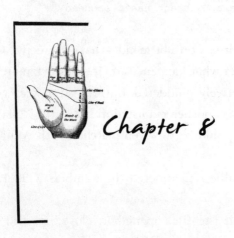

Chapter 8

C33-1780—George—Dad—had undergone many treatments, therapies, tests, and surgeries. It was strange to read what I knew to be the essential facts of my dad's character written out as "Talents," but here they were: Support of Others, Consistency, Strength, Endurance, Affability, Getting Along in a Group. His write-up read as follows:

```
C33-1780 was designed to be fighter-follower
soldier prototype to work in conjunction
with C33-2990, the fighter-leader prototype.
As expected, 1780 and 2990 have created the
kind of bond that would underscore a band-of-
brothers commitment on the battlefield or in
covert or POW military contexts. Typical of
```

the "number two" personality 1780 exemplifies,
he is an important force in the social fabric
of the subjects, providing a sounding board
for others as they react to the invigorating
and inspirational 2990. Recent experiments
in training the tone-deaf 1780 in music to
attempt to enhance his inherent empathetic
abilities has failed. No enhanced auditory
capacity, such as that displayed in C33-3496,
was established.

Breathe. It took me a second to lift my eyes from the page. That was my dad. Tone deaf, but a great listener. Someone everyone felt they could talk to. Happy to let other people call the shots, and always there for you. He never, ever gave up. I was trying not to cry before I closed the folder. I almost succeeded.

"How can I find my mom in here?" Nia said. "Callie, do you remember—"

But just then, Hal put a finger to his lips. "We've got to move *now*," he whispered urgently. "Two guards are in the dormitory, heading this way."

"Which way do we go?" Callie asked, her eyes wide in panic.

Hal stopped for a moment, then pointed to the end of the room, farthest from the door we'd come through on our way in. "There're stairs there," he said—this was when having a psychic on the team was a real asset. "Let's go."

Trying to be quiet, we ran through the creepy hospital room and through a set of unlocked double doors. We flew down the set of stairs that, as promised, were on the other side of the doors. I was just thinking about what a genius Hal was becoming with his hunches and premonitions saving our butts time after time, when the four of us skidded to a halt at the bottom of the steps. I guess the bright lights coming up the stairs should have tipped us off, but we weren't thinking. And now we were completely in for it.

Because, while upstairs, we'd just been wandering around a deserted lab and human-experiment chamber that had been defunct for twenty years, now we were in the basement, standing inside a fully operational laboratory.

I guess it should have occurred to us—what with the guards and all—that this facility might still be active. But we'd been so focused on the past that what we saw in front of us was a complete and utter surprise.

The room was enormous—it must have been as big as all the rooms upstairs put together. It was so huge we couldn't see the end of it beyond the hospital beds, lab stations, metal hoods that looked like huge versions of the one over the stove in our kitchen, lots of shiny equipment that I had no idea how to name, except to note that some of it was the size of a small car. Computers were humming, readouts were flashing, machines were beeping. Men and women in white lab coats were poring over folders, piping things into bubbling test tubes, and sitting on tall stools pulled up to computer stations clustered around a set of monitors in the center of the room. Shockingly, no one happened to notice us in the two seconds we were standing there before Hal did a one-eighty on one shoe and dragged us into a room with a glass door marked REFRIGERATION.

It was good that he found a way for us to hide so quickly. But note to self: You can only spend about seventy-eight seconds in a refrigerated chamber before you begin to turn into a human popsicle. It was freezing and dark. There was enough light coming through the glass door to make out that there were racks filled with miniature test tubes, each one covered with a rubber seal. It was Nia who realized what the glass vials were.

"We have a situation here," Nia said, pulling her hand away. "A blood situation."

She was right. The vials here were just like the ones Callie and Hal had found in the Braggs' secret home office. Except now we knew what the coded C33 numbers affixed to each vial meant. I know we should have concentrated on getting out of there...but blood? There was just too much of it to ignore.

"And look at this," said Hal. He touched a screen on the wall and activated a computer, which at first touch seemed to control the temperature of the room. As soon as it turned on, we saw a readout for current temperature, a temperature log, and statistics about humidity and barometric pressure. But then, when Hal clicked DATA we saw the same database we'd been looking at on the Bennett computer just the day before.

Except now, when Hal clicked on a person's name, he was connected only to a status on their blood collection.

"Okay, this is all fascinating," Callie said. "But what's the plan for getting out of here?"

"Maybe we just run?" Hal said.

"We were pretty darn lucky not to be seen the first time," Callie said. "Hal, can you try to see if anyone's coming?"

"Let's all hold hands to give him more power," Nia suggested. Hal and Callie must have picked up her hands right away, because in a second she was looking around. "Zoe," Nia said. That was when the other three noticed I wasn't with them.

"Where'd she go?" Callie said.

They couldn't see me because I was in the back of the room, blending into the shadows. I was squinting at the racks of blood vials. I'd managed to find the one where my dad's blood, Vial C33-1780 was stored.

You see, when we'd first stepped into this room, I'd had a thought. I'd always hated how we'd left my dad's body behind in California. I wished I'd seen him laid out in a funeral home. Or at least had an urn of ashes to scatter. Anything at all.

But now, I had something. Maybe it was a little creepy, but I didn't care.

My fingers closed around the vial of my father's blood. I

reached for the pendant Amanda had given me and rubbed it between my fingers to soothe myself for a moment. I squeezed it and thought hard about my dad, trying to remember the exact color of his eyes, the little crinkles in the corners of his smile, the sound of his laugh, how his shirt smelled when I hugged him . . . I could suddenly feel him all around me, and the tears started to come. I looked at the pendant in the dim light, and it came to me. *Tears, blood, it's all the same.* I realized I could slip the vial right into the pendant. A perfect fit. Had she somehow known that I would find his blood at some point? I felt weird taking it, but knowing the vial fit into the pendant made me feel better. This place had stolen my dad's childhood. And then they'd stolen his life. All I wanted to do was to get him out of there.

I stepped out of the dark and showed myself to my friends.

Callie had one arm hooked through Hal's. I took four steps toward them and grabbed his other elbow. Nia locked arms with me. And we waited for Hal to see.

Only nothing came. I was watching him, wondering how I would know what he was thinking. I believe he would have shifted. His face would have changed. Something.

But he was perfectly still.

What finally broke the silence was the buzzing of Hal's phone. "Sorry," he mumbled like he'd been caught getting a text in class.

Nia let go of Callie's and my arms. "Do you want to check it?" she asked sarcastically.

Almost as a reflex, Hal said, "What if it's important?" glancing at the screen.

Nia rolled her eyes.

But the second Hal read the text, his face wrinkled and then it opened up. Before he even said a word, I knew we'd been offered a lifeline.

He showed us the text. I didn't recognize the number.

```
44355512123      17:48:22              1K
GET OUT NOW. GUARDS CHANGING SHIFT
IN 60 SECONDS. CAR WAITING.
```

I closed my eyes, trying to find a window when everyone working in the lab would be looking the other way. And I got it. I whispered "Now," opened the door, and we hustled silently through the lab, staring straight ahead. Up the stairs we went, fast as we could without running, though somehow, by the time we got up to the hospital ward, our pace had accelerated to an all-out sprint. We made it out the dormitory door, down the hall, into the ordinary classroom, through the window and then, still managing to duck around the corners of buildings and behind trees, we made it to the gate, around the garage, into the woods, and out to the road.

It wasn't until we were leaning against a brick wall,

waiting for a guard to turn his head that Hal caught his breath enough to say, "Isn't someone going to ask me who sent the text?"

"It wasn't Amanda?" Callie asked.

"She was my guess too," Nia answered.

"No," said Hal. "Believe it or not, it came from my dad."

It's hard to imagine a moment where the sight of Hal's mom's minivan complete with its MY HONOR ROLL STUDENT CAN KICK YOUR HONOR ROLL STUDENT'S BUTT wouldn't be completely mortifying for Hal.

This was the moment.

The sliding door slid open and we piled in. He started pulling away before the door had closed. The van was fast and Mr. Bennett pushed it to its limit, taking corners on two wheels and running red lights without even blinking an eye. Who knew?

"Dad, *what* are you doing here?" Hal said.

Mr. Bennett's face was pale and drawn and he looked nothing like the calm man we'd seen yesterday reading the paper and relaxing on the patio. "Are you kids all right?" he asked.

"I'm fine," said Hal. "We're all fine. But I don't get it—how did you know where we were?" You could literally see his brain straining to reconcile everything we'd just seen at the pharmaceutical college with the current reality: his dad, the minivan, the text. "Am I—" Hal

85

started. "Am I in trouble?"

"You're not in trouble," Mr. Bennett said, laughing in spite of the tension. "You guys—all of you—you're brilliant, is what you are."

"Come again?" Hal said.

"I'll explain in a minute," said Mr. Bennett, and he pursed his lips like he was about to begin. He did a massive screeching U-turn in the middle of the intersection of Astoria and Miller and took us back toward the college for a quarter mile, then turned left, driving in silence now to a destination he did not name.

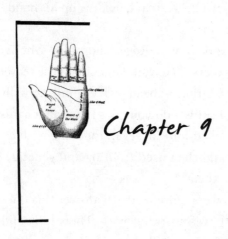

Chapter 9

"Brewster's?" Hal said, when we pulled into the parking lot of Orion's best ice cream place. They make all their own flavors—sometimes they don't even have the standard chocolate and vanilla—and I think they even invented the dirt sundae.

"Get sundaes," Mr. Bennett said. "Or whatever you want. It's the least I can do. And then we can talk."

I hadn't thought I could eat, but once I had a peppermint sundae with hot fudge sauce and crumbled cookies in front of me, I realized I was ravenous. I was about a third of the way through it when Mr. Bennett, carefully licking his single-scoop mocha cone, started to talk.

"Look," he said. "I—we—I think I speak for all your parents. We're worried sick. When you became friends with Amanda, when she disappeared, when you found each other . . . I've been watching you."

"Wait, wait, wait," Hal said, holding up his hand. "You know about Amanda?"

"I've been working with Roger Thornhill," Mr. Bennett explained, "for years. The work I'm doing is the reason our family moved to Orion—ahead of Thornhill, actually. My particular set of skills—do you guys know about this yet? How Dr. Joy looked for kids, even toddlers, with certain innate talents and then used training and genetic therapies to enhance them?"

None of us were quite ready to answer this question. If Mr. Bennett was working with Thornhill, and was watching us...if he knew all about Dr. Joy . . . why hadn't he stopped us? Why had he let us do all those dangerous things? There were so many times when we could have been hurt.

"It's a little shocking, isn't it, that your parents would knowingly let you partake in any of this," Mr. Bennett said, obviously understanding from our silence that he would need to backtrack. "What responsible parent—hey, what somewhat negligent parent—would ever allow his kid to walk into the kind of danger you have been exposed to?"

"The question did just cross my mind," Hal said sourly.

"As well it should," Mr. Bennett went on. "And all I can tell you is that I am more worried than I ever imagined I could bear to be. But I am also impressed. I've been astounded, actually, by the things you four have been able to achieve. And now it is important that I give you whatever information I can to help you. Because Thornhill is convinced—and I believe he is right—that you four are the only ones who can help Amanda, and Amanda is the only one who can help us all."

I looked at Hal, staring dumbstruck at his dad. Callie's mouth hung open as well. Only Nia was able to calmly ingest the news. She was all business now. "Okay, then," she said, leaning forward. "You were telling us about Dr. Joy's therapies. We read some of the files inside. And we know that you were in there. What happened to you?"

"As you know, I was one of those kids. Dr. Joy wanted to turn my brain into a computer. As much as was possible, he expanded my capacity to store data and to analyze it."

"That's why you became an accountant?" Hal said.

"Accounting is easy for me." Mr. Bennett smiled. "I can manage inflows and outflows for a multinational corporation with the earning capacity of a small country in my head. There aren't too many people out there who can do that."

"And that's why you travel so much?" Hal asked. "Because Dr. Joy trained to you be a really excellent—" I think Hal was thinking about Thornhill, his talents as a soldier, his fierce fighting skills, his ability to strive heroically and sacrifice all for a cause he believed in. "You got trained to be a kind of genius *accountant*?"

Mr. Bennett laughed. "Well, that wasn't exactly Dr.

Joy's aim. But that's what happened in the end. Accountants never starve during tax season. And it's been a great cover for the work I've been doing for Thornhill. I've been helping him identify and protect as many former C33s and their families as we can possibly reach. I've been creating a database. But it's not what you saw on Thornhill's computer."

"How'd you know what we were looking at?"

"Because I have my laptop set up to view the home computer remotely."

"And you didn't make us stop?"

"I needed you to have that time. Because of your connection to Amanda, your talents . . . you guys are the only ones making any forward progress to find her, and she's at the heart of any attempt to stop what's going on. Why do you think I raked the lawn for you?" Mr. Bennett smiled.

"Yeah, okay," Hal said, shaking his head. "Wow."

"I knew after what you found yesterday you'd go to the college, and trust me, I did everything I could to keep you safe. We have a network watching that place—and you guys. That's how we knew about the guard shift and exactly how long you'd been inside. Anyway." Mr. Bennett took a small, neat bite of his cone. "The material you were looking at is actually a copy of the Official's database. We managed to hack into it, although I'm sure that's been updated since we downloaded it about a month ago."

"So, wait," Nia said. "What *was* that place back there? You lived there when you were a kid? With Amanda's parents? And Zoe's dad?"

"And your mom," Mr. Bennett said gently.

"But I've visited the place where my mom grew up," Nia said. "In Colombia."

"Your mom was the youngest of our group, only ten when we were released, so she was able to have a somewhat normal childhood after that. She was placed in Colombia because she was of Colombian heritage, but nothing more about her biological family is known. For her, her years in the program were fuzzy. A nightmare, really. She was not one of the fighters, the older kids who worked hard against what Dr. Joy was trying to make us become."

"So he performed experiments on you?" Hal said. "And it was legal?"

"That's right," Mr. Bennett said. "At the time, our government lived in fear of becoming subordinate to the Soviet Union. Dr. Joy pitched his research to a Congress desperate enough to endorse secret programs like his to give us a better chance against the Soviets."

"So did it work?" Hal asked. "Did you all turn out to be superheroes?"

Mr. Bennett laughed bitterly. "Hardly," he said. "A few of us are quiet geniuses, like your mom, Callie, or have skills that we use in our work, like me. But most C33s are barely able to function in society. They've either worked very hard to reintegrate themselves or they've died, or they're living entirely off the grid. I can't tell you how many stories of C33s end with them abandoning their car on the side of the road and just disappearing."

"Whoa," said Hal.

"You guys—you kids—have turned out to be the ones with the extra-human capabilities."

"You mean—?" Hal began. "You know?"

Hal's dad nodded. "There are others like you out there. I tracked down a family living in Alaska who has a seventeen-year-old who communicates with animals— we believe Amanda already tracked him down before she came to Orion. His powers manifested during a window of time when we didn't know where she was. Another child of a former C33 in Japan started programming multiplayer video games when he was eight—again, we think it likely Amanda was on the scene while on vacation with Amy. This guy doesn't just program computers. He has some strange way of communicating with machines and creating artificial intelligence in them. Now he's eighteen and has gone underground, using his self-learning computers for a criminal franchise. We're trying to track him—this kid is incredibly intelligent but naive to the danger he might be creating for himself."

"A criminal franchise, huh?" Hal said. "I guess that makes all the lies I've told Mom in the last few weeks seem like less of a big deal."

Mr. Bennett cleared his throat. "You should never lie to your mother." He sounded like he was making the statement in case Hal's mom might have a surveillance video.

Mr. Bennett might be a secret agent fighting the forces of evil, but that didn't change one important fact: You never cross Mrs. Bennett.

"How you kids developed—that's what Dr. Joy has always been after."

"Really?" I said. "What about the whole soldier-prototype thing we read in the files?"

"Yes, initially, that was Joy's plan. You know how every now and then, human beings emerge who are capable of great things—genius, you could say, but it goes beyond intelligence. Abraham Lincoln was a genius statesman. Martin Luther King Jr. a visionary and a born leader. Joan of Arc the perfect soldier—unflinching in her commitment to her ideals, strong, able to endure, persistent. Beethoven . . . he composed his three greatest symphonic works when he was completely deaf. Can you imagine a world in which you could engineer that kind of power? That's how Dr. Joy envisioned his program. At first.

"Then, as time went on, he grew more ambitious, pursuing the kinds of abilities you four have. He never achieved this in the lab."

"What finally made Dr. Joy stop?" Nia asked. "Before? When the original program disbanded?"

"Oh, he didn't want to stop. But the Cold War was ending. Under Reagan, the focus was shifted to space-based missile defense. Joy's funding was cut by the government and we were all released. But then we had to attempt to live normal lives after having been raised without families or parents, all within the walls of one building. For years he followed us around the country. We'd see him sitting in his car in a parking lot outside our jobs or churches or homes. He was watching us, keeping tabs, working illegally. For a while I think he was put behind bars, back before . . . well, before Amanda."

"It always comes back to Amanda, doesn't it?" Callie said wistfully.

"Amanda," Mr. Bennett repeated. He sighed. "Yes. Amanda is an anomaly. By the time the program was disbanded, Max and Annie had fallen completely in love. For life. They were married within months of the program's termination. Amanda is the only one who is a child of two C33s."

"So what happened?" I asked. "Max left, right?"

"He had to," Mr. Bennett explained. "You see, Max and Annie didn't think they could have kids. They assumed that all the damage that had been done to their bodies under Dr. Joy's care would make it impossible. They had adopted Amanda's older sister, Robin, and were seeking to adopt a second child, when to their very great surprise, Annie realized she was pregnant."

"That's an amazing story," Callie said.

"Dr. Joy had been hanging around their lives for years at that point," Mr. Bennett went on. "He was out of prison. I don't know what he was doing for money. I think he was sleeping in his car a lot of the time. He must have had an address, though, because in an act of extreme generosity, or extreme stupidity—I've tortured myself and I still don't know which one I care to attribute it to—Max and Annie decided to share their joy with good old Uncle Joy, as he made us call him, though we nicknamed him Uncle Joe after one of the most vile dictators of all time, Joseph Stalin. Anyway, Max and Annie sent Dr. Joy a birth announcement."

"So?" said Nia. "What harm could that have done?"

"All the harm in the world," Mr. Bennett said, shaking his head sadly. "Because Dr. Joy realized the potential in Amanda's birth immediately. We believe he used the fact of it—her direct biological link to two genetically modified former C33s—to make a pitch to the Official to get the facility up and running again."

"The Official," I said. "Who exactly is the Official?"

"That," Mr. Bennett said, "is a very good question. Unfortunately, we don't know. We haven't found out his name—all records or memoranda we can get our hands on refer to him as the Official. We believe this derives from his line of work. He has some ties to the federal government, ties that allowed him to direct all kinds of funding into restarting Dr. Joy's research. We don't believe it's actually sanctioned, even in a top-secret capacity, by Congress, but we're not sure. The way these things work—it's complicated."

"It's depressing, is what it is," Hal said.

Mr. Bennett smiled ruefully. "Just after joining up with the Official, Dr. Joy made an enormous tactical error," he went on. "You see, he'd always overestimated our loyalty to him. I think through some massive delusional fantasy, he convinced himself that he really was our uncle, that the gifts he was bestowing on us would make us grateful to him. So, rather than simply kidnapping Amanda in her infancy, Joy approached Max and Annie and flat-out asked them to give him their baby.

"He showed up on their doorstep and told them of the great life he had in store for Amanda. First, there'd be the testing. She'd be scanned, quizzed, opened up, bled—all this as a baby. Then she'd be altered—of course. Then she'd be studied some more. And finally, she'd be launched into the world. She'd be a diplomat, a world traveler, rich beyond belief, powerful, and good. This was Dr. Joy's vision. Unbelievable as it sounds, he thought they'd be thrilled.

"Max and Annie's response was to go into hiding. They split up as part of the disguise. Eventually, Max came here, to Orion, once he'd realized that to save his daughter, he was going to have to unite all the former C33s, or as many as he could gather. After Annie's death, he'd realized hiding was no longer an option. He was going to have to bring Dr. Joy and the Official down."

"Wow," I said. Through my shirt, I fingered the pendant. I couldn't believe my dad had known about all this, had lived with this secret, this fear, and never let on.

"Why didn't you ever tell us any of this?" Hal said. "If you knew we were looking for Amanda, why didn't you help?"

"That was Max's idea."

"Who is Thornhill, right?" Hal said.

"Exactly. Max is an amazing leader—always has been—it's like he has a sense of what people are capable of even before they know it themselves. He told us that if we let you discover the mystery for yourselves you would learn and grow in the process, and gain the skills that you needed to save Amanda. To save all of us.

"God, I wish we could just keep you hidden from the Official and Joy, keep you safe." Mr. Bennett looked so distraught, for a second I thought he was going to choke on a sob. He brought himself quickly back under control. "But unfortunately, your abilities, and Amanda's, the things you can do—not only are they what Joy is after, they seem to be our only chance of finally stopping his project, of putting all this to rest. Your powers—your connection with Amanda—they allow you to go farther than anyone else."

"Wow," Hal said. He looked as overwhelmed as we all felt.

Later, when we were back in the car, almost at the public library where our bikes were waiting, Callie said, "Do you know where my mom is?"

Mr. Bennett shook his head. "She isn't working with

Thornhill, or even in communication with him. But I know her. She wouldn't have left you without a very good reason, and I believe she's still alive.".

"We've all been trying to help out with what your family's been going through," Mr. Bennett went on. "Ramona—Nia's mom—I don't know if you realize the extent that she has been looking out for all four of you during this adventure. She's been using her volunteer commitments as opportunities to pave the way for your investigation as much as she can."

"My mom?" Nia said. "Really?"

"Well." Mr. Bennett smiled. "She talks a lot about keeping you all safe. Feeling secure and confident so you can reach your potential, which is not a feeling we ever got to have. And well-fed. She dropped off many a casserole at Callie's after her mom left, made sure there was milk in the fridge. She's been sending extra portions of food in your lunch."

"That sounds like her," Nia agreed.

"Does my dad know?" Callie asked. "He doesn't, does he?"

"Very little. For everyone's safety, we've been communicating on a strictly need-to-know basis," Mr. Bennett said, peering up at us in the backseat through the rear-view mirror.

"What about my mom?" I asked.

"She knows more than she used to, but I can't go into details," Mr. Bennett explained. "I know this is hard, but

Thornhill thinks it's best that you not discuss this with anyone, including your parents. We all know the pieces that we know, but he doesn't think it is safe for us all to be talking openly—at least not yet."

"I don't mean to buck Thornhill," Hal said, "but does he remember that we're only ninth graders?"

"He does, but he told me that if I ever had the chance, to tell you there's something he wants you to remember instead. He said to remember that not all C33 offspring have powers," Mr. Bennett said. "Despite her obvious talents, Cornelia doesn't show any signs of it." He looked at Nia. "Neither does Cisco. And, Zoe, your sisters, too—nothing. Saving Amanda—saving all of us—is truly up to you four."

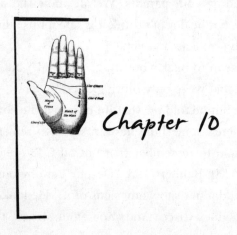

Chapter 10

Sunday night is always the best night of the week in our house. Whatever scarcity of food there is during the rest of the week, my mom makes up for it on Sundays. She sets the radio to the jazz station, cooks something delicious that's bound to make lots of leftovers, and the four of us eat together in the dining room. With candles.

When I pulled up to the house on my bike, it was great to see that all the lights were on downstairs—but it was weird. I felt like I was a visitor from another planet. I felt like I'd been gone for years, not just a day. I knew so much now. About my dad. About what had happened to him and to us.

Inside the house, it was warm. I smelled onions and garlic frying in olive oil, the sweet aromas released by cooking tomatoes. And some kind of meat? I knew we had some kind of ground beef in the freezer—my mom has been too busy to grocery shop for the longest time, which usually means there's not much to eat around the house, but when she does take the time to cook, she is amazing at turning whatever random piece of zucchini or crust of Parmesan cheese and half a box of pasta into a meal. And usually that would be a Greek meal. To me, home is all about the smell of moussaka, lemon and rosemary-scented olives; yeasty, stretchy flatbread; thick, creamy yogurt with just the right kind of tang. And baklava. When my mom invests the time to layer nuts and phyllo dough and butter, the house smells like cinnamon all day—yum. One of the first pictures I took and really loved was of Iris and Pen licking the honey sauce off their fingers when they were four. The print used to hang on the wall by the stairs in our old house. I wonder where it is now?

I felt so different I half expected my mom to be able to tell just by looking at me, but she glanced at me hurriedly and said only, "Hey, Zo, great you're here. Can you set the table quick for me?"

My mom has never looked like other people's mothers. She's kind of like a bird—her legs are little sticks and her neck is graceful and long. Her hands are so small she can hardly span an octave on the piano, but she can—she plays beautifully. I've never seen her dress casually, except in the early days of the RV trip, when she wore my dad's old sweatshirt every day and alternated between crying and driving. Usually, she wears silk and finely woven wool jackets with tailored dark jeans and cute shoes. I've seen her mow the lawn in an angora sweater.

Now, she wore a vintage top, skinny jeans, and suede ankle boots that drooped at the top. My sisters were sitting across from each other doing their homework in the breakfast nook, and while I hung up my jacket, my mom stepped away from the stove to lean over them, checking Pen's math sheet as the wooden spoon in her hand dripped red sauce onto the paper.

"*Think* about it. Half of the factory's output is four hundred and sixty-eight apples. So what's a third of the basket? How would you figure that out?"

Because she's a tiny person, you don't expect it, but when Mom opens her mouth she sounds like Billie Holiday. Sings like her too.

Pen looked up at her now. Both twins have huge brown eyes set deep into their faces. My mom calls them "Greek eyes," which always made my dad laugh out loud.

"There's two ways to do it," Iris prompted.

"Don't help me," said Pen. She doesn't like it that Iris has a great math brain and finishes her math homework in half the time.

"How was the library?" my mom said, glancing up at me as she went back to the stove.

"It was great." By this point, I was pulling out a stack of plates. Brown with wheat stalk designs on them. Chipped. When we first moved to Orion, my mom rented this house and bought everything we needed to furnish it at an estate sale. It all belonged to an old lady named Eunice—we ended up with five yellowed notepads that say at the top, *From the Desk of Eunice P. Clarke*. Amanda loved Eunice's things, but I didn't.

"Mom," I said, laying down Eunice's nasty old polyester napkins and her long-dulled stainless steel forks—also patterned with a wheat stalk on the handles. "Do you ever think about Pinkerton?"

Mom froze in place over the stove, oven mitt poised dramatically. She put one hand out in front of her to grasp the oven's handle, as if to steady herself. There are silent rules in my house: We don't talk about Pinkerton. We don't talk about my dad. "Do you think we'll ever go back?"

My mom's eyes begged me not to ask. The skin at my mom's temples constricted, and she clenched her jaw, I could see that the topic was causing her pain.

But I needed to ask. I need to ask now. "Did Dad—?" I said. "Did Dad tell you about where he grew up?"

"Oh, Zo." My mom can sing in one note what it might take other people a hundred pages to put into words. And she was almost singing now, so in the lilting way she spoke those two syllables "Oh, Zo," I could hear what she meant: I can't talk about it. She meant: It doesn't mean I love you any less. She meant: You forgot spoons.

And I got it, I really did. She just couldn't go there. For years, things had been hard. And now, our life had settled into a routine. Mom actually likes her job, or should I say her two jobs: music teacher at the high school and jazz singer two nights a week. For Pen and Iris, Pinkerton was a vague memory. Orion was home now.

But not to me, I wanted to say. I touched the pendant under my shirt. I knew the vial was still inside it. I didn't know if I would ever do anything with it . . . but I wanted it. I needed it with me the way I'd needed—insisted—on our dining room table having five chairs when my mom had bought only four. Four chairs would have made it feel more real that my dad was never coming back.

The next morning I was already awake when my mom came into my room.

"Zoe?" she said, shaking my shoulder. "Time to wake up—you're leaving for Washington extra early, remember?"

"Hmm," I said.

"Want me to drive you?" she asked.

"No, that's okay. You stay here and get the girls up . . . I can ride my bike and meet my friends." Easier this way. I could slip off and she could stay here, have a few quiet moments before the twins roared away.

Usually it was me wrestling my sisters into readiness, all of us in the kitchen, bumping into each other, pulling glasses down for OJ, or shoving sandwiches into lunch bags; but once I'd stumbled downstairs at this extra-early hour, only slightly more alert after my shower, it was just me and Mom. She still smelled of the perfume she wore when she was getting ready to go out at night. I couldn't help but wonder if *she* had slept at all. What time had she gotten home?

She set the kettle on to boil, and laid out on the table a package of Carnation hot chocolate powder and a single-serving box of corn pops—the cereal that, in a variety pack, everyone in my family leaves for last.

"You'll have to eat the cereal dry," Mom said now. "We're out of milk. I meant to get to the store yesterday, but I got busy—"

"That's okay," I answered. For a while after my dad died, we didn't have the money for food—we ate a lot of tomato soup and mac and cheese from a box. Now, my mom was making okay money, but almost never had the time to shop.

"Hot water?" she said, as the whistle in the dinged-up kettle blew. I pushed my mug across the table so my mom could pour.

Eunice P. Clarke was really fond of small mugs the color of polluted pond water. We have, like, twenty-four of them, and not one is large enough to accommodate a whole packet of cocoa. If you wanted to even get close to the right proportion of water to powder, you had to mound the cocoa on the water's surface, so that it looked kind of like a volcano waiting to blow. A volcano with mini marshmallows on top.

"I found this in the mailbox last night," she said. "You forgot the street number when you wrote out the address."

"What?" I said, racking my brain to remember the last

time I'd written anyone a letter. "Are you sure it isn't a letter *to* me?"

"You're the return address," she said. "And it's your handwriting as well."

I reached for the sealed envelope Mom slid across the table. Already, there was a hollow feeling in my chest. Surprises, I'd come to learn, were never good.

From the moment I touched the envelope, I was sure it was from Amanda. This might sound dumb, but even if she's running for her life, Amanda loves paper. Every letter I'd ever gotten from her—before and after her disappearance—had been transformed by her into something beautiful. She'd mark it with her coyote totem, or even just distress it a little with an interesting tear or an artful ink stain. She wasn't afraid of cheap paper—half her journals were plain old copybooks—but she decorated them with ribbons or glued-on buttons or pictures from magazines. Everything she'd ever touched she'd made her own.

This envelope was made from paper that was thin, almost more of a gray than a white, like the sky on a day that can't quite decide whether to rain. I could see that someone had used white pastels to draw rain clouds. It was a funny kind of chalky pastel marking. But there was no denying that it was beautiful once you'd seen that it was there—a drawing of a chameleon, like the one she'd chalked on my locker the morning she disappeared.

My mom was right about the address. It *was* written in my handwriting, made out to Constitution Avenue in

Washington, D.C. But it was weird. There was no street number on the address. The post office had stamped INSUFFICIENT ADDRESS—RETURN TO SENDER. In the upper left hand corner of the envelope, where the return address belongs, was my name. Again, in my handwriting.

But I had never seen this envelope before.

With shaking hands, I tore it open.

"What is it?" my mom said.

"Umm . . . ," I said. There was nothing inside.

Part of me was so disappointed, I didn't even want to bother making up a story. But I did. I lowered my voice, took a deep breath, looked my mom right in the eye.

"I think it's this chain letter thing a bunch of friends at school are trying out," I said. I sometimes hate how good I am at lying.

"Is it connected to the D.C. trip?" my mom said.

"Not really," I said, but then wondered for a second if maybe it was. As with the postcard, it was leading me to Washington D.C. Could that mean something? I stuffed the note into the pocket of my vest.

My mom raised her eyebrows. She leaned back in her chair and sighed. Usually she's too busy, but when we do sit down together and actually talk I am always startled by how little she lets you get away with.

"Mom," I said. I wanted to tell her that I knew. About Dad. That she didn't have to hide it from me anymore. "Yesterday—"

But she hadn't heard me. When I looked up, she was

staring out the window, lost in thought. Or maybe she was half asleep. She was out so much at night these days I'd seen her drift off at the dinner table, and once, when I went by her office at school to ask a question, she had her head down on her desk with her eyes closed.

The cocoa was starting to sink into the water, and as I watched it drop, I gave it a stir before looking at my watch, seeing how late it had gotten, and running out to get on my bike so I could meet the heinously early bus to D.C.

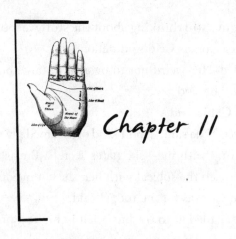

Chapter 11

The sky was just starting to get light as I pulled into the Endeavor parking lot, and I noticed that no one but me had come on a bike. There were Heidi Bragg and the I-Girls shimmying out of the back seat of Heidi's mom's BMW SUV. I caught a glimpse of Mrs. Bragg—hard, beautiful, amoral. Another fine product of the C33 program. What does that mean for the rest of them? And wait a minute, what were Heidi and the I-Girls even doing here? The History Club was for brainiacs—had they talked their way into this trip last minute just like we had?

Meanwhile, Nia and her irresistible brother Cisco were emerging from his Honda. Cisco was coming along on the trip as a peer chaperone. The girls in the History Club were going to be very excited.

Nia came over to the bike rack and we quickly found Callie and Hal.

"Are you guys still thinking about the stuff we found?" Callie asked as soon as we'd said hello.

Hal nodded. "It's weird not to be able to talk about it with my mom," he said.

"I know," Callie said.

"I told Cisco," Nia said. "And I kind of assumed my mom would bring it up with me—she hates secrets. But when I started to approach the subject with her, she cut me off."

"That's how it was for me too," I said.

Mr. Fowler called us to the bus. I felt in my vest pocket for a stick of gum—I always chew gum on buses to keep from getting sick—and I felt the folded corners of the little white envelope that had come for me.

"Did any of you get any messages?" I said. "Or mail?"

"Oh," said Callie. "I almost forgot." She pulled an envelope out of her bag that looked just like mine. It had been opened. She said, "It looked like I was the one who mailed it. It's my handwriting. But it's not from me."

Hal reached into his back pocket. "Here's mine," he said.

"I got one too," Nia said, pulling out hers. Hal's and Nia's were identical to Callie's and mine. The same strange chalky drawings of their totems, marked in such a way that you could only see them in a certain light.

The four of us got on the bus in time to get seats together. Heidi and the I-Girls boarded after all the seat pairings were gone, and asked people to move to let them be together.

"Am I the only one who thinks it's strange that the I-Girls are on an academic club trip?" I said.

"Yeah," Callie said. "What's going on?"

"How did they even talk their way into the club?" said Nia. "Eliza only let me join because we're friends. She hates Heidi as much as I do."

"Hey, Wynne," we all heard Heidi say in a sticky-sweet voice, addressing a girl with bushy brown hair, who always wore hooded sweatshirts and read romance novels under her desk during class. "Since you're all alone in your seat, would you mind if people who have friends sat there instead so they could be together?"

Nia made a clicking sound with her tongue against the roof of her mouth, and I agreed with what she was thinking. What was Heidi's problem? Heidi was a girl who had it all—she was gorgeous, and she was smart as a whip—last year she won a schoolwide literary contest for her poem "Fashion Pollution." People fell all over themselves to help her out, and her police chief dad and quasi-celebrity news anchor mom basically ran the town.

"Why do people obey her every command?" I said, leaning across the aisle so that the other guides could hear me.

"Yes!" Callie whispered. "Even if they only spend a few minutes with her, people feel like they're her best friend."

"I'm guessing she's like us . . ." Hal suggested. "That

she has a power—to make people do what she wants?"

"Oh, no," Nia said, putting her head in her hands. "The idea of that girl being given special abilities on top of her extreme good luck in life makes me ill."

"It kind of makes me afraid," said Hal.

Just then Cisco and the other peer chaperones began handing out the scavenger hunt forms. Looking it over, I forgot all about Heidi for a moment. In fact, my jaw literally dropped. The sheet listed dozens of landmarks we were supposed to visit in Washington. The U.S. Capitol, the White House, the Vietnam Memorial, the Lincoln Memorial. . . . But then there was the extra credit, which listed a bunch of places that were totally obscure. Why would Thornhill want a bunch of high school students looking for the National Institute of Health's Capitol Hill offices? And the Office of Management and Budget? Was it even safe for us to get out to Langley, Virginia, to take pictures of the CIA?

I saw surprise on the faces of the other kids on the bus, and a lot of eye rolling—so much for scavenger hunts being "fun."

All except Heidi, who looked smug. She clearly was not prepared to do much, with her minions there to do it for her.

t was sixth grade. The concert band at our school had won a trip to the state championships. We were staying at a Days Inn near the community college where the competition would take place the next day.

After dinner at an Applebee's, the band met in one of the hotel rooms, and spread out on beds and chairs and the floor to watch James Bond movies and eat popcorn. There wasn't anything else to do.

Or at least I thought there wasn't, until Arabella pulled my sleeve. She raised her eyebrows. "There's a bar mitzvah going on in the ballroom," she said. "DJ, free food?"

"Are you thinking what I'm thinking?" I said.

"I have no idea what you're thinking," she lied. But we both knew what we had in mind.

We waited until the trip chaperones and other kids' eyes were all fixed on the TV. I didn't even need to look at Arabella to know that this was the perfect time. But I looked anyway, because that was more fun. Our eyes met. "Now," Arabella mouthed.

We'd packed dresses to wear to the evening portion of the concert the next day. We went back to our room down the hall to change—our other two roommates were watching the movie. I followed her into the elevator, through the lobby with its mirror-clad columns and fake fireplace, and down a hallway to Banquet Hall A.

We could hear music and then we were standing at the open doors to a the ballroom. There was a disco ball hanging over a dance floor, round tables being cleared of dinner dishes by waiters, and up on a platform a long rectangular table decorated with stuffed animals and canopied in balloons— a giant floating balloon ceiling. The guests were dressed up, some sitting down, a few dancing, others talking or milling about. There seemed to be a lot of kids—maybe a few years older than we were.

Arabella pointed out a sign and slowed down to read it. "MAZEL TOV TO JONATHAN SCHWARTZ TODAY. I love bar mitzvahs,"

Next to the board there was a table laid with a white cloth. People had been sticking half-empty glasses, crushed cocktail napkins and used toothpicks on it, but earlier it displayed fancy calligraphied place cards for the tables. A few unclaimed cards remained.

"Only four no-shows." Arabella picked up the cards and fanned them out like she'd been dealt this hand. "So who do you want to be? Shelley and Gale Scott at Table Four? Or Myra and Gary Levine at Table Twelve?"

"Um . . ." I was suddenly nervous. "Do you think this is a great idea, sneaking in? What if we get caught?"

"What's sneaking?" Arabella said. She looked to the left and right to make sure no one was watching as she pocketed Shelley and Gale's tags and laid Myra and Gary's back down. "For Jewish people, going to a big celebration like this is technically a mitzvah."

"What's a mitzvah?"

"It's brownie points with God." Arabella smiled. "And by the way, if anyone asks, just say you're a cousin from Ohio. Everyone has cousins in Ohio they never see." She laid a hand on my elbow. "Look," she said. She pointed to a table at the far end of the room set up with platters and piles and towers of different kinds of desserts—éclairs, molded ice creams, miniature cakes shaped like soccer balls, a chocolate fountain, cut-up fruit, and a bowl of candy big enough to make Halloween blush.

I guess I must have been staring in disbelief. "Come on. This is nothing. My mom and I once attended an insurance convention in Las Vegas for three days and had prime rib for lunch. That hotel room had cable and a pool, too."

"You did that with your mom?" I gasped.

"Only because we had to," Arabella said. I didn't understand her comment at the time, but I thought about it constantly when we were traveling from campground to campground in the RV.

I remembered something else in that year about Arabella— once, when we went camping with the Girl Scouts, she'd gathered wood, started a fire, hung up a tarp, and laid out her sleeping bag before the rest of us had figured out where the bathrooms were.

I must have fallen asleep on the bus, because I woke up when we were pulling off the highway outside Washington, D.C., starting our lumbering ride on one of those main avenues heading toward the center of the city, where there's a massive stretch of grass dotted with monuments—the Mall.

"Okay, everybody," Mr. Fowler announced, standing up in the front of the bus, clutching the sides of the seats to keep his balance. "I'm going to explain the rules of the first part of your trip. So listen up."

Mr. Fowler teaches gym but has always wanted to teach history. The school lets him sub when history teachers are absent, but when Mr. Fowler subs, you have to be careful about what he tells you. He's big on "teachable moments," i.e. self-involved tangents, but he's not much for "factual accuracy," as in he once told my class that The War of 1812 referred to the U.S.'s record of victories versus losses in battles. We won the battles 18–12.

"As you know," Mr. Fowler said now, "this day has been set up as a scavenger hunt. You're going to be divided up into groups of four, and each group is going to find all the landmarks on the list. Take pictures. We know most of you have cameras on your phones. If you don't, grab a disposable camera from the front seat on your way out.

"When you find the landmark, write a few lines on the paper explaining something about it—its function, how it was built, what it represents, some of the inscriptions you read there." He checked his watch. "By the time we get out of the bus it should be just about nine thirty. We'll meet back here at noon and again at three. Here is a list of the cell phones numbers for me and the other chaperones, as well as your classmates, in case you are running late to the rendezvous point. Use it *only* in an emergency. I don't want calls asking me where to find the restrooms or snacks or other nonsense.

"If you miss any of the check-ins or if you fail to find every landmark on your scavenger hunt sheet, you will be required to create a bulletin board for the History Club. These are time-consuming bulletin boards and you can expect to spend a full weekend on the project. You will also receive a letter home to your parents."

There were shouts and complaints, calls of, "No fair! That's crazy."

"Hey, don't look at me," Mr. Fowler said. That's another one of his favorite tricks—to try to be friends with us, acting like we're all on some big team and the *other* teachers are the ones who are making our lives hard. "Mr. Thornhill planned this whole thing. And obviously, he's not here to complain to, so just keep it to yourself. Any questions?"

The four of us stared at Mr. Fowler. Then turned to each other.

"Thornhill planned this trip?" Hal said.

"Is the whole scavenger hunt a clue?" Callie asked.

"Amanda was still here when he put the trip together," Nia said, thinking out loud. "He wouldn't have had much of a chance to make changes since he was assaulted not long after she left."

"That's right," Nia said. "He must have planned this trip with Amanda in mind."

"Great," said Callie. "So now, not only are we supposed to be decoding Amanda's clues, we're also supposed to be cracking the code someone else has left for her?"

I took the pendant out from under my shirt and ran my fingers over the filigree.

"Do you guys think *Amanda's* in D.C.?" Hal asked. "Do you think she's living here now? Has she left Orion for good?"

"Obviously, we don't know," Nia said. "But it would make sense. Thornhill planned this trip before he knew Amanda was going to disappear. He'd have thought she'd be on it. He must have wanted to lead her here—"

"Listen up," Mr. Fowler said, raising his voice to quiet us all down—everyone was talking loudly at this point. "I'm going to read out the groups."

Suddenly: silence. Forget the bulletin board. Forget the letter home. What would be worse than anything was getting stuck for the day in a high-pressure scavenger hunt with someone you could not stand?

"Group one," Mr. Fowler began. "Jerry Miller, Hank Albright, Stef Stone, Kendall Minovi. Group two," he continued, working his way down the list. As he read, there were whoops and groans as people registered their fates. I noticed two important things. Number one: friends were generally being split up. That was not good for us. Number two: the I-Girls got to be together as usual.

Mr. Fowler had gotten about halfway down the list when he read, "Nia Rivera." I don't think he actually paused before moving on to the next name, but at the time, I felt like the moment between when he read Nia's name and when he read mine lasted an hour. "Zoe Costas, Henry Bennett, Callista Leary."

Almost immediately my sigh of relief transformed into

a lump in my stomach as I realized what our names being together meant.

Nia must have had the same thought, because she leaned across the aisle to whisper, "The scavenger hunt really is for us."

"I know," Hal said. His face was white and his voice sounded thin, like a reedy sax playing out of its range.

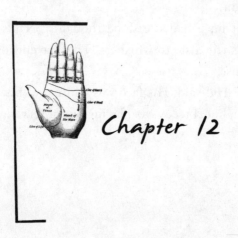

Chapter 12

Callie was scanning her copy of the scavenger hunt sheet that had been passed back. "There's a lot of stuff on here," she said. "I'm not sure we're going to be able to do it all and still have time for anything extra, like looking for Robin." She pointed to Nia and Hal, and her tone became very businesslike. "You two are the ones who will really get in trouble if we don't finish the hunt. Maybe Zoe and I should look for Robin while you guys make sure you pass the assignment."

"No way," said Hal.

"Yeah," Nia concurred. "Remember—'Come Together'?" One of Amanda's messages to all of us when I was still hiding from the other guides was an in-code version of the Beatles song that she'd loved. It was clear Amanda wanted us all working together—not on our own.

"Yeah, okay," Callie agreed. "I didn't relish the idea of splitting up either, just wanted to put the suggestion out there."

Cisco stood and started making his way down the aisle, telling kids that this was the time they should start planning out their scavenger route, if they hadn't already. "There's not a lot of time to get all these places in," Cisco said loud enough so that everyone could hear. "You should map out how you'll fit in the minimum of fifteen you need to visit." It's amazing how quickly people got to work the second he spoke.

Girls kept making up stupid questions to ask him, just to enjoy for a moment the feeling of having him look straight into their eyes as he answered them patiently. "I thought having Cisco on this trip might be helpful," Nia groaned. "These girls are so ridiculous."

When Cisco got to our seats, he crouched down in the aisle and said, low enough so that only we could hear, "You guys ready? You have a plan?"

Nia had told him all about our mission for the day. To find Amanda's sister, Robin, who could be anywhere in this city of six hundred thousand.

"But we also need to finish the scavenger hunt," Callie said, still scanning the list.

"I was looking at the layout of the monuments," Cisco said. "And I was thinking strategically, about the best way to hit as many of these places as we can."

"Using your soccer field sense?" Nia said.

"No." Cisco laughed. "This feels less like soccer to me and more like bowling. The idea is that you only get a set number of tries to knock down as many pins as you can."

He spread out the rough map of the D.C. area that was on the back of the hunt packets across his thighs. "Look," he said, "the bus is going to drop you off here, right? And Nia said you're heading for the World War Two Memorial at nine thirty? If you sweep up here, you can snag a picture of the Washington Monument. Then, standing on the hill just in front of it, use the zoom on your camera to shoot up toward the White House and get a shot of that. By then it will be time to head to the World War Two Memorial. After that, you can scoot down to the Jefferson Memorial—get a picture of that across the tidal basin, don't walk all the way up there. But do walk around close enough to get in the FDR Memorial."

The scavenger hunt sheet had spaces for writing down a quote from each Memorial. "You'll be most efficient," Cisco went on, "if you work together as a team. One of you should use the camera—probably best for Zoe to do that, since I am pretty sure she is the photo editor of the yearbook. Nice photos of the soccer team in that last issue, by the way! One of you should carry the map. Callie? You are good with maps and abstract concepts, right? Somebody told me that . . . and Nia, you should be the one to jot down the quotes. You're good with literary references." He was so disarmingly charming it was almost hard to look into his earnest brown eyes.

"And me?" said Hal. "What's my job?"

Cisco raised his eyebrows. "You, my friend, will take on the bad guys."

Hal flexed his scrawny runner's arm muscle. Cisco laughed and shook his head.

"Stick with the psychic premonitions, dude. Focus on your strength." Cisco chuckled.

Hal laughed, as unnerved by Cisco as all those girls who were still asking him where the National Mall was, even though it was clearly marked out on the map.

As Cisco continued to make his way down the aisle, checking in and reassuring kids, I wondered if what Cisco did was a talent. I thought about Heidi again, how maybe her power was a similar thing.

And then I tried to imagine Cisco convincing a kid to give over his wallet, or getting Wynne to move out of her seat, and though I knew that he was charming and persuasive, what Heidi had the power to do was more extreme. No, I realized glumly: In terms of having a super power, Heidi was definitely one of us.

The bus came to a groaning halt at the side of the road. I could see the green grass of the Mall stretching on either side of 15th Street.

"We're here," I announced. I checked my watch. "And it's already nine fifteen."

"We better get moving then." Nia pursed her lips. She does this thing, which I think of as putting on armor—her face shuts down into a mask. When she looks like that, no one messes with her. Hal shifted in his seat. Callie tucked a reddish curl nervously behind her ear. And me? I got so still that nobody could see me. Even now I was ducking behind the seat in front of me so the kids filing down the aisle couldn't see me.

Once we were off the bus and Mr. Fowler was out of the way, Callie looked at the map. "Okay," she said. "Cisco said to start with the Washington Monument. But do we even have time?"

"We have ten minutes," Nia said.

"But look up," I said. Because there it was, a giant needle reaching into the sky, twenty feet up a hill to our right.

I snapped a picture. We ran up the path and ducked inside—Mr. Fowler trotting behind us, marveling at the fact that, for once, there was no line. Quickly we all scanned for some kind of quote. I was taking pictures at the same time, which is why I noticed that when I looked through the lens of the camera, some of the words in one of the lines inscribed in the wall took on a glow, almost as if someone had painted over them with a gigantic highlighter.

"Do you see that?" I said, showing it to Nia. She looked at the letters, then looked through the lens of the camera. "I wonder if it means anything," she said. Just in case, I snapped a picture and she wrote the words down.

Train up a child in the way he should go and when he is old, he will not depart from it. Proverbs 22:6.

She underlined *Train up a child*, as those were the words

that, when viewed with the camera, seemed to glow.

The souls of efficiency, we turned on our heels and left. Three minutes total, and now it was 9:23.

The White House was next. Even with the digital zoom opened up all the way you could barely see it in my image, but that was nothing a little cropping couldn't take care of. The assignment said "photo." It said nothing about the resolution.

"Time check?" Hal said.

"Nine twenty-four," Nia answered.

"We're here." Callie was checking her watch and looking down at the map. "The World War Two Memorial is . . ." She looked up at the street signs. "Fifteenth Street and Constitution."

"Time is nine twenty-five," Hal warned.

We set off walking fast, noticing that a few other teams of students were headed in the same direction.

"There it is," Hal said, pointing about twenty yards ahead, where we could see columns and a fountain just across the road.

I recognized the World War II Memorial from the postcard Amanda had wedged inside the sunflower purse—it is a large plaza sunk into the ground with a fountain in the center, a wall in the back and curving rows of pillars on either side.

We had to cross 17th Street to get to the monument. While we waited for the light to change, Callie pointed to one of the other teams from our class. They were talking to a pair of park rangers. The way the rangers were standing, leaning forward on their toes—the kids on the team weren't asking the questions. The park rangers were.

"Are those guys in trouble?" Callie said, squinting.

Then suddenly, one of the rangers was staring at us. He was pointing, and I did what came naturally. I kicked out a foot to trip Hal and then scooted four steps to the left, whipping out my cell phone and pretending it had rung. Actually I pressed the speed dial for Hal.

"What the—?" Hal said. Callie bent down at his side.

Nia plowed over to me, irate. "You're on the phone?"

"Good," I said, glancing back at the rangers out of the corner of my eye. "Did you see how that one was pointing?" She nodded. "We're not close enough for him to see our faces, and there's a crowd. All he could tell is that we're in a group of four. I needed to break up our line, but more quickly than I could have if I'd told you all to move. Callie went to Hal. You followed me." I couldn't help smiling.

"You're kind of obnoxious," Nia noted, eyeing me up and down. I smiled even more.

By now my call had gone through. I had Hal on the line. "Sorry about that," I said, explaining.

Nia got out a map and pretended to examine it. "What should we do? Should we try to sneak away?"

"But Amanda might be there," Hal protested. "It's already nine thirty-four."

"We're never going to see her if we get stopped by

those two park rangers first," I said.

Callie said something to Hal I couldn't understand, but after, she bit her lip, obviously disappointed. I knew how she felt.

"What if you guys go around," I suggested. "Separately. Hang out at the back. Find someplace you can't be seen."

"What about you?" Hal sounded concerned.

"I can find out what the rangers are carrying on their clipboards," I said. "And you never know. Maybe Amanda's in there, in disguise. It's worth the risk."

"But you're not actually invisible," Nia warned. "I've been watching while we stand here. The rangers are checking every kid who goes in there."

"Don't worry," I said. "They'll see me. But what's important is—"

"—that they won't *know* they see you?" Nia said.

"Exactly," I answered, sounding way more confident than I actually felt.

After Nia, Callie, and Hal disappeared into the trees to the left of the monument, I made my way toward it. One of the rangers started to head toward me as I meandered down the shallow steps into the plaza. I took a good look at him. He was keyed up, edgy, on a mission. He was probably singing Nirvana in his head right now. If I even thought about Nirvana, it would be like attaching a loudspeaker to my face. He'd notice me for sure.

But spunky, early Beatles? If I could turn myself into

the lightly flying and swaying "Love Me Do," this guard would not be able to see me. I could tell just by the way he rolled his shoulders defensively that he was one of those boneheaded morons who don't understand what 90 percent of human beings love about the Beatles.

So I hummed as hard as I could. The music made me feel lighter, almost like I was floating on my tippy toes, barely touching the ground. I felt like my body had grown wispy, a lightly dancing cloud. I didn't look at the ranger directly, but I could see his legs and they were stopped as if he'd remembered something mid-stride.

He was working. Another student, Hannah R., was approaching, and he moved toward her. She wore leggings and a hoodie and chewed on her nails, covered in a pale pink polish, as she asked the ranger a question. I walked past and he didn't give me so much as a look.

I turned, as if admiring the majesty of the Washington Monument behind me, but really I was looking at his clipboard. He wasn't hugging it to his chest as carefully as he should have been.

Especially given that the photograph I saw on it was so incredibly large. It covered the entire board, and was something I recognized right away.

It was Amanda.

Not a great picture of her. And not a recent one. But it was still Amanda. Her hair was its natural light brown color, hanging down against her face. Her large gray-green eyes stared out at the camera and her mouth was turned up just enough so that I could see she didn't care much for the person taking the shot. School portrait? At Endeavor, she'd managed to be absent when they were taken, but at some other school in some other town, she must have not yet perfected her absenteeism.

Quickly, I turned my head to see if I could catch a glimpse of the other ranger's clipboard—but he was too far away.

Were these guys even park rangers for real? Or were they working for the Official, part of the group that was after Amanda?

Stepping into the monument, I kept my face toward the ground, covering it with my hair. Other kids from school were there, but I didn't look at them directly, giving them no reason to acknowledge me.

I pretended to read a quote engraved into one of the walls, inching my way closer to a third ranger, this one standing at the back of the monument. I took a bottle cap out of my pocket and tossed it behind me into the fountain.

The ranger I was near was not one of the pair I'd seen at the entrance. He had a clipboard though, so I assumed he was working with the other two. When he turned to see the splash, I followed his gaze, looking at his clipboard. But there was nothing on it except a stack of brochures about the memorial. As I was looking, this kid Sean Divine went up to the ranger and asked for one.

Was this third ranger for real? Were *all* the rangers for real? Because of the Smokey the Bear hats and the whole campfire talk association, park rangers have always seemed to me even more trustworthy than police officers, but now I didn't know what to think. If regular rangers were out to get us—if there was some sort of version of a Wanted poster up in the park rangers' office with our pictures on them—we were not going to be able to get away.

Did this Official—the one Hal's dad had told us had all those government connections—have that kind of control? Could he control the police? How about the army? Okay, that's ridiculous. He only had a couple of rangers, and not even all of them.

But how had he managed to find out that Amanda had sent us that message?

This was not a good time to be working these thoughts out in my head. I could feel myself starting to panic. I had to get myself under control.

I noticed a woman dressed in jogging clothes, standing on the other side of the fountain from me. She was watching me. Or at least I thought so. I couldn't see her face under her baseball cap, but she had her hands on her hips and was positioned with one heel perched up before her, stretching out the back of her leg. I caught her glancing up in my direction.

She wasn't Amanda—Amanda had at least three inches on this woman.

So why was she looking at me?

Pushing my panic way down deep inside, I forced

myself to go perfectly still. With my whole body I sent the message: There's nothing to see here. This body will do nothing interesting. I made every joint in my body—elbows, toes, neck, you name it—assume a neutral position. I took long, slow, even breaths. If the jogger was really just a jogger—if this whole ranger thing had just turned me paranoid—her gaze would move away from me.

I channeled Feist—you know, deep and mellow—music that makes me think about the feeling of being deep under water.

The jogger didn't look away.

This whole setup was starting to feel like a trap.

And speaking of traps, this memorial—the shape of it—suddenly struck me as a total disaster. It was sunk into a hollow in the earth, surrounded on three sides by ten-foot walls. The rangers were guarding the only way out.

And I had to get out.

I had to run.

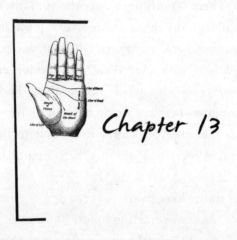

Chapter 13

"When you're in danger," Amanda had whispered when we were kids, playing games, following strangers at the grocery store, "think in opposites. When you want to run so badly you can feel the muscles in your legs actually starting to twitch? That's when you need to make your body perfectly still."

Boy, did I want to run now. It was like I'd already experienced it, so vivid was my understanding of what the hand clamping down on my shoulder would feel like—rough, not like a teacher, but like someone who didn't care that I was a kid.

This might be my last chance to make a break for it.

But I forced myself to stand still by reading the quotes in front of me. I picked up my camera to take a picture and I noticed that some of the words carved into the wall were glowing when I looked at them through my camera's lens. Just like at the Washington Monument, the letters had been treated in a way that was not visible to the naked eye. I snapped a picture of the inscription—the words, *The eyes of the world are upon you*, were highlighted—like some sort of blacklight chalk, not visible except through a camera's lens . . . but what did the highlighting mean? I read the inscription in its entirety in an attempt to understand.

D-DAY JUNE 6, 1944
YOU ARE ABOUT TO EMBARK UPON THE GREAT CRUSADE TOWARD WHICH WE HAVE STRIVEN THESE MANY MONTHS. THE EYES OF THE WORLD ARE UPON YOU. . . . I HAVE FULL CON-FIDENCE IN YOUR COURAGE, DEVOTION TO DUTY, AND SKILL IN BATTLE.

—General Dwight D. Eisenhower

I had to read through it three times before it penetrated my panicked brain, but for some reason, once I understood it, the quote gave me courage. My dad had told me about D-Day, so I knew it was the turning point in the war, with 5,000 boats transporting 150,000 men to the French shores in one day. Nine thousand of those men died before sunset.

The idea of the scene at the beach—the men leaping off the boats under machine gun fire, rushing the embankments topped with gun towers made of reinforced concrete (okay, I've seen *Saving Private Ryan*)—made the three park rangers seem a little less terrifying.

Sort of. They were still watching, though at least the jogger was gone. It was everything I could do to hold still long enough to evade their notice. I made sure to keep my head down. My hands were shaking, and I guessed that my whole body looked alert and tense—not good.

What had that quote said? *The eyes of the world are upon you.*

That's exactly what I'm worried about! I wanted to scream. Slowly, not breathing, I inched backward and forced myself to walk not toward the nearest exit, but away from it, strolling as if I was looking at the memorial. The second ranger from the front of the memorial began heading in my direction. Was he wondering why he hadn't had a chance to check me out on my way in?

Opposite, opposite. I didn't correct course. I didn't shy away from him. To keep calm, I counted the columns in my head over and over. And when he was close enough to me to really see, I pulled out the last trick that was up my sleeve. I stared. At the Washington Monument in the distance. Hard. I made my whole body tense up. This was a subtle equivalent of the old, "made you look" trick.

He bought it. For a hair of a second he looked where I'd been looking. But when he looked back to wonder why I'd been staring—and it was quick, it's not like the Washington Monument was on fire—I was gone. I'd used the moment his attention was focused elsewhere to slip between two columns—finding to my relief that a pavilion in the middle of the row of columns was open in the back. Before I exited the memorial through this lucky doorway, I looked back toward the guard, keeping myself hidden behind a column. I had a good view of his clipboard, which I was expecting to hold another giant picture of Amanda.

But instead I saw a series of smaller images. There was one of Hal. One of Nia. One of Callie. And one of me.

Seeing my own face—and those of the other guides, knowing that we were all being hunted now—my breath caught in my throat. Not that I wasn't already scared.

But I didn't have time. Because there was one last picture on the board blocked by the ranger's shoulder. I was waiting for him to turn so I could see it. Soon enough, he did turn, and there was a picture of Amanda's sister. The one Thornhill had told us to come to Washington to find. He'd called her Robin, and I knew that was the name she was born with. But when I knew her, she had been Ravenna.

In the picture she was wearing a high ponytail, a white vest, and a black-and-white-striped skirt. She was smiling forthrightly at the camera, her big blue eyes open wide. When I'd met her she'd been a ninth grader, like I was currently, and now she would be in college. But the years that had passed didn't matter. I'd have known her anywhere.

The same wide eyes, open forehead, a smile that was hard to resist. Robin was adopted, but still, she and Amanda looked a lot alike.

I remembered the last time I saw Ravenna. It was just before Amanda's family left Pinkerton. She'd come home from cheerleading practice, all excited to have been elected team captain. What was she doing with her picture next to ours—how did the rangers know that she might be here too?

As soon as I was out of the view of the rangers, I broke out into a run, all the panic I'd been fighting inside the monument boiling over within me. When I didn't see Callie, Hal, and Nia right away, I could feel my breath coming faster.

How stupid, I thought. If there were fake rangers inside the monument, of course some would have been patrolling the outside of it. Callie, Hal, and Nia had probably walked right into them. I'd been worried for myself, but actually it was they who hadn't been safe.

Nia's hissed "Zoe" was the happiest sound I'd heard that day. I turned to see her crouching in an alcove that must have led to some kind of service entrance to the monument. Hal and Callie were there too, ducking behind the little wall. I ran to join them, and not a minute too soon.

Peeking over the wall, I heard and then saw the two rangers from the monument walking by.

"Oh no," Callie said, seeing them. "Those rangers— they're the guards from the airstrip. Didn't you notice the one with the tattoo on his face? That's hard to miss."

"Right," I said, seeing the tattoo for the first time. "I guess I was doing everything in my power *not* to register them—I never got a good look at their faces."

I saw the guard's face now, though. The one with the tattoo was the angry, jittery one—the Nirvana guard. The guard we'd seen eating crackers and sleeping on the job was the other, the one holding the school pictures of the four of us and Robin.

I explained that having the Official's guards disguise themselves as park rangers was better than having the Official be able to commandeer actual rangers.

Nia understood right away what I was getting at. "Can you imagine how easy it would be for them to capture Amanda if they had access to law enforcement in the city?"

"Was Amanda out here?" I breathed.

They shook their heads. "She wasn't inside the monument either," I explained. I told them about the pho-tographs. About the jogger who seemed impervious to my ability to hide.

Callie drew her arms around her body like suddenly she felt cold.

Hal ran his hands through his hair. "This is getting—" he began. "This is all getting so real."

Nia pursed her lips. Her eyes narrowed into slits. Her signature glare. "I don't like whoever is doing this to us," she said. "And to Amanda."

"Me neither," I said, but I let the rest of what I wanted

to say drift away, because I'd just noticed something carved into the wall.

For a second I wondered if it was a mistake.

"Look at that," I said, pointing.

Nia nodded quickly. "I was wondering about that too," she said. "I have a feeling about it. When I touch it, I don't know—it's like I can feel Amanda here somehow."

I put my fingers on top of the carving, a simple cartoon of a face peering over a wall next to the words KILROY WAS HERE.

"I know what this is," Nia said.

"Care to explain?" Callie inquired.

" 'Kilroy was here' is a famous piece of World War Two graffiti," she began. "A ship inspector named Kilroy chalked it on boats he'd inspected. The thousands of soldiers who were transported to war on those boats remembered it and started putting it everywhere. By the end of the war the words 'Kilroy was here' had been scrawled, engraved, painted, and otherwise applied to hundreds of thousands of locations in Europe, North Africa, and the Pacific—in village churches, on cave walls, in prison cells, in bombed-out barns and submarine bunks and foxholes."

"That's cool that they included it in the monument," Hal said.

"I know," I said. "And it's also really cool that they hid it."

"Yes, it is cool," Callie said. "Maybe you guys should

actually join the History Club for real. But me? I'm more interested in why Nia had a feeling about it."

Nia shrugged. "I don't know. It wasn't a feeling that was very strong. Mostly what I was thinking was that Amanda would have liked this—a cartoon face carved in a hiding place where everything else is so formal and grand."

"Let me see something," I offered, lifting my camera to my face. I explained how the words inside the monument had glowed when I'd done this. Sure enough, *Kilroy was here* glowed in the same way.

"Look," Hal said. There were old dead leaves collected in the alcove, piled up against the back of it, right under the Kilroy cartoon. As Hal kicked the leaves away, we saw some more graffiti. Newer graffiti. Graffiti all four of us understood instantly.

Chalked onto the wall were drawings of a bear, a cougar, a night owl, and a chameleon. The shapes of their bodies were elongated in the drawing, so that they twisted into one snakelike shape—a vine, or maybe a string worked through an invisible maze.

"*This* is from Amanda," I said. I could hear the sound of triumph in my voice. Nia nodded.

"How could that be, though?" said Callie. "How could Amanda have known we'd end up here?"

"Maybe she left this drawing to show us a safe place to hide," I offered.

"But we wouldn't have seen the drawing until we'd already found the hiding place," Nia said. When she is figuring things out, she has a hard time keeping the arrogance out of her voice—though she isn't arrogant deep down.

Hal only shrugged. "Maybe she figured we would. Maybe it was farfetched but she went with it."

"Everything with Amanda is farfetched," Callie said.

"Wait!" Hal pointed at Nia. "Do you still have the D.C. postcard?"

She pulled it out of her pocket and passed it to Hal.

"Look," he said, pointing to the V mark we'd noticed before. "This V is right where we're hiding." He pointed with his finger and scrutinized it, but it was still hard to know if the shadow on the outside of the monument was an alcove.

"But we didn't figure that out," Nia said. "No one could have."

"And yet we're here," said Callie. "We found it."

"She knew we would," I said. "It's the only place to hide. She knew that I'd figure out how to keep us from being seen. Or that you would, Hal. She knew Nia would be drawn to the Kilroy. I think these guys are really close on her heels and she just wants us to know that she is still with us. She can't come out here, but she is close. Or maybe that's what I want to think."

For a minute, as we digested this new understanding, we all just sat staring at the animals drawn on the wall. I knew we needed to keep moving, that it wasn't safe to stay at the monument too long, but still, I didn't want to go.

"They're beautiful, you know that?" said Hal, pointing to the chalked drawing. "It reminds me of Thornhill's car. I mean, on the one hand it was an act of desperation, a message, a clue, a start to all of this. And on the other hand, it was a work of art. Everything she touches just seems to radiate with Amanda-ness."

Nia sighed, and I recognized in the sadness of that sigh my own sadness about Amanda. I missed her. All of this would seem less scary, and I would feel less lost, if only she were here.

"When I was with her," Callie said, blushing, "everything felt like it was going to be okay. Everything that I thought was bad about myself seemed, well, seemed kind of cool."

Hal traced a finger along the outside edge of Amanda's swirled drawing and without thinking about it too much, I followed the train his finger left in chalk dust. The overall shape. Was it important? Was it a letter? It was hard not to follow the animals' eyes, all of which were directed toward the ground, as if they were looking for something to burst from a cavity in the earth.

Just as I was about to suggest that maybe we should try to break open the alcove's door, or look for a key, or something, Hal kicked aside the last of the leaves collected on the grate, and exclaimed, "Hey, guys, look, I just found five dollars!"

"Really?" said Callie.

"How often does that happen?" said Hal. "I've found

quarters and stuff, but I don't think I've ever found a five-dollar bill lying on the ground."

"It's found money," said Callie. "That's good luck."

"I guess," said Hal.

"Or maybe it's more than good luck. Maybe Amanda left it here," Nia said. "Maybe it's part of the clue."

"But what does it mean?" said Callie.

"Wait a minute," I said. "Can I see it?"

Hall passed me the bill. I smoothed it out across my knee. A five-dollar bill. I looked into Abraham Lincoln's chiseled face, his impassive gaze, his firmly set mouth. And then I turned the bill over, and there it was, as plain as day.

"I've got it," I said, and showed them what suddenly seemed like the most obvious thing in the world.

"Got what?" said Nia.

"Yeah," said Hal. "What are you talking about?"

Pinching the bill on both sides, I put my hands together and drew them apart again quickly so that I could hear the paper snap.

"Check this out," I said. "Look right here!"

It was so obvious to me, I couldn't understand at first why Hal, Nia, and Callie were looking at me with blank faces. "Don't you see?" I went on. "It's a picture of the Lincoln Memorial. Amanda must be waiting for us there."

"That's the Lincoln Memorial?" Callie asked.

"It looks so familiar," Nia said. "I thought it was the Parthenon."

"That's because your mom isn't Greek," I said. "It

may have been inspired by the Greeks, but if you had pictures and little replicas of the Parthenon surrounding you since birth, you'd never be confused. And the Lincoln Memorial, my friends, is something like three hundred yards over there."

I pointed, and without even having to speak a word, Nia and I erased the chalk with the sleeves of our jackets, and the four of us started off.

As we speed-walked alongside the reflecting pool that separates the World War II Memorial from the Lincoln Memorial, I couldn't help thinking of a scene in that '90s movie my mom likes to watch when it comes on TV—*Forrest Gump*. When Forrest is speaking at a rally in front of the Lincoln Memorial, love-of-his-life Jenny runs through the reflecting pool in her eagerness to reunite with him. Part of me wanted to jump into the pool too, I was in such a hurry.

But if you had a list of ways of remaining unnoticed in our nation's capital, jumping into a fountain would not be on it anywhere. "Slow down," I warned the others. "We're supposed to look like tourists, remember?"

We slowed our pace and walked in silence.

I snapped a few shots with my camera as we were walking, partly to make it look like we really were tourists and partly out of habit.

I scanned through the pictures I was taking, and in one of the images I'd just shot, I saw something in the top right corner. Something that gave me pause.

Highlighting that quadrant of the picture and then zooming in, I was able to make out the shape that had looked like nothing more than a slash of black before.

It was a jogger. The one from the Memorial. She was running, but the light was shining on her face and I could see she'd been looking. At us. She'd been watching. She knew where we were.

I looked up, scanning the path where she'd been running but it was empty now except for a little girl riding a bike, and her dad jogging along at her side.

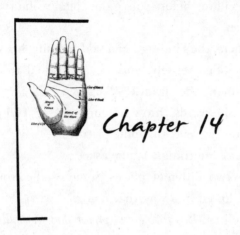

Chapter 14

Here's the thing about the Lincoln Memorial. It is simply very large.

The columns alone are forty-four feet tall, and as you climb the five flights of steps on the front of the building, you feel smaller and smaller. Once you get inside, forget it.

Abraham Lincoln was the tallest president in history to begin with, but this statue is nineteen feet taller than he was in real life. I was so jittery I would have felt intimidated by a life-size sculpture of a squirrel.

Fortunately, the only park ranger we saw was talking to a bunch of old people, and there was no clipboard in sight.

I scanned the crowd for Amanda. If you're looking for someone in a wig, suddenly everyone's hair looks fake. It testifies to her penchant for elaborate costuming that

I spent a good minute looking at an old man wheeling around an iron lung before ruling out the possibility that it could be her.

"If she's here, she's hiding," Nia said, keeping her voice low. Callie nodded tensely, and we all started to walk around and among the gigantic pillars.

"Look at the words through your camera," Hal said, and I lifted it to my eye, snapping pictures.

"Do you see anything?" Callie asked.

I did. In two different places, some of the words I was reading glowed in a way that matched what I'd seen before. In the line, *It is fitting and proper that we shall have here a new birth of freedom,* the words, *we shall have here a new birth of freedom* were highlighted.

And then I put the camera down. Fast.

I grabbed Callie's arm. But when Nia said, "What is it?" all I could do was look at her and try to communicate with seriously raised eyebrows that something was very wrong. Which helped not at all.

Because I had seen something. Or rather, someone. It was the jogger. She was close. She had seen us. And now she was headed straight in our direction.

There are some situations were even all my invisibility tricks just don't work. With my unobstructed view of the floor, I could see the jogger's sneakers moving swiftly toward me. Purposefully striding. This was not someone pausing in the midst of a run to admire the monument's grandeur. This was not someone stopped to stretch. This was no jogger.

When I heard my name, I think I jumped out of my skin. "Zoe?" the jogger said, and as I looked up three things happened simultaneously.

The jogger took off her baseball cap.

I felt the words *It's okay, it's okay, it's okay* pulsing into my brain like they would after you have a bad fall but realize you're not bleeding and you haven't broken anything.

And I said, "Ravenna," because I knew then who the jogger was. It was not someone to fear. It was one of the people we'd come here to find. And once I saw her without her cap, I realized it was someone I would know anywhere.

I wondered how I could ever have been afraid of her. She looked so, well, so normal in her yoga pants and sweatshirt, her iPod buds hanging down from her shoulders, her dark ponytail springing to life now that her baseball cap was removed. Ravenna Bruyere. Robin Beckendorf. Amanda's sister.

Ravenna was the kind of older sister who had always made me feel like I was special. Back when I was ten, I thought she knew how to do everything my ten-year-old self thought a girl in high school should be able to do: track team, yearbook staff, algebra, field hockey. She'd been a cheerleader, an honor student.

Compared to Amanda, she was resolutely normal. But there were also things about her that weren't. When

Amanda fell off her bike and gashed her knee, Ravenna spoke briefly to their mom on the phone, then scrubbed her hands very carefully, put on surgical gloves, cleaned out Amanda's wound, injected a tiny shot of anesthetic and gave Amanda a stitch. What normal teenager can do that? What normal household has that on hand? Theirs did.

"You know how to do that?" I'd said, my jaw hanging open.

Ravenna had grinned. "Mom hates doctors," she'd explained. Later, when I asked my mom and dad about it, they'd exchanged significant looks, sighed, and hadn't answered my question.

"Zoe Costas?" Ravenna called out now softly. She was speaking in a low voice and checking over her shoulder to make sure no one was watching, but she couldn't keep the enthusiasm out of her voice. She opened up her arms and before I knew it, she'd pulled me toward her. "How are you? Girl, I missed you. How's your mom? Iris? Pen?"

I quickly told her that everyone was fine. I couldn't stop looking at her, though. There were things she did—a way of crinkling up her eyes when she smiled, moving her hands when she talked—that reminded me of Amanda. And her smell—part drugstore hand cream, part musky body spray, reminded me of home and my life before Orion. Of my dad.

"I'm so sorry about—about everything," she said into

my ear as she hugged me again. "Someday we're going to have to talk all about it."

"Okay," I mumbled. I didn't trust myself to say much else without crying. In fact, I was already sniffling. I wiped a tear away with the back of my sleeve, hoping the others wouldn't see. A totally ridiculous idea, as they were all staring at me.

Though they weren't staring because I was crying.

"Um, Zoe?" Nia said. "Why are you hugging my brother's girlfriend?"

There was a second where I was so confused by Nia's question I didn't even understand what she meant. "Cisco's girlfriend?" I repeated. "I don't think so. This is Amanda's sister, Ravenna."

"No it's not," Nia said. "That's Rosie. Rosie O'Connor. She's a college student in D.C. She met Cisco when he was at some soccer clinic near her dorm. They've been going out for months."

"Yeah," said Hal. "I've met her." He looked at Ravenna. "I mean, you." He turned back to me. "At the *As You Like It* performance at school."

"She's been to my *house*," Nia said.

Openmouthed, I turned to Ravenna. "Is this true?" I said.

She nodded. And then she smiled. This huge, light-up-the-sky smile that made me remember why everyone had always wanted to be her friend. "My name is Rosie

149

now." She turned to Nia and Hal. "But Zoe's right too. I *am* Ariel's, I mean, *Amanda's* sister."

"But how—?" I started.

"The Cisco thing?" Rosie laughed. "I wasn't looking for anything like that—it just happened." Of course. Ravenna had always dated the cutest guy in her grade when we lived in Pinkerton. She had that wholesome, J. Crew, straight-A-student thing going on—no one had been able to resist it. Even in undercover mode, dating probably did "just happen."

"But you're in college," I said. "Aren't you too old for him?"

"My mom thought so," Nia said. Hal snorted a laugh into his hand, pretending to pass it off as a cough. Mrs. Rivera is awesome—warm, protective, supportive—but if she doesn't like something one of her kids is doing, she doesn't make a secret of it.

"Cisco's only two years younger than I am." Ravenna seemed not in the least bothered by Nia's attitude or Hal's barely disguised guffaw. "He's a junior and I'm a freshman. And look—"

We all turned to see Cisco climbing the last of the steps into the temple, leading a few teams of students, his face showing first surprise, then confusion, then confused happiness. "Guys," he said to the students he was leading. "Go write down some quotes. I need to check in with my sister over there."

"Hey," he said, shooting his butter-melting smile

at Ravenna, then Nia, then the rest of us, then back to Ravenna. I'd never seen Cisco look at anyone the way he was looking at Ravenna. *Wow*, I thought, he really likes her. "What are you doing down here in tourist-land? I thought campus was way up there." He gestured in a northerly direction.

"Oh, you know," Ravenna said. "Internship stuff."

"In your jogging clothes?" Cisco raised his eyebrows.

"Cisco!" Nia said, her voice a whisper that was also, somehow, a shout. "Do you realize that your girlfriend also happens to be Amanda's sister?" If she'd said, "also happens to be a two-headed bullfighting leprechaun," she wouldn't have needed to adjust her tone of voice.

Cisco's eyes grew wide. "Rosie?" he said. I don't know what reaction Nia was expecting him to have, but Cisco seemed, more than anything, to be impressed. "Really?"

She nodded. "Sorry," she said. "I couldn't tell you. You understand, right?"

But Cisco couldn't even take that question in yet. "Really?" he repeated. "You've been Amanda's sister—" He paused. "The whole time?"

"Well, since she was born." Ravenna laughed.

"I guess that would be true," he mused, running his fingers through his gorgeous dark hair. "And you just happened to run into these guys? Because you're working at your internship?" You could hear the doubt in his voice growing as the startling coincidences started to mount.

"No," she said, her voice serious now. She smiled at

him. She held his gaze, making sure he knew she was sincere. "Of course not . . . you *do* understand?" she said. "You don't think I was using you, do you?"

Cisco ran his hand through his hair. "Look, Rosie. I don't care what your name is, I know who you are."

"Okay," she said smiling in relief. The two of them just stared at each other that way a couple of beats until Nia said, "Guys?"

"Right," Rosie said. She ducked her head, indicating that we should step out of the way. We followed her to a relatively hidden spot to one side of Lincoln's seat.

"Is Amanda coming?" Callie asked.

Rosie shook her head. "I don't think so. She told me to find you at the World War Two Memorial, but when I got there and saw the guards, I followed you here."

"Amanda told you—" Nia said. "Does that mean you've seen her?"

"No," Rosie said. "I wish. She sends me notes. In code. I haven't seen her since we chalked my dad's car."

"That was *you*?" Hal said. "We saw another figure in the surveillance video, but didn't know who it was."

"And hello?" Callie said. "Thornhill *is* your dad?"

"You didn't figure that out already?"

"We knew," Nia said. She doesn't ever like to admit she doesn't know something. "But we didn't *know* know. I mean, for sure."

"What happened to your mom?" I said. "We saw a

newspaper clipping about a car accident—was that real?"

"It was," Rosie said, swallowing hard.

"Your mom was killed?" I said. "By the Official?"

"For what it's worth, I don't think he meant to kill her," Rosie said. I could tell that this was painful for her to talk about. She slowed down as if she couldn't tell this story without going into all the details. "She was running. We were always running, except for the time we were in Pinkerton. There, we were happy. We knew we had to leave, but we didn't want to. We stayed too long, and when we learned it was time to go, we didn't want to leave. We waited . . . too long. We let the guys who were after us get too close. We got away that time, then later, they found us again. My mom was trying to lose the Official's people one night. She was driving. It was late. Roads were slippery. I think her death actually set Dr. Joy back, because with Mom gone, Amanda just took off. She was just starting to come into her powers, realizing what she could do, and she freaked out. And of course, with her abilities, she was able to disappear totally. I think she would settle somewhere for months at a time, but then she'd take off again. Even knowing all the tricks my mom taught us over the years, I couldn't find her. I'd get a clue as to her whereabouts, I'd come running, but it seemed that when I got to wherever she last was, the trail was always cold. So I set out to find my dad. That's how I ended up out here."

"Do you think my dad was killed by accident too?" I said. "Or do you think—?" I could barely speak the words. It was something I hadn't let myself say out loud before. I know it may sound obvious. If I was reading a book or watching a show on TV, I would have assumed that the bad guys did it. But this was my dad. *My* dad. The one with the saggy belly I'd laid my head against when I was sick. The one who used to sing "Swing Low, Sweet Chariot" when he washed dishes after dinner. The one who used to love to tell stupid jokes. How could he have been murdered? How could the life he was supposed to have, the life he deserved, how could that have been stolen from him? From me?

Rosie put her hands on my shoulders, looked at me hard. I could see in her eyes that she understood what I was feeling. "All I know is something I heard *my* dad saying one time. He said there are lots of ways of making it appear as if someone had a heart attack, when in actuality he was poisoned. Also, he said your dad had to be killed. He said your dad was like him—a soldier. They'd been raised together. As a team, they would have been impossible to stop. For a long time, George didn't want to get involved at all. He didn't want to put you, your mom, and your sisters in danger. But in the year before he died, he and my dad had been in communication. They'd decided to work together. My dad said George had been getting ready to move your family underground, and then join him."

"So he was murdered," I said. "And your dad—he's in captivity."

"His life isn't in danger yet, though. My understanding is that they want to study him." Rosie's pretty blue eyes had filled with tears. "Look," she said. "There's a lot I wish I could tell you about what my father believes is going on. But I'm worried about our time."

"Who's following you?" Cisco looked protective. "Want me to take care of them?"

Rosie smiled at Cisco wistfully and I saw in that smile that she really was older than him. Or maybe it wasn't the years—it was what she had seen. "I want you to stay as far away from them as possible," she said. "Believe it or not, my little sister is our best protection these days."

"Protection from whom, exactly?" Nia said. "This goes beyond Dr. Joy now, doesn't it? Who is sending the goons after us today?"

Rosie's lips tightened into a narrow line. "You've heard of the Official, right?"

"My dad said he was working with Dr. Joy to revive the C33 program," said Hal.

"That's right." Rosie sighed. "He's in charge of the government agency where I'm interning. The agency is supposed to be monitoring the testing of experimental vaccines, but actually it's administering a secret project with only a few top people in the know."

"You work right under their noses?" I said. "But the

photos . . . the rangers . . ." Suddenly, I put two and two together. I put a hand up to cover my mouth.

"You can't go back there."

"Why not?" Rosie looked at her watch. "They'll notice if I'm gone much longer."

"But the pictures," I said. "They know." Nia drew in a breath—just those few words were enough for her to connect the dots. "Did you by any chance get a look at the rangers' clipboards back at the World War Two monument?" I said. Rosie shook her head, and I explained what I'd seen. I could see from the look on her face that she was starting to understand.

"They must have known for some time," she said. "Maybe that explains—"

"Explains what?" Cisco said.

She looked away from us, as if she had forgotten our presence, and was just thinking aloud. "Explains how I can't get anywhere near whatever it is they're really doing. I see Dr. Joy, but no matter how many excuses I come up with, I can't even get into the hallway near his office."

"Rosie," Cisco said, concern wrinkling his forehead—I caught myself wondering for an instant if anyone would ever look at me in the way Cisco was looking at Rosie now, like all he wanted in the world was to protect her. He put a hand on her arm. "Don't go back there. It's just not safe."

But Rosie didn't even register his warning. "I'd been hoping to at least find out who the Official is. A name, anything. With Amanda on the run . . . it's not right. My mom is gone and my dad is who-knows-where. I should be looking out for her."

"You are," I said.

Rosie smiled at me, back to being an older sister.

"Have you seen him, at least?" Nia asked. "Thornhill told us he was in charge. Do you know what he looks like?"

"I don't," Rosie said. "But I hear him referred to all the time. He has ties to the government, but I haven't been able to figure out what the connections are."

"Wow," I said, "I thought it was bad enough that Chief Bragg was involved. But now it's like the actual federal government."

"Oh, no, not all of it," Rosie said. "And you know, it's funny. My dad suspected Chief Bragg of being involved but that was not confirmed—now, of course, who knows what my dad thinks. There's something strange about the way the Bragg family keeps turning up. But anyway, the Official isn't the president or a Supreme Court justice or anything. What he's doing is illegal, and with the right kind of evidence we could bring him down. As long as he doesn't get whatever it is before then—we think he will be harder to stop them."

"What is he looking for?"

"I don't know," Rosie said. "I don't think anyone knows for sure. And I guess now I'll never find out." The cloud of frustration reappeared on her face, and then she clearly willed it away. "Okay, let's focus on what we do know. We know that whatever the Official is up to, it has something to do with Amanda. Something to do with the way she is. Amanda told me that I should be watching you guys," Rosie went on. "She said you might all be learning from her. Do you know what that means?"

Hal blushed. Callie looked up at the ceiling. Nia looked down at the floor.

"Sometimes," I said. "We do things that we really shouldn't be able to do."

Cisco was nodding. "Nia's been telling me about this," he said. "It's crazy."

"You have powers like Amanda's?" Rosie said. "My dad said you would."

"Mr. Bennett told us that kids of C33s sometimes have them," I said. "Do you?"

Rosie shook her head. "No chance. I'm adopted, as you know. But even if I weren't, it's more likely that children of C33s have no superhuman talents." She smiled. "Cisco here . . . he's just naturally handsome and athletic and charming."

"What?" Cisco said, his huge "Who me?" smile making us all relax.

"What about Heidi Bragg?" Cisco said. "She's always struck me as having some noteworthy . . . talents."

"Heidi Bragg's an interesting case," Rosie said. "My dad was trying to figure her out when he was abducted. Brittney was always a disappointment as a C33, but then Heidi emerged with her take-no-prisoners personality—but no one's been able to figure out what, if anything, she can really do."

"How did Amanda know how to find *us*?" Nia asked. "Did she know what we were going to be able to do?"

"No," Rosie said. "Amanda knew the children of a lot of former C33s were living in Orion. So she went there, started school, and made friends with the kids she wanted to make friends with. She told me she was letting the friendships come to her, actually. And I guess yours did."

"I guess so," said Callie.

We were quiet a minute, letting all this new information sink in. I had to admit, I liked the idea that Amanda and I were friends not because she needed me, but because she liked me. She used her instinct for friendship as a divining rod.

"Here," Rosie said, passing two purple envelopes in our direction. "Amanda sent these to me. I have no idea what they are, but I think she wanted me to pass them on to you."

Nia took the envelopes and immediately went white, grabbing her brother for support.

"What is it?" I said.

"Did you see something?" asked Hal.

"Yeah," said Nia, rubbing her fingers over the envelopes' sides. "Thornhill. These envelopes were in his office on the night he was attacked."

"Can you see who attacked him?" Hal asked.

"Not yet," said Nia. "It might work better if I had some extra hands."

We didn't want to draw attention to ourselves by looking like we were forming a prayer circle, so we touched casually—I bumped shoulders with Hal, who put his hand on Callie's back. She hooked a finger through the edge of Nia's pocket and Nia stretched her foot toward mine so we were touching.

Maybe because we weren't actually holding hands—I don't know—but this time, we did not see Nia's vision as she did. We held the linked pose a few seconds, then Nia broke away.

"Amazing," she said.

"What?" said Rosie.

"It's Amanda. She was with Thornhill on the night he was attacked. Amanda was holding these envelopes and then someone was coming, so he shoved them under the top of the desk and pretty much pushed her out the window."

"Wow," said Callie.

"She snuck back in there?" Rosie said. "I told her not to. It wasn't safe. But I guess she must have. And then mailed them to me. You'll see they're postmarked. She must have gotten them in the mail from someone originally, and brought them in to show Dad."

The seal on both envelopes had been broken and Hal dumped out their contents—two credit card–sized pieces of plastic, one red, one blue. "Do you think they're gift cards?" he said.

"Gift cards?" Callie teased, because, yeah, it did seem completely crazy to think that Amanda would have gone to such lengths to get us gift cards. "Like . . . to the Gap?"

"Okay, I get it, dumb idea," Hal said.

Nia took one of the cards in her hand. "Are you seeing any images?" I asked.

Nia shook her head.

A ranger stepped into the monument. He was leading a school group, so I assumed he was not one of the false rangers, but still, his presence was enough to remind us that they could find us here at any time. "I have to go," Rosie said. Her eyes were filled with regret, as if leaving us when we clearly still had a lot to talk about was a repeat of her having to separate from Amanda.

"Not back to your internship," Cisco said.

"No," she answered. "I've got other things to do." She situated her ear buds in her ears, pulled her cap down, and looked as grim as someone as nice as she is possibly can. "Guys," she said. She looked into each of our eyes for a strong and steady beat. I wanted to give her one last hug, something, but she'd already turned away. I squeezed my hand into a fist. One more connection to my old life—gone. Ravenna transformed to Rosie transformed into another anonymous runner in the city.

Hal's eyes suddenly opened wide. "We've got to get going too," he said. *"Now."*

Then, whispering, "Follow me."

"I have to check in with other groups," Cisco said. "But I'm not going to be happy if you guys don't make the lunchtime check-in, you hear?"

"Got it," Nia said.

We sped after Hal down the first flight of steps and then around to the other side of the memorial, where there was a little lawn dotted with shrubs large enough for four of us to hide behind. We couldn't see the steps from where we were hiding, but we could hear what sounded like guards—were there three of them? I wondered. Four? The tempo of their boots on the steps matched the rushing beat of my heart. As soon as they'd passed us, Hal stood and beckoned for us. We jogged down the stairs as quietly as we could.

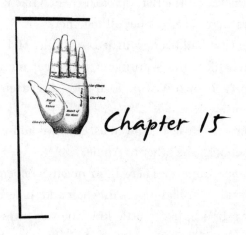

Chapter 15

As soon as the Lincoln Memorial was out of sight, we stopped to catch our breath under a cherry tree that was in full bloom.

I had a feeling in the pit of my stomach that wouldn't go away. My body was itching to disappear, to fade away, or wait out the rest of this Amanda adventure under the cover of the nearest rock. I reminded myself: Amanda needs you.

To steady myself, I turned to the nearest map posted on a kiosk next to our bench. According to the map's "You Are Here," we were on the western end of the Mall, heading north to Constitution Avenue.

"If we keep walking in this direction, we'll reach the Vietnam War Memorial," I said. "It's on the scavenger hunt."

"First we need to look at the envelopes," Nia said, laying all of them out on the flat top of the bench like it was a table. There were six envelopes all together.

The ones that had been returned to Callie, Hal, and Nia all looked like mine—no name, no street number, addressed in their own writing as if they'd written the envelope themselves.

There were two Rosie had given us. One was addressed to Max Beckendorf, the other to Annie.

I picked up Annie's. "There is so much I remember about her," I said. "She had super-curly hair and sometimes wore it in two braids, like a little kid. She was awesome with accents," I said. "She could do any of them. And she could tell what you were thinking. We never got away with anything when she was around."

Nia laid the pieces of plastic on top of the Max and Annie envelopes.

"Okay," Hal said, looking at what Nia had laid out. "This remains completely confusing."

I didn't say anything because I'd stopped thinking about the cards. I was looking at our envelopes and thinking about the "You Are Here" map.

"What a minute," I said out loud.

"What?" Hal said.

"Look at your envelope," I said. "It's addressed to 20th Street NW. Shouldn't it be significant that Callie's is addressed to 21st Street NW?"

I grabbed Nia's note, addressed to C Street NW, and I went back to the posted map. "C Street . . . that's just up there, on the other side of Constitution. It intersects with both 20th and 21st Streets. And—"

Nia was getting what I meant. She grabbed the envelope addressed to me and ran over to the map. "Constitution Avenue itself."

Callie and Hal joined us at the map. "It's a city block," Hal breathed. "The four streets on the envelopes outline a city block."

Suddenly all the exhaustion we'd felt after running from the park rangers was gone.

Callie looked at her watch. "We only have an hour until we have to report back to Mr. Fowler for lunch."

"Wait," said Hal. "Look at the scavenger hunt list. There's something on that block on our list."

"Where?" said Callie, leaning over his shoulder.

"It's extra credit," he said. "It's called the Natural Sciences Institute—it's some kind of museum, I think. Plus it's a research facility."

We didn't have time to discuss it. If we wanted to make it to the block the envelopes described and then get back to the Washington Monument in time for lunch, we had to fly.

The Natural Sciences Institute took up most of the block described by C Street on the north, Constitution Avenue on the south, and 20th and 21st Streets on the east and west. It looked like a smaller version of the Museum of Natural History in New York. There were steps in the front where people were sitting and soaking up some sun. I saw some kids from our grade—science geeks mostly—running down the steps. They'd already been inside.

Brian Bellaronda and Ally Kline stopped to ask us how many monuments we'd seen. "We've only got twelve so far," they said. "We're so going to fail."

We showed them our hunt list. We only had four.

"Wow," said Brian, looking at Ally like suddenly they'd noticed we were sick and they didn't want to catch what we had.

Once they'd left, we took a second to look up at the imposing front of the museum looming over us at the top of the long flight of steps. "Do you think that whatever we're looking for is inside?" Callie said. "It's going to be pretty tricky to find anything in there. It's huge."

"And we don't even know precisely what we're looking for," Nia added.

"I thought we were looking for Amanda," I said. "I thought she was finally going to show herself."

"Maybe," said Nia, bitterly. "But more likely there's some song lyric she wants us to find and be inspired by." Nia sat down on a bench, as if to catch her breath. But then she jumped up, saying "Hal, Zoe, Callie—come here. It's this bench."

She was holding out her hands so I took one, Callie

took the other, and Hal stood in between us. An image rushed up before our eyes. A woman, sitting on the same bench that Nia was sitting on now. You could tell from the way the woman's long legs were tucked to the side that she was tall. She was older, too—the age of one of our teachers maybe—and beautiful, her blond hair shot through with a few streaks of silver, her eyes big, though sad. The sky was gray and low and the woman was picking off pieces of the sandwich she was eating and tossing them to the hungry pigeons.

I opened my eyes to see that Callie's face had gone white. "That's—" she said. "She's—she's here?"

"Who is here?" I said. Callie had dropped hands with us.

"This is why Amanda brought us here," Callie said. "It's my mom." Callie gave us all about half a second to digest this information before she started asking Nia questions she couldn't possibly answer. "What is she doing here? Is she looking for me? When was that image from?"

Nia shook her head. "I don't know."

"She was wearing an ID, did you see that, though?" said Hal. "On a cord around her neck, like you see doctors wearing in hospitals."

"Maybe she works around here."

"She works?" Callie said. Mrs. Leary had left a note for Mr. Thornhill saying she had to leave because it was the only way to keep Callie safe. I could tell that Callie was doubting that statement now. How did having a regular job fifty miles away serve that purpose?

"It's lunchtime," I said, looking at my watch. "Or almost. Maybe we're supposed to wait here for your mom. We have a few minutes still until we have to check in with Mr. Fowler."

"Yeah, maybe," Callie said, crossing her arms in front of her chest.

"I don't know if you could tell from the expression on your mom's face," I said, "but she's sad."

"Really?" Callie said.

"You couldn't see it?" I said.

"Well, she wasn't jumping for joy. She just looked kind of blank to me."

"Not to me," I said. "Her mouth had this little tremble to it, like she was about to cry."

"Really?" Callie said again.

"Her gaze was unfocused too," I said.

"I thought she was just feeding the pigeons," Callie said.

"She was," I explained. "But her attention wasn't on them. She didn't move her head as they moved. She was thinking about something," I ended.

"What was she thinking about?" Callie asked.

"Why don't you ask her yourself?" Nia said, a huge but somewhat worried smile spreading across her face. "She's coming right now." While Hal and I had been focused on Callie, Nia had been looking up at the museum, and we followed her gaze now to see the woman from the bench in Nia's vision coming down the museum steps.

"So are a pair of rangers," Hal said. "Any minute now. They're hot on our heels. We need to hide."

"But my mom—" Callie began, torn at having her so close.

"Zoe," he said. "Can you get to her without the guards seeing you?

I nodded. "Then you get Mrs. Leary," he said. "Nia, Callie, follow me." He started heading for a series of large bushes that were big enough to stand behind and still not be seen. Just as the three of them ducked away out of sight, the rangers Hal had predicted rounded the corner and started looking up and down the stairs, checking clipboards, radioing in a conversation I was not close enough to hear. I flipped up the hood of my sweatshirt, and I know this time it's going to sound crazy, but I think I managed to camouflage myself on the gray stone steps by simply thinking the word *gray*. Or rather, singing it inside my head, imagining the low tones of the dirge-like vowel played on the sax. I felt a sleepy, sinking feeling like you do on a rainy, gray morning, when you're staying hidden beneath your comforter.

I was lumplike enough to pass under the rangers' radar—they were looking for four of us as usual, not one. And certainly not a one who looked like she maybe lived on these steps, who looked so connected to the place that the idea of her being a visitor was impossible for them.

Mrs. Leary passed not three feet from where I was standing. She did not see me either. I was looking down, so all I registered were the hems of her somewhat too-short wool pants, her striped socks, rubber-soled clogs like nurses wear in hospitals. As soon as the rangers looked away, I stood.

Breaking into a run, I caught up with her on the sidewalk. "Mrs. Leary," I called out.

She turned on her heel, and I realized the way her eyes narrowed into slits and her throat went tight that I had scared her. "I'm a friend of Callie's," I said. "I'm here with her. She needs to speak to you."

Where Mrs. Leary's face had been a tight mask, ready for a fight, it now went slack. "Callie?" Mrs. Leary said. "She's here?" She looked to the left and then to the right eagerly, her breath coming quickly.

"She's just over there," I said. Mute, Mrs. Leary followed me back to the entrance to the museum. The rangers seemed to be gone so I brought her up the stairs and behind the bushes where the others were hiding.

As soon as Mrs. Leary saw Callie she rushed to her, her hands out to cradle Callie's face. She held her, looking at her, then drew Callie into a hug, then pulled back so she could look again.

The rest of us kept our distance, trying to give them their moment alone and watching out for any sign of ranger activity. How many times had I imagined just such a moment with my dad? It wouldn't be exactly like this one, of course. I always imagined it happening in a car wash or a hardware store, the kind of place my dad would have taken me on a Saturday afternoon. I had this scenario worked out in my head where he'd gotten a job at one of these places and he was hiding out there. He wouldn't cry, but he'd have his own way of letting me know that he'd been missing me the whole time, that nothing had been the same without me. Maybe he *would* cry, but a Dad cry—muted, disguised by frequent fake coughing. He'd grasp me not by the face but the shoulders. He'd hold me out at arm's length, and then he'd lift me up and spin me around like when I was little.

Watching Callie and her mom, I felt myself smiling. I felt so good it was as if everything they were experiencing was really happening to me.

But it wasn't. Callie's mom had been *missing*. My father was *dead*. I would never see him again. I would never have what Callie and her mom had right now.

t was 7:25. Amanda's and my first set as the Bruella Duella at Arcadia was supposed to start at 7:30, but Amanda was nowhere to be seen.

I was waiting, trying hard to actively trust her. I wanted to. I wanted to believe that she'd walk in at the last minute, with a good reason for being late.

I wanted to have that kind of confidence in her, but

instead, I sat at a table, drinking seltzer and thinking bitterly, *She* was the one who set this whole thing up. *She* was the one who talked me into doing it. Just the night before, she'd come over and, with glitter and silver poster paint, we'd transformed the back of Pen's old science project into the elegant black-and-purple sign propped on an easel on the stage, to one side of the piano: It promised The Bruella Duella, alluding, Amanda had told me, both to jazz great Dave Brubeck, to her former last name Bruyere, and to her favorite villain of all time, Cruella de Vil.

"How can you hate a woman who is so good with a cigarette holder?" Amanda had said, as she'd put the finishing touches on the *a*'s at the end of *Bruella* and *Duella*. At the time, I'd laughed along with her, but now I was thinking, *How can you like bad people? Maybe only if you yourself are partly bad.*

If this sounds harsh, trust me, Amanda deserved it. Because just then Arcadia's manager was coming over to tell me it was time to get up on stage. The manager was a guy named Bobby who had only ever dealt with Amanda, and from the way he was looking at me, was probably just realizing now that we were under twenty-one—by a lot. Bobby looked at his watch. He pantomimed the international gesture for "What's it gonna be?"

I slowly mounted the three shallow steps to the stage. I was holding the sax in my right hand, kind of out in front of my body so my knees wouldn't bang into it as I walked. I tried to pretend it was just another concert at school, but the difference here was the stage lights. Blue and pink. Every time I looked out into the audience, I had to squint. The feeling of not being able to see anything beyond the stage was disorienting.

I looked down at my toes. I was supposed to be looking at Amanda. We started playing the same way every time—I'd look at her, she'd look at me, I'd kind of count a beat inside my head that she'd be following because she's very good at following people, and then I'd raise my eyebrows on the upbeat and we'd both dig in.

I counted out the beat alone then, tapping my toe. Just imagining the music as I laid down the rhythm it would follow was reassuring, and by the time I blew the first notes into my sax, I knew that I could carry this song by myself.

"Stormy Weather" is one of the songs that the saxophone was made to play. But it was different without the piano. It was more raw. It was more sad. I had the words in my head as I started, the line, "Can't go on / Everything I have is gone" and I just breathed all the sadness and disappointment I was feeling in Amanda—in everything—into that one line. I could feel the sound swinging out into the room. Even though I couldn't see the people in the audience, I could feel that they were with me.

And then, as I ended to applause, Amanda jumped up onto the stage.

She was dressed all in black like someone who wants

to dematerialize in the dark—black jeans, a black turtle-neck, and a beret worn not like a French person would, but pulled down over the top of her head to her ears. I would have wondered if she'd been breaking into a bank if I hadn't noticed her eye makeup, which seemed to capture the stage lights—it glowed and sparkled, white with hints of pinks and blues. On the stage she looked like nothing but a pair of eyes.

Sad eyes. Eyes that were hard to read. Eyes that refused to be questioned.

Why didn't I say something? Why didn't I stop the show and demand to know where she'd been? Maybe if I'd tried, she would have told me some of what was going on. She might have told me who was chasing her, or why she needed to disappear. Maybe I could have helped her somehow.

She raised her eyebrows. "What's next?" she said, and instead of answering her, I started to play a song we hadn't practiced. It was something that back when my parents used to sing to me at bedtime, was the song my dad always chose. It started with the line "Every time you say good-bye" and was all about the sadness of saying good-bye.

It was a song no one had dared to play in our house since my dad died, but I played it now. It was a song that would have made Amanda sad even if she hadn't known it was one of his favorites. A song that we never knew why he chose, but maybe he'd been able to presage his own early death. Amanda was nodding as she came in after the first four sad lines, and I knew I would never call her out on being late. Because late, or even missing from my life, she was still here, and when your father is gone, you know that here and gone are two very different ways to be.

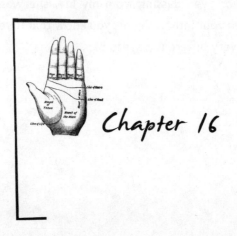

Chapter 16

Callie and her mom stood crying and hugging each other for a very long time. Eventually, Mrs. Leary started asking questions about how Callie had found her, and what she was doing here. We didn't have even a fraction of the time they needed to catch up on everything that had happened to Callie, so Callie told her the quick version, about Amanda, about her disappearance, and about what we'd learned about the C33s when we broke into OCP.

"You grew up there, didn't you?" Callie said. "I saw that puzzle—the Water Lilies one you said you loved when you were a kid."

Mrs. Leary was nodding. She squeezed Callie's hand then looked at all of us. "And so you're all Amanda's guides?" she asked. "Hello, Nia," she said. "Hal."

Never one to hold back, Nia jumped in, "When you

were growing up, did you know my mom?"

"Of course." Mrs. Leary chuckled, wiping her damp face. "From our early years. She was the first baby I ever got to hold. As she grew, we older girls used to fight over who got to pretend to be her mom and brush her hair and all that. Your mom was also class parent when you and Callie were second graders, and Callie would bring home cellophane packages with hand-calligraphed recipe cards."

"That sounds like her," Nia smiled.

"Since I left, your mom has been wonderful, looking after Callie and keeping her safe."

"I know," Callie said. "Mr. Bennett explained."

"Good," said Mrs. Leary. She turned to me. "And you're Zoe?" she said. "You're George Costas's oldest?"

"Yeah," I said. "But my dad—"

"I know, sweetheart," Mrs. Leary said. "I heard about what happened to him and I'm just so, so sorry. You know, I used to look up to your dad. When we were growing up, he and Max, there was just nothing they couldn't do."

"Mrs. Leary," I said, "we believe we're here because Amanda wanted us to find you. Do you know why that would be?" I thought about Rosie and the mysterious red and blue plastic cards. "Did she give you something to give us?"

Mrs. Leary shook her head. "I've never even seen Amanda," she said. "Only heard about her from other C33s. But I do have something for you to give her."

"What is it?" Callie asked.

Mrs. Leary ran a hand through her hair, further disturbing her bun. "This is going to take some explaining," she said. "It's hard to imagine, but there was a point in my life when I wasn't afraid of Dr. Joy. After the C33 program was disbanded, after I began publishing and receiving grant funding for my own work, and he was so down and out, I began to feel like he was benign. Pathetic even.

"He was still coming around a lot. Every time I published a paper or won a prize, he'd be there, either sending a little note of congratulation or, worse, showing up on our doorstep 'just for a chat.' We had him in for dinner sometimes. This was all before you were born. I felt sorry for him, honestly. He didn't have a steady job, and any money he did manage to come across he poured into this sad little underground lab he insisted was thriving, though I have my doubts—it was nothing compared to the setup he had with C33—mostly he was just tinkering with blood work. In any case, I wasn't sure he always knew where his next meal was coming from, so when he showed up, I'd make him a bowl of pasta and invite him to sit at our dining room table."

"Which is gone now, by the way," Callie said. "Dad had to sell it to pay the mortgage." Callie swallowed. "Is that really bad?"

Mrs. Leary did a double take. "Is that *bad*?" she said. "No, no—it's the least bad decision he could make. Callie, please understand that I left knowing full well how horrible things were going to be for your dad, that he would be shaken to his core. It's killing me, how much I miss both of you. I knew you were strong, but still, the burden I was asking you to shoulder—I know it was a heavy one."

"So how could you leave, then?" Callie said, sounding more like she needed to know than like she was accusing her mother of something terrible.

"If I had thought I could stay without putting your life in danger, there was nothing that could have possibly induced me to leave you and Dad," Mrs. Leary said. "You understand this?" She waited for Callie to answer.

"I understand," Callie said, almost reluctantly.

"Okay." Mrs. Leary looked hard at Callie, then returned to her story. "When word got around that I was pregnant, there Dr. Joy was with a chintzy rattle made out of plastic so thin who knew what chemicals would have leached into your mouth if I'd allowed you to suck on it. That went into the trash, but I made sure Dr. Joy stayed for dinner and even as he was pumping me for information about how my pregnancy was going—he practically begged me to let him take a look at the ultrasound—I took my turn pumping him. A little wine helped, and by the end of the night I had a very rough, very vague idea of what some of the therapies Dr. Joy had developed and tested out on us. I understood how they worked and I had enough knowledge of the human genome, brain plasticity, and the vascular system for it to scare the pants off of me.

"That very night, I started my research. I had to teach myself a lot of biology, but by the time you were born, I developed some theories about how to reverse the effects of what Dr. Joy had done. You see, Dr. Joy told the government, which was funding his research, that he was developing human prototypes, genetically superior models who could be endlessly reproduced and sent out into our society to, well, conquer the world—he had a vision of an army made up of perfect soldiers, an orchestra composed of only virtuosic players, an Olympics where the United States could claim gold in every single sport, and doctors whose practice combined a rigorous approach to science with a nuanced appreciation of human nature and the ability to inspire their patients to better health.

"Did Mr. Bennett tell you how, as his project developed, he grew even more ambitious?"

Callie nodded.

"That night over the pasta and the wine, he explained it all to me, the top-secret part of this top-secret project. I mean, get the man on the subject of the lost potential of the seventy-five percent of the human brain that neurologists don't understand, that doesn't seem to be actually used for anything, and he can talk for hours. It was his dream, he said, to build a person who tapped into all that lost brain potential. It explained a lot, actually, about how miserable it was to grow up under his care. Aside from the experimentation, there was the simple hard-driving rigidity of his parenting style—if you could call it that. No matter what we did, no matter how successful we were, he was never happy. He was always pushing for more."

"Good old Uncle Joy, right?" I said. "Or would that be Uncle Joe?"

Mrs. Leary smiled. "I guess you heard that nickname from your dad?" she said.

"And Amanda's mom, a long time ago."

Mrs. Leary shook her head. "Annie McLean. Who became Annie Beckendorf." She sighed. "Such a fire-cracker. You know, when I heard about her accident, after knowing what happened to your dad, Zoe, it was the final straw that sent me underground.

"You see, Callie," she said, "my basement lab was not enough. By chance I ran into Falk, another former C33, at a conference and we realized we were working on the same idea. He invited me to join him at the lab he had set up here, at the Museum of Natural Sciences. He's suppos-edly mapping the genome of a tribe of chimpanzees, but in reality, we're trying to crack Dr. Joy's code.

"I didn't join right away. I stayed in Orion as long as I could, hoping we'd be able to come up with a solution working from there. But then—"

"But then what?" Callie said. "What happened?"

Mrs. Leary pushed a hand through her silvery hair again. "You became friends with Heidi."

"What?" said Callie. "That's why you left? Because of Heidi?"

"No. I left after what happened to Annie Beckendorf.

That scared me. But your friendship with Heidi was a factor. She had such an effect on you. Just as I was starting to suspect you were developing an unusual power."

"You left because of Heidi?" Callie said. "You could have just said—"

"It wasn't the friendship per se," she said. "It was the vulnerability. I could see what a huge influence she had on you. And I knew that you were special.

"Have you four learned about how some of the offspring of former C33s have . . . powers?"

We nodded.

"You all have them, don't you?" she said.

We nodded again.

"Callie," Mrs. Leary said. "Do you remember that day when I was repairing the garden fence and there was that boulder in the way? Do you remember how you easily kicked it aside? Or when Dad needed wood moved and you could tuck it under one arm some days, but others it was really heavy? I could tell something was going on, that as you were coming of age, some sort of power was developing, too."

"Yeah . . . ," Callie said slowly.

"I was looking for something like that, some power to emerge that was out of the ordinary and that was it. I'm sure it's grown, also. One of the things Falk is working so hard to describe and explain is why C33 offspring powers seem to intensify when you are grouped together. It's sort of the next area of research, though I'm hoping it will remain theoretical. Our only advantage of course is that Dr. Joy did not have access to any of your blood."

"He didn't?" Nia said.

"Has your mother ever allowed you to have blood drawn at a doctor's office?" Mrs. Leary said.

"Now that I think about it, no," Nia said.

"Mine neither," said Hal.

"Since my dad died, my mom hasn't even let me or my sisters go to the doctor," I added. I'd thought it was because we didn't have insurance.

Mrs. Leary opened her mouth as if she was about to explain more about our blood when Callie interrupted her.

"I still don't understand what Heidi had to do with all of this," Callie said.

"Her mother, Brittney, was an original C33. Did you know that?"

"Yes," we all said.

"Did you know that Thornhill believes that she was working with the Official?"

"Like we couldn't have seen *that* coming," Nia said.

"You're not surprised?" Mrs. Leary asked.

"Not after we found all those blood samples in her house," Hal said.

"Oh! That was what happened to them!" Mrs. Leary said. "Hal, your dad uncovered computer records referring to a backup blood storage bank in Orion. Of all places, it was being stored in a refrigerated room in the back of a travel agency."

Nia's eyes opened wide. "We know that place," she said.

"But before Thornhill could send in some people to destroy the blood bank, it was moved, and no one could figure out where. Brittney had the blood."

"So Brittney is a bad guy," Hal said, shaking his head. "It explains a lot."

"Yeah, like why Heidi tried to run Amanda down with her car," Nia said.

"Heidi did that?" Mrs. Leary said.

Callie nodded. "But she ran over this other girl—Bea Rossiter—instead," she said. "And I helped her cover it up."

"But you also power-played the Braggs into paying for Bea to have reconstructive surgery," Nia added.

"And you dumped Heidi," said Hal.

"You did?" Mrs. Leary said. "You were able to do that?"

Callie nodded. Mrs. Leary shook her head in disbelief. "I can't believe you were able to outmaneuver the likes of Heidi Bragg."

"I can't believe I let her manipulate me for so long." Callie said.

"Callie," Mrs. Leary said, "look at me. Heidi has a talent, just like you do, just like Zoe, Nia, and Hal. Do you know what her talent is?"

Callie shrugged. "Being popular?" She was joking.

"That's actually close," Mrs. Leary answered. "Her

talent is for making people do what she wants them to. It was something Dr. Joy was trying to do with Brittney when she was in C33, but it never took. He ended up just making her beautiful and then when the beauty treatments had such a detrimental effect on her character, he tried therapies to make her more likable. He made her into someone the average American would identify with even if she's richer, thinner, and better informed than they are. He built, ironically, the perfect anchorwoman, which is of course what she became.

"But what he wanted was more like what Heidi has become. Someone deft at using all those attributes to build power, who doesn't just persuade others to follow her example, but seems to be able to co-opt their own thoughts and instincts—convince them for brief periods of time that their only chance of happiness flows through her."

"Wow," said Hal. "That's so evil."

"It is," Mrs. Leary agreed.

"It's what happened to you," Nia said to Hal. "When Heidi sweet-talked you into handing over Amanda's box."

"Now you know," Callie said. "That wasn't your fault."

"No," said Mrs. Leary. "No one can resist her. Or at least, it is very, very difficult." She turned to her daughter. "But you, Callie, apparently you can?"

"It wasn't that big of a deal," Callie said.

"It was a huge deal," Nia insisted. "Remember what happened to me when I tried to stand up to her in middle school?" When Nia had exposed Heidi's cheating, Heidi retaliated with cruel public humiliation for Nia, involving a boy Nia had a crush on. It had long-lasting effects on Nia's social life.

"Whatever," said Callie, blushing.

"I hate to say this," I said, checking my watch. "But if we don't head back to the meet-up with our group, Nia's brother is going to call the police or send out the cavalry or something. There have been some guys following us around all morning," I explained to Mrs. Leary.

She closed her eyes like she was fighting off a sudden headache, then opened them again. "If there was any way to do this that wasn't putting you in danger, all of you, believe me…"

Callie took her mom's hand. "Mom," she said. "I know." I could see that Callie was fighting back tears. But also that she was going to be strong. She was going to summon all her strength to convince her mom she was going to be all right, even if she wasn't sure of that herself.

"Before you go, take this," Mrs. Leary said, passing Callie a bottle that looked like cough syrup.

"What is it?" Callie asked.

"It's the result of nearly a decade and a half of research. I call it the enhancement eraser. It's a liquid—I hope it's effective—that identifies and targets any synthetic or introduced genetic material in your body. Not to be too technical, but it then triggers an immune response against the foreign or enhanced material."

"Huh?" Hal said.

"The tricky part of it was finding the enzyme that could distinguish between your body's regular DNA, and DNA that has been added on. Chromosomally, of course, they're distinct, but the trick is to synthesize a material that will correctly identify and unbond from those materials."

"Was that explanation supposed to help make this more clear?" Callie asked.

"Okay," her mom said. "Drink one tablespoon of this liquid, and everything that came from work Dr. Joy did to your parents will be erased."

"So we should drink it now?" Callie said, laying her hand on the bottle's lid as if to unscrew it.

"No," Mrs. Leary said, laying her hand on top of Callie's. "Not yet. You need your powers still. To help Amanda. To protect yourselves. What I want is for you to give this to Amanda. If Amanda no longer has her powers, she can no longer be of any use to the Official. His interest in her will evaporate, as will Dr. Joy's funding. Imagine our lives without this mess." We could see Mrs. Leary's eyes glowing with the excitement of her idea. "Gone," she said. "Poof." She snapped herself back to attention. "Now," she said, lifting her chin in an attempt, I could see, to be brave. "It's time for you all to go. You'll need to run."

"Mom—" said Callie. You could see how almost impossible it was for her to leave her mom now. As if there were a string of rubber cement stretching out between them, the longer she stayed, the harder it was going to be to separate.

"Callista, go!" Mrs. Leary said, and she turned on her heel, left us in the bushes, and walked briskly back up the Institute steps to return to her secret lab.

Then we started to flat-out run.

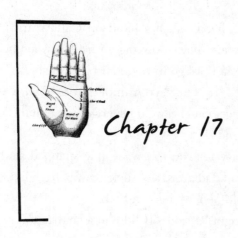

Chapter 17

Before we'd gotten down the steps, Hal had a hand on my arm. "Wait," he said to Nia and Callie. "Go back."

Nia looked at her watch. "We have to be back at the bus for lunch in ten minutes," I said. "And it's a fifteen-minute walk. Cisco—"

"Just wait a second," Hal warned, and sure enough, we'd just made it back behind the bushes where we'd been talking to Mrs. Leary when a shiny black SUV pulled up at the curb at the base of the museum stairs. Two men in dark suits hopped out.

"They'll be gone soon," Hal said. "They won't see us."

"Do you think they're here for us?" Callie asked anxiously. "Or for my mom?"

Hal shook his head. "I can't tell."

"We have to go help her." Callie started to poke her head out.

Nia shook her head, her hand on Callie's arm. "We can't. Chances are they're looking for us. We won't be able to help Amanda if we go in there and get caught."

"You need to trust your mom, too, Callie," Hal added. "If we get caught, we'll never get the enhancement eraser to Amanda."

"That's easy for you to say," Callie snapped at them. "Your mom and dad are safely tucked away back in Orion. My mom could be in danger in there."

"Callie's right," I said. "If I'd had a chance to save my dad, I would have wanted to be able to try."

"Thanks, Zoe." Callie looked at me with big sad eyes and it was like Amanda was here—there weren't too many people who could see deep inside me the way Amanda could, but Callie was seeing deep inside me now. I think she got it then—the feeling she'd just had, of seeing her mom again after not knowing where she had gone, not knowing if she was even alive…the intensity of that feeling allowed her to understand what it was like for me, to have my dad completely gone.

I don't know what she would have ultimately decided to do—whatever it was, I am sure Nia and Hal would have joined me in backing her up—but just then the men in suits came jogging back out of the museum, their open jackets catching the breeze. When one spoke into his walkie-talkie

I could see that he was saying the words *searched*, *no evidence*, *kids*.

"They were looking for us," I breathed. "Not your mom."

Callie pulled down the hood of her jacket and let her long hair tumble out. She had to give it a good shake to set it free. "Sorry," she mumbled.

Hal knocked into her shoulder, a playful bump. Nia touched her arm. "It's fine," Nia said.

"But now," said Hal, "we really have to get going."

Callie was holding her back straight, her muscles clenched—seeing her mom and then having to say good-bye was almost worse than not seeing her at all.

Cisco's face was pale and his mouth set in a determined line. I felt immediately bad for how worried he must have been. Nia had called him to tell him we were fine and just running late, but still . . . I don't think he believed we were okay until he saw us. Nia went right to him and pulled him aside, I'm sure to tell him about finding Callie's mom and what she'd asked us to do.

Next Nia needed to check in with the one Rivera who was probably most anxious to hear she was okay: her mom. She'd promised to call her during lunch.

"I've got to call my mom too," Hal said.

"And I have to call my dad," Callie said. "Though I'm still not sure if this phone call is for my dad to make sure I'm okay, or for me to make sure *he's* okay."

Suddenly, I felt like an orphan. I mean, I have a mom and everything, but she'd sent me off on my bike this morning knowing I'd be in a strange city all day long. Trust is one word for it. But more likely, my mom was just too busy with her jobs to have much of a choice. My mom assumes I can take care of myself and, because she has so much going on, she cannot deal with the alternative.

But I pulled my phone out of my pocket anyway because I didn't want Callie, Hal, and Nia to feel sorry for me, and I actually dialed my mom's cell. As soon as the phone started to ring on the other end, I felt good, too. Having lost my dad, I never forget how lucky I am to at least have a mom.

I knew she must be at work, so at first I wasn't surprised to hear laughing in the background when she picked up. She was probably in the faculty break room eating lunch.

"How's the trip?" she asked.

I thought about everything that had happened to me that morning—the guards at the World War II Memorial, seeing Ravenna, meeting Callie's mom. I couldn't help it. I choked on a sob.

"Zoe?" My mom's voice rose. "Are you okay?"

I took a deep breath. "I'm fine." I said, getting myself under control.

But then I heard laughter in the background again. I heard a teakettle whistle that sounded way too familiar for my mom to be at work.

"Are you at home?" I was shocked.

The whistling abruptly ended and then I heard a low voice say something that I couldn't quite decipher through the phone. But it didn't really matter what the voice said. What mattered was that it was a man's voice.

"I came home for lunch," my mom explained.

"Really?" I said. My mom never comes home for lunch. She doesn't think much about food—usually she'll skip lunch and practice instead. "Is anyone sick?"

I heard another rumble in the background—it was *definitely* a man. "Iris and Pen are fine," my mom said. "I just had something I needed to do."

"Who's with you?"

"No one," my mom said.

"I *heard* someone."

"No one you know. Look, I'm so sorry, Zoe. I can't explain now but I have to go. Please be careful on your trip. You will be okay? Promise me?"

I promised, and then, without further ado, she was gone. I stared at the phone for a minute.

"Are you okay?" It was Nia asking, and her question made me realize my face must be betraying my thoughts. I quickly composed it.

But then, when I met Nia's eyes, a confession poured out. "My mom basically hung up on me," I blurted, half hoping Nia would think I was joking and laugh.

She didn't laugh. She squinted the way she does when she's reading and gets so absorbed she doesn't realize her face is essentially talking back to the book.

"I think she's dating someone," I went on.

"Uh-huh," Nia said.

"She's staying out late," I said. "I don't think she's telling the truth about where she goes."

"That doesn't sound good," Nia said. I was glad she didn't try to tell me that I should be happy for my mom, that she was starting to make a new life for herself. I'd tried hard enough to convince myself of that inside my own head.

"Just now," I said. "I heard a man's voice over the phone."

"But isn't she at school? It could have been another teacher."

"No," I said, and I wished now I hadn't started to tell Nia any of this. "She was at home."

"Oh." The way Nia said it made me realize it was as bad as I thought. To her credit, she didn't look away from me. She kept our gazes locked, her dark eyes unflinching.

"My call home was weird too," Callie said when she and Hal joined us and I found myself telling them about what was going on with my mom. She was looking at her phone as if it had tried to bite her.

"You mean because you couldn't tell your dad you saw your mom?" Hal said, a step behind.

"He could totally tell something was up," she said. "He kept asking me why I sounded so different and I kept saying, 'Do I sound different . . . ?' I mean, he might not be the most successful single parent, but he *is* my dad."

"Next time, tell him you're in love," Nia suggested.

Callie's face went beet-red.

Hal stared down at his shoes.

Nia looked at me, shrugged, and rolled her eyes. Nia has very little patience for beating around the bush.

"Let's get some lunch," Hal said to change the subject, and grabbing the lunches we'd brought with us out of the cooler, we found a spot on some benches under a tree in a picnic area near the bus. Except for me. I hadn't packed a lunch. I wish I could say I'd forgotten, but really, it was because when I'd opened the fridge, there hadn't been any food that I could take. My mom's moussaka from the night before wasn't something you could really expect to eat cold, out of a Tupperware. There had been potatoes, uncooked. A half-rotten onion. A jar of mayonnaise. And just enough peanut butter and bread for the twins to pack lunches for themselves. I'd thought long and hard about the banana that was black on the skin from being in the fridge, deciding eventually that it wouldn't survive the trip.

"You didn't bring anything to eat?" Nia asked. Leave it to Nia to ask.

"I'm . . . uh . . ." I had a bunch of easy lies I could have used here. I've heard people say, "I don't eat breakfast" often enough to claim I didn't eat lunch, like it was some kind of principle of my existence. I could have said, "big breakfast," and pretended like the four sips of hot chocolate and the tiny box of corn pops had been enough. But lying to these guys, the way I'd been lying to everyone since my dad died—strings of tiny, insignificant lies—felt wrong now. I just sighed. And then my stomach growled.

Callie passed me a cheese stick. "My dad finally started going to the grocery store again, so I don't have the heart to tell him he's buying food I haven't eaten since kindergarten."

Nia offered me a homemade empanada. "But that's your lunch," I said.

"My mom packed extra. She's been packing extra for weeks. I guess it's for you." She wrapped the empanada in a napkin and handed it to me. "These are corn and bean, but my mom uses pancetta. You're not a vegetarian, are you?" I shook my head. "Of course you're not," she muttered. "My mom would have figured that out about you."

"I can't take your lunch," I said.

"Of course you can," Hal countered as he cut his candy bar in half with a plastic knife and gave me an exactly even share, wrapper still intact. "Because you know, Zoe." He held up his half as if he were an announcer on TV. *"Snickers satisfies."*

I had to admit that it did. And it also felt nice to be taken care of. By my friends.

Once we'd had a chance to eat a little bit, Nia pulled out the scavenger hunt sheet and looked at it. Scanning the crowd, I noticed that everyone in our grade was doing the same thing. Except for one person. "Guys, look," I said, pointing across the lunch scene to the I-Girls. Lexi and Traci and Kelli were poring over their scavenger hunt sheet—I could see their sheets were covered in pen and they were looking at their camera phones and then writing. But where was Heidi?

"That *is* weird," Callie said, but we didn't have a chance to speculate further. Just then, Cisco came over and took the scavenger hunt sheet out of our hands, shaking his head.

"This is impressive," he said, "in its blankness."

"Tell me about it," Nia agreed.

"You only have four out of the twenty-two places," Cisco pointed out. "You need fifteen."

"I think we should resign ourselves," Hal said. "We're just going to fail."

"Ramona Rivera does not accept failure. Figure something out, dude, or Nia will have to tell our mother what's going on here. And if my mom had any inkling about the goons dressed up like rangers chasing her daughter, I'm afraid Nia will be put under lock and key for the rest of her life. Then where will you be?" Cisco sat down heavily.

"But I think Thornhill and Amanda are using the scavenger hunt to tell us something," Nia said. "Whatever we get from it is what we're meant to get from it."

"Very deep, Ni-Ni," Cisco said. "But Mr. Fowler's still going to fail you if you don't come up with more pictures and quotes."

"Speaking of quotes . . ." Nia explained to Cisco about the quotes that were highlighted in some way.

"Do they mean something?" Cisco asked. "Do you

think they come together to work as a code?"

I pulled out my camera, setting it to view mode and looked back for the highlighted quotes we'd found. From the Washington Monument, I read: *Train up a child.* From the World War II Memorial: *The eyes of the world are upon you.* From the Lincoln Memorial: *We shall have here a new birth of freedom.*

"Wait a sec," Cisco said, getting out his own camera. "I just remembered. I saw something like that in a picture I took when I went out to Arlington—the Tomb of the Unknown Soldier is one of the stops on the scavenger hunt, but there's a whole lot of other stuff out there that's pretty fascinating." He flipped through the images on his phone until he found the one he wanted. "You know how I feel about JFK—I had to get a picture of his tomb. This is it."

He passed the camera to Nia, and we all looked at it together. It was a picture of about fifteen girls with Cisco smiling haplessly from the center of their group.

If you were looking at the picture casually you might just think that the highlighted words were simply catching the sun's rays in a certain angle, but to us, it was obvious. They were intentionally treated. From the line, *The torch has been passed to a new generation,* the phrase *The torch has been passed* was highlighted. And then, in a different part of the picture, from the line, *Bear any burden—meet any hardship—support any friend—oppose any foe to assure the survival and the success of liberty,* the phrase *Bear any burden—meet any hardship—support any friend* glowed in the same way as the other words we'd seen.

"That's from Kennedy's inaugural address," Nia murmured. "It's the one that has the line in it, 'Ask not what your country can do for you. Ask what you can do for your country.'" Nia was almost as good at quotes as Amanda.

"Do those words mean anything to you?" Cisco said. "Do you think you could scramble all the letters and spell out a meeting place Amanda has in mind?"

Callie looked exhausted. "That's two hundred and forty letters," she said, coming up with the number so quickly I realized she must have counted them out of habit. "Do you know how many possible permutations there could be?"

"Do you think they're the words Amanda was hoping we would find?" Hal said. "There could be more of them out there. We've barely scratched the surface of all the places Thornhill wanted us to see. Did she highlight words on every spot on this list?" He waved the scavenger hunt sheet and I immediately began to feel overwhelmed.

"The ones on the World War Two Memorial make sense," I suggested. She *sent* us there, with the postcard."

"She sent us to the Lincoln Memorial, too," added Callie. "And the Washington Monument's a given since it's right where the bus parked, she could assume everyone would go there."

"But JFK's tomb?" Hal said. "That's random."

"Not necessarily," Nia mused. "If Amanda knew Cisco

was coming on this trip, she might have remembered that JFK was one of his personal heroes. It makes complete sense that he would take a picture of his tomb—and she knew Cisco would get that information back to Nia."

"Am I that obvious?" Cisco asked. Nia raised her eyebrows. "Okay, I guess I am." He shrugged and gave one of his trademark sheepish Cisco smiles. And then his face lit up. "Dude!" he said. "Maybe I'm not that transparent. Last fall, I saw Amanda at this party—I was there with my friends and she was hanging out with a crowd of seniors. We got to talking and it turns out we *both* were huge JFK fans. We talked about how Vietnam would have been totally different if he hadn't been killed. But how would she *know* that I would go there?"

"She wouldn't know," I said. "She'd guess. I think she's used to guessing. She trusts her own instincts. And usually they're right on target."

Hal shook his head—I couldn't tell if it was in resignation or admiration. "Amanda had been in control of our movements all day. Everything we've seen, she's *wanted* us to see?"

"She must be nearby," Callie added. "She's probably just a few steps ahead of us. Maybe we're supposed to use the quotes to find her—maybe they're laying a path."

Nia picked up the sheet again. "They must mean something," she said. "I can feel it. They're like a poem or song lyrics or something. Where you feel like you get it, but you can't say exactly what it's about."

Together we all looked down at our sheet and read the quotes to ourselves in silence.

Train up a child . . . The eyes of the world are upon you . . . It is fitting and proper that we here shall have a new birth of freedom . . . The torch has been passed . . . Bear any burden— meet any hardship—support any friend.

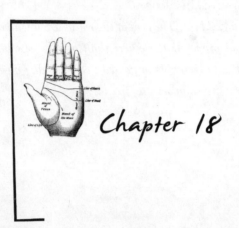

Chapter 18

One of the things my dad was always really good at was telling stories about misunderstandings. His favorite kind of story was the kind where someone says "I want hotdogs," but someone else hears "Terrible hot rod," and all sorts of confusion ensues. He collected these stories the way some people collect stamps, or snow globes, or salt and pepper shakers in the shape of cows. My dad told his stories to people when he was selling cars on the lot, told them to other parents during our music recitals, told them to my mom when they were doing the dishes and we were in bed, told them on car trips, he told them to my friends when they were over (embarrassing!), and he told them to Amanda.

And once, he told one when our two families were out to dinner together. It was the night of elementary school graduation and we were at the Greek pizza place, my dad leaning back in his chair with a very sleepy Pen slung over his shoulder. Iris was already asleep on my mom's lap. Mom was chatting with Amanda's mom as Amanda and I were asking for our zillionth quarter to play the car driving video game they had next to the door. Rosie, or Ravenna as I called her then, had gone to the movies with a friend. To keep our attention and give the moms more time to talk—and because he was running out of quarters—my dad said he would tell us a story instead.

I rolled my eyes. I was a rising middle schooler by then, so I was making like I was sick of his stories. Dad said, "All right, Miss Smartypants, how about a scary story?"

Well, I totally wanted to hear that, and I looked at Amanda, hoping we'd be able to exchange a glance that said, "Awesome." But she didn't seem excited by the idea of scary. If I had to name a feeling to match her deadpan gaze, screwed-up mouth, and raised eyebrows, I'd have said she looked a little bit bored, but she was too polite to say so.

My dad started in on his story anyway—all about the legend of some kind of monster named Bloody Fingers. Two Boy Scouts were camping in a tent, when they heard a voice in the wind, calling and howling and getting closer and closer, "I'm Bloody Fingers and I'm a mile away!" Then, "I'm Bloody Fingers and I'm twenty-five paces away!" But then, when Bloody Fingers got to the Boy Scouts, he turned out to be a five-year-old Cub Scout, who announced in a cheerful voice, "It's Bloody Fingers. Can I have a Band-Aid?"

Amanda laughed really hard. She always loved my dad. It was hard to be in a bad mood when he was around.

But then she said, "I have a scary story too. Do you guys want to hear?" After we'd nodded, she started in on a story that still, even today, sends shivers down my spine. I thought about it all the time when we were on the road in the RV. I'd thought Amanda somehow had been able to predict the future. That she'd sent me a secret message.

The story she told was about a girl whose dad had died before she was born.

"Like your dad?" my dad had interrupted Amanda in the pizza place, switching Pen over to his other shoulder, shaking out his arm, using his concerned adult voice. Later I've realized he would have known Amanda's dad was alive. I guess he was just thinking about what Amanda was feeling back then.

"No," Amanda said, her voice calm, her gray-green eyes looking up over his shoulder as if she could see something in the room that we could not. Thinking back to the story after Amanda disappeared, I realized—or wondered—if she was really talking about my dad. If the whole story was about me.

In Amanda's story, the girl doesn't believe her father really is dead. All the girl knows is that her mother was pregnant with her at the time her dad died, and that her mom destroyed every picture of her dad and never mentioned his name. The girl has always assumed this is because her mother can't bear the pain of losing him. So every year on her birthday, the girl waits until her mother has gone to sleep, and she sneaks outside into her yard. She looks up at the stars and feels the night air cooling her skin and she just knows that he is out there, watching her.

And then she starts to get secret messages that only she can understand. That make it clear her dad is watching her, and knows things about her. She loves making drawings of trees, and in her tree drawings the trees always look the same—a maple with a thick trunk; spreading, low-hung, heavy branches; a swing made out of two ropes and a plank.

After the girl's art teacher hangs up her tree drawings and paintings at the school art show, she gets a photograph in the mail. It has a date stamp on it that shows it was taken the week before. When the girl's mom sees the photograph in the girl's hand, she sits down hard in one of the kitchen chairs. "Where did you get that?" she asks the girl and her mom says, "That's your father's tree swing. At the house where he grew up. The house was torn down, but see that fence? That hillside? It's definitely the one." Her mom doesn't notice the date stamp. "Where did you find this?" she asks. "In the attic?" The girl nods. If she tells her mom the photograph arrived in a plain white envelope with no return address, her mother will start watching the mail, and the girl has a feeling there will be more. She doesn't want to miss any.

A month later a wooden cigar box appears on the floor of her room. Inside is a deck of cards missing the jack of diamonds. A few weeks after that she's in the library, reading, and she leaves her book open on the table to ask a question at the reference desk. When she returns, the book is closed, but her place has been held with a bookmark. The bookmark is a playing card. The missing jack of diamonds.

She tears through the library looking for her father, and it is only then that she realizes she has no idea what he looks like. She has only one picture of him, a blurry shot taken at a distance, and he would have aged since it was taken. She looks at every man in the right age range, but all of them are impossible. She wonders why he would hide from her? Why would he tease her with all these subtle clues?

And then the next clue arrives. This one comes in the mail again, in a plain white envelope. Inside are two yellowed newspaper clippings, one his obituary and the other an article published a month after his death. Reading them, the girl comes to learn that he died in a car accident—his car drove off a bridge and his body was never found. The investigation was eventually dropped when the girl's mother pleaded with the police to have the search called off. She was eight months pregnant at the time and needed closure.

She doesn't understand any of this, but one night when her mother is out for the evening she has all the clues she's been collecting spread out on the kitchen table and she's poring over them, trying to find a solution in her mind, when she hears a hand on the doorknob. Someone is about to enter the house. She knows it isn't her mother. She would have heard her car in the driveway. Come to think of it, she hadn't heard any car in the driveway. Her dog hadn't barked. Who could it be?

The whole time Amanda had been telling the story, she

hadn't broken her concentration or lost track of the story the way I always did when I was that age. My dad and I were staring at her, totally transfixed by what she was saying, and when she got to this point and stopped, my dad, at least, had his mouth hanging open.

Now, Amanda looked at each of us long and slow, dead in the eye. "Do you think you know what's going to happen?" she said. I had an idea but I didn't say it out loud. It was too terrible. I was really worried about that girl. My dad slowly shook his head too.

"Well," Amanda said. "No one knows. The police found the door open, the materials on the table, the girl gone. The mother too. They were never seen or heard from again."

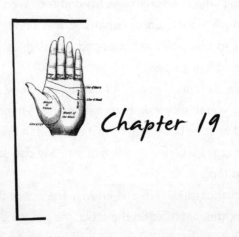

Chapter 19

As we were finishing up our lunches, Cisco left to help Mr. Fowler. We were starting to think about the next step when the shiny black SUV we'd seen in front of the Institute for Natural Sciences pulled up a few feet away from where we were sitting. An image flashed before me: the rangers in their dark suits coming toward us, their strong grip on our upper arms, their dragging us into their car and gunning the engine before Cisco or Mr. Fowler could even see.

But that wasn't what happened. The guards or rangers or whatever they were stayed behind the car's tinted windows and the only person to emerge from the car was Heidi. We saw one long leg, a high-heeled ankle boot, her skinny jeans, her leather jacket, her slouchy bag and then her pretty face, twisted into a frown. She saw us watching. She waved like the person driving the car was her mom, not some henchman working for the man who tortured our parents when they were kids and was now coming after us.

Ignoring her I-Girl toadies, Heidi strolled toward us, like we'd all come to this party together.

"Hey, guys," she said, in a good imitation of a languid, bored, and impartial tone. She looked us up and down like we were wet dogs about to tramp mud into her white-carpeted living room and then she turned her head so she could get a view of our scavenger hunt sheet. *"The torch has been passed,"* she read. "Where's that from?"

Nia opened her mouth about to tell Heidi about JFK's inaugural speech being inscribed on his tomb, but when Callie elbowed her in the ribs, she shut it. But still, she didn't hide the scavenger hunt sheet—it was hard with Heidi. You get this feeling when she's talking to you, like she's your best friend, and you don't want your best friend to think that you're suspicious of her, do you?

"The eyes of the world are upon you?" Heidi read. "That's deep, right?" she giggled.

"What do you want, Heidi?" Nia said, but she let an almost imperceptible stutter betray the fear she still had of the girl. I saw Hal sigh the tiniest bit. He was still intimidated too.

Heidi turned to Callie. "I'm sure you've been diligently

checking landmarks and historic monuments off your list?" she said.

"And I'm sure you've had somebody do that for you," Callie snapped. "Let me guess—Lexi, Kelli, and Traci have been scurrying all over D.C. while you got your nails done."

"Funny," Heidi said, without laughing or even cracking a smile. She reached to pick up Callie's phone. "Can I see your pix?"

Callie quickly pocketed it. Whatever Heidi wanted, Callie was strong enough to know not to give it to her.

Heidi giggled. "What?" she said. "Do I have the plague or something? Are you afraid that if I touch something that belongs to you, you'll turn into me?" She made a pouty face, and turned back to Nia, whom she'd had better luck with. "Don't you *want* to be popular, Nia?" She whispered now so that only Nia and I could hear. "Like your brother?"

Nia shook her head. I could tell from the way she was holding her chin stiffly that she was getting angry. Fortunately, she had the self-possession to stand up and walk away. "I'm going to throw away my garbage," she said, looking pointedly at Heidi when she said the word "garbage."

Callie and Hal got up to throw their bags away too.

Heidi sat down in the vacated space the other guides had left. Next to me. And suddenly I wondered if this had been her plan in being so awful to Nia. For us to be alone.

She looked down at the empanada I was still eating

as if it were a dead animal, then she passed me a bag of potato chips. "Here, have something that's *not* cold and congealed," she said. Her voice was smooth and I couldn't help feeling warmed by it. I knew all the things Rosie and Mrs. Leary had told me about her, but somehow they didn't seem to matter so much right now. I actually caught myself wondering if, aside from the attempted murder and likely involvement with Dr. Joy and the Official—if she wasn't all that bad.

"I can't eat potato chips because I'll get fat, but my dad packs them for me anyway." She giggled. Heidi often laughs at things she says as if they're jokes in a way that makes me wonder if she knows what a sense of humor really is. "*You* don't need to worry, though," she went on.

"Uh . . . thanks," I said, deciding to leave unsaid that I could not have gotten one leg into Heidi's super-skinny jeans. But then I suddenly realized that I really, really didn't want the chips anyway. When I think about Heidi, what she did to Bea Rossiter, I think about what happened to my dad and everything that's *been* happening—and I couldn't bring myself to eat her chips.

"Keep the chips," I said. "I'm not hungry anymore."

Heidi gave me a look. Not a dirty look. Well, not exactly. It was more appraising. She usually has completely unambiguous body language. I think it's actually the secret to her power. When she's walking across a room, every single part of her body is pointed toward the destination where she's headed. She doesn't overthink.

But now, one toe was pointing back to the I-Girl group, and one toe was pointed to me. She didn't know which way to turn. And in this moment of hesitation for her, I took a chance. Maybe it was stupid. Maybe not.

"What are you getting out of all of this? What did he promise you?" I said.

I could tell from the way her pupils didn't dilate that she wasn't surprised by my question. Still, she did the best job of pretending she could. "What are you talking about?" she said.

"You know," I said. "The Official. What did he say he'd give you?"

Heidi sighed and rolled her eyes. She was half turned away from me, but I knew she didn't want to walk away. She wanted to tell me. "Was it money?" I said. "Something else?"

Heidi stood, all ambivalence gone. "You don't know what you're doing, Zoe Costas. And you're never going to find your friend. No one is. She's as gone as your dad."

I just sat there, my only thought being not to let her see that she had gotten to me. Hands shaking, I picked up the scavenger hunt sheet. I could hear it rattling as Heidi walked away.

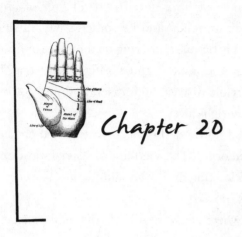

Chapter 20

To get away from Heidi's prying, we left lunch and started back on the hunt, all agreeing that what with its proximity to the Lincoln and World War II Memorials, plus its war/battle theme, the Vietnam Memorial would make the logical next step on Amanda's Washington D.C. tour. We were just discussing our options when I heard a voice behind me.

"Hey, you up there, hold up!"

I felt like all the organs inside my belly had been replaced with rocks. They'd found us. It had to be one of the guards from the airplane hangar.

So you will understand the enormous sigh of relief I breathed when it was just a guy in a suit, carrying a soft briefcase and a coffee in a to-go cup—clearly, a businessman. He was holding the scavenger hunt sheet. I must have dropped it, though I couldn't remember doing that.

The man must have noted that all four of us were smiling at him in relief, and he smiled shyly, raising his cup to us in a little toast, offering us the sheet in his other hand, taking a look at it and saying, "Field trip?" like we had a terrible disease he himself had just got over. I liked this guy right away.

He looked down at the sheet, where we'd circled the Vietnam Memorial. "The Vietnam Memorial's just up that way if you're looking for it," he said.

"Thanks," I said.

"Is that where you're heading?" the man pressed. "It's definitely not one to miss."

"Okay," I said. There was something about this guy. Did I know him? I couldn't look away from his eye. I wished I could spend more time with him. He just seemed . . . well, comfortable. Normal. He reminded me of how nice it would be not to be running all over Washington, but to feel like a kid again.

But then Callie pulled at my arm. "We gotta go, Zoe," she said. She smiled a nice-girl apology at the man.

I had to drag myself away. Something about seeing him was reassuring, a little slice of normal pie. But as soon as he was gone, I could feel our pace increasing.

The Vietnam Memorial was the first place we'd visited that day that didn't have columns and steps. It was just a slowly sloping wall inscribed with the name of every single serviceman who died fighting in Vietnam. As usual, we didn't know exactly what clue we were looking for, and there weren't any park rangers watching—or at least there weren't any that we could see—so we wandered up and down the monument's length, looking at the names. I took a lot of pictures.

And then suddenly I was looking at an inscription that made me stop. "Guys," I called out to the others. "More highlighting." The inscription read:

IN HONOR OF THE MEN AND WOMEN OF THE ARMED FORCES OF THE UNITED STATES WHO SERVED IN THE VIETNAM WAR. THE NAMES OF THOSE WHO GAVE THEIR LIVES AND OF THOSE WHO REMAIN MISSING ARE INSCRIBED IN THE ORDER THEY WERE TAKEN FROM US.

Only the words, *The names* and *are inscribed* and *they were taken from us* were highlighted.

Nia reached out her hand to touch part of the inscription. All those lists we'd been seeing—of the C33s. Thinking about my dad. About Amanda's mom. Mrs. Leary. The former C33 Mr. Bennett had told us about who'd left his Volkswagen at the side of the road, never to be heard from again.

Suddenly, Nia shivered. She dropped her hands from the wall.

"She's been here," Nia said.

We didn't need to ask who.

And we couldn't if we wanted to, because suddenly, one of the guards we'd been seeing all day was strolling down the path toward us. "Don't look," I said. "Just turn slowly and follow me."

Which they did. I scanned the simple wall and the path before it for somewhere for us to blend in and disappear, but there was nothing. I could have really used some columns just about now. "Do you feel Amanda anywhere else?" Hal whispered to Nia as we continued to move slowly, walking away from the guard.

Nia put her hand out on the wall, touching names one at a time. "Here," she said on the fourth name. "This one. She was here."

The guard was closer. A few other groups from our school were standing on the path with us, and I think their presence was protecting us from the guard to a certain extent. Callie waved to one of the girls from the mathletes, and when the guard saw this he slowed his pace.

"Zoe," Callie said, speaking to me between nearly closed lips, not turning her head to me. "Is there anything more you can do to keep him from seeing us?"

"Not when it's like this," I said. "He already *has* seen us. And he's already really close."

"Oh, no," said Hal. We didn't even have a chance for him to tell us what he saw before we saw it too. The other guard—the one who'd fallen asleep at his desk in the airplane hangar—coming into view from the opposite direction.

Nia had her hand on another name—Nia was like a bloodhound now, following Amanda's path along the monument, touching every name Amanda had touched. "She was here too," Nia said, stopping in a new place. "I think more recently than the other ones. I think we're close."

"Do you think she's here?" Callie asked.

"Or do you have a sense of where the trail is going?" Hal said. "Because I'm *not* getting a good feeling about the place we're in right now."

I turned my head fast—a bad idea, as I saw out of the corner of my eye the guard who had newly appeared, the one with the tattoo on his face. He was taking a step closer to us, as if he was poised to pounce the second we made any gesture toward trying to run. Stay calm, I warned myself.

As Nia continued to lead us down the monument's side, blindly feeling her way forward, Callie stood right behind her like she was going to shield her from whatever danger was approaching. Hal looked stressed. He was probably having a premonition of what was about to happen to us, and from the look on his face, I had a feeling that whatever was in store for us would not be good. Hal's fingers were drawn up into fists; even the muscles in his neck were tight. He swallowed hard.

"What do you see?" I hissed. The guards were getting

close enough now that I thought they might even be able to hear.

Hal just shook his head.

"Hold my hand," Callie said to Hal. Without questioning her, Hal took it.

Hal flushed. Just the act of flushing made him look healthier. He looked at Callie. "Your strength," he said. Callie smiled. Hal smiled right back her and both of them seemed to glow.

I saw what Callie must be doing. She must be using the connection that existed among the four of us to pass onto Hal some of her own strength. It must work in the same way it did when we were all holding hands to share Nia's visions.

Just to see what would happen, I put a hand on Callie's elbow. I was suddenly flooded with a rush of something I couldn't name, but it reminded me of being on the playground in elementary school. All I could think about was how great it would feel to run. I remembered when I was a kid, running so hard I'd kick my heels into my thighs, and I'd never get tired.

And in this rush of energy I said, "We have to run. We have to get away from these guys."

But at that same moment, Nia whispered, "Here! I have another one."

"Too late," I said. "This isn't safe."

Nia shot me a look. "I'm so close to getting something." And then she put her hand on Hal's shoulder and suddenly, we could all see what she did.

It was Amanda. In the vision, she had her back to us, a shadowy figure in a hoodie, bending down in front of the Vietnam Memorial, touching the same name that Nia was touching now, then leaving something at the base of the memorial wall.

Nia lifted her hand off Hal's shoulder. The guards were no more than ten feet behind us now. The groups from our school were on the opposite end of the memorial—it was about to empty out completely except for the guards and us.

We looked down. There, at our feet, was a bouquet of dyed green carnations, wrapped in purple cellophane. Tied at the base of the bouquet was a card, and drawn on the card in purple ink was a coyote. Amanda's totem.

She'd been here. Maybe only minutes before we'd arrived.

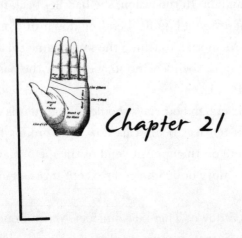

Chapter 21

Nia picked up the bouquet and flipped the card over. We saw words:

Bear any burden—meet any hardship— support any friend.

"JFK's inauguration speech," Nia said. "The lines Cisco saw etched on his tomb at Arlington National Cemetery."

"I guess we know where we need to go next," Callie said.

"I don't know if we're going to be going anywhere," Hal said.

Something happened. The last of the other tourists and kids from our grade dispersed and the guards made their move.

Then Rosie was suddenly there. I don't know from

what bush or tree she must have jumped out, only that she and Cisco were running toward us and she was calling our names. It took me a second to even register that she was Rosie—her jogging outfit of the morning had been replaced by a tight ribbed tank underneath a slouchy green shirt, dark jeans, combat boots, and a black pixie wig.

"Run!" Rosie shouted. But it wasn't necessarily that easy. I hadn't realized until we were inside it what a perfect trap the memorial makes—the sides of the wall converge into a V—the guards had set themselves up so that they were blocking us into the point.

I don't know how we would have made it past them if Cisco hadn't run interference for us, using his soccer moves to literally block the guards. They could not work their way around his fakes. No wonder he wins national titles every year. "Go!" he shouted.

We did, following Rosie back out onto the Mall, heading north into the streets of D.C.

When I looked back, Cisco had climbed up and over the wall itself. He was sprinting away from the guards, headed south. They weren't following him.

Because they were focusing all their energy on chasing us.

We only had about five seconds of a head start on the guards, but Rosie knew the city well, and she led us down one side street after another until I was totally turned around and had lost track of where I was. We finally stopped running when we were sure we had lost them.

"How'd you find us?" I said.

"I was worried," Rosie said. "I went back in to get some files out of my desk. The office is crowded enough that I thought I could sneak back in with this disguise. I was on my way out the door, when I overheard someone talking on the phone. I heard them use the word "kids" and I started to listen—it was something about bringing you guys in. They were sending a van to the Vietnam Memorial. I called Cisco's cell and when he told me you had headed in that direction, I met up with him and we rushed over. Just in time, too, I guess."

"Yeah, thanks," Hal said. "While we were there, I was seeing what they had in mind once they caught us. I saw their plan all laid out. They had an unmarked van. They were going to inject us with tranquilizers. Scary stuff."

I felt myself shiver. Callie hugged her arms across her chest. Nia ran her hand through her hair.

"Turn here," said Rosie, directing us down a narrow street, which led to a public square. We jogged across it. At the other side, Rosie dipped into what I thought was going to be a store—it was a doorway in the side of a building—but turned out to be nothing but an alcove with a huge escalator leading down underground.

"It's the Metro," Rosie explained. "One of the greatest hiding places in Washington." She passed us all fare cards. "These will get you in and out no matter what station we go to," she explained.

But when we were about a quarter of the way down the escalator, I looked up to the top, and pointed. There, muscling their way onto the crowded escalator, were the two guards who had been chasing us. My heart sank. Was it possible we would *never* get away from these guys?

We started to push our way past people who were standing on the escalator, reading their papers and checking their phones. The guards were gaining on us. We started to run, not bothering with the fare cards as we hurled our bodies over the turnstiles.

In front of us, another escalator led down to the train platform. We could see a train just stopping on the platform below us.

"We're not going to make it," Callie warned in a low, shaking voice.

I checked behind us and saw that, in addition to the two guards chasing us, there was a third man I recognized from the airstrip. He had the husky body of a football player or former marine, and he was lumbering down the escalator toward us. Fortunately it was crowded, and our pursuers had to duck around the other commuters in front of them and sometimes even wait, standing, impatient and furious.

Just as a warning bell let us know that the train doors were closing, Hal hit the platform at a sprint, with Rosie and Callie right behind him, then Nia and me tearing for the doors. Hal made it to the train doors just as they closed in his face. People just getting off the train streamed toward us. We used them as cover, their bodies a human barrier between us and the beefy guard who had reached the bottom of the escalator.

"What now?" Hal asked Rosie, but I could see that she had run out of options. I remembered seeing the same look in my mom's eyes toward the end of the year we spent driving around in the RV.

Hal took over. The crowd was heading back up onto the escalator, and I guess for lack of a better idea, we followed. The men spotted us and got on the escalator again too, about ten feet behind us. We couldn't push past people on the escalator now—it was far too crowded for that.

There was no way out. At the top of the escalator, we'd get nabbed like fish in a net. The way the security guys behind us were holding their bodies, you could tell they knew this. They were relieved, confident. You could see it in their mouths—their jaws were set in a look almost of boredom, like they were just as convinced they only had to wait a few minutes and this would all be over.

I was just as convinced as they were that we were going to get caught. I mean, we were just kids. They were adults, trained for this sort of work.

I wondered where the guards would take us. That van Hal had seen? Would Dr. Joy be waiting for us in the backseat? What would he do to us? I felt my skin recoiling against the idea that he would take blood from my veins and lock it into a refrigerated tank. I clutched the pendant holding my dad's blood like it was a talisman, like he was here to protect me in some way.

Just then, I heard the squeaking whine of another train pulling in. I felt every cell in my body jump at the thought that there was hope. Maybe we could evade the three guards—and get onto that train! But even as I was getting my hopes up, Callie was doing the math, estimating the number of seconds the train would take to stop, to unload passengers, to let passengers on, to close its doors—and she was comparing that number to the pace at which we were traveling up and the pace at which we'd make our way down. "We can't do it," she said. "We won't make this one either." Hard to believe she could do this with mental math—that's Callie for you.

But Rosie took Callie's calculation and turned it on its head. Catapulting over the side of the railing, she landed in between the up and down sides of the escalator, balancing on the polished steel slope between them, her knees bent like she was surfing a wave. Hal was right behind her, and then Callie, and me, and Nia. It was really hard to balance, especially as we were trying to get down the slope as fast as we could. We half crab-walked, half slid over to the down escalator.

At first, the guards who were on their way up the escalator seemed frozen in place. As I passed Falls-Asleep-on-the-Job I made eye contact with him. He had piercing blue eyes and he was looking at me like there was a sheet of bulletproof glass between us, like if he tried to reach out for me, he would only hurt himself. Tattoo Face was quicker, but not quick enough. He reached out and he grabbed the tail of my shirt. But I yanked it out of his hand.

We stepped through the train doors, just as the chime sounded to let us know they were closing. Our car was heavily graffitied—S.HE.B.LIE.VD was scrawled in spray paint across one of the windows. I looked back at where we'd come from—the guards were struggling to push their way down the up escalator. One climbed up onto the metal slide where we had gone. But he seemed unable to let himself tumble down the way we had, so he was too late. The doors had just closed with a slap of rubber when the guards reached the platform edge.

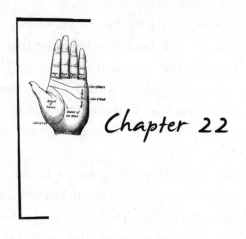

Chapter 22

Hal looked like he might be going into apoplectic shock. His eyes were bugging out and his skin was the color of paper. "I can't *believe* that," he said. "That was cutting it so close!"

Nia was looking around, walking from one end of the car to the other, peering through the windows into the cars on either side of ours. "I'm still not convinced they don't have people on the train."

"Are you any closer to getting to Amanda?" Rosie said in between panting breaths. "Is there anything I can do to help?"

We explained about seeing Callie's mom, the enhancement eraser she'd developed, and about finding the green bouquet.

"Well, you've got one piece of good luck," Rosie said,

digesting the new information. "This Metro line goes right out to Arlington National Cemetery."

Nia sighed. I could see that she was scared and tired, and also exhausted, both from the chase and from the effort she'd expended at the Vietnam Memorial—for the encounter with Amanda had used a good deal of energy. Nia sat down next to Callie and the two of them stared straight out into space. How much more could one day hold?

But Hal was not tired. He was holding onto a strap as if he had too much energy to sit down. His mind must have been turning faster than the train wheels because suddenly he turned to Rosie, and as if he were taking up a conversation that they had just left off he said, "How did Amanda find us?" Rosie didn't say anything, waiting I think for Hal to explain his question. "You said before she just made friends naturally, but doesn't that seem a *little bit* coincidental?"

Rosie shrugged. "I told you—all Amanda said to me was that there was something she recognized in you. She told me she'd come looking for guides, and I asked her how she knew when she found one. She said it was just like making friends in any new town. You kind of wandered around, going from place to place without knowing anyone until suddenly, you meet someone and you feel a connection."

"Are you thinking she felt the connection with us, the

way we feel it with each other?" Callie said, looking up at Hal from her seat.

"You guys have really bonded, haven't you?" said Rosie.

"No," said Hal. He blushed. "I mean, yes, we're bonded. But it's more than that. We have this thing. When we get together. We can kind of see into each other's heads."

"We make each other stronger," said Callie.

"Stronger how?" Rosie asked.

So we told her. About how our strange abilities seemed to work better when we were touching. How Callie's strength had passed to Hal. How Nia's visions were stronger and could be shared when we were holding hands.

When we'd finished talking, Rosie just stood there, shaking her head. She was quiet a good long time and I felt kind of guilty, as if I were burdening her with too much information. I wished I could take it all back. Amanda must have felt this way all the time.

Our train climbed out of its tunnel and began crossing a bridge over the Potomac River. For a time, you could see all of D.C. through the train's rattling windows. I took my camera out and snapped a few shots, mostly to calm myself down. I focused in on the sunlight gleaming on the dome of the Jefferson Memorial, the pillars of the Lincoln Memorial, straight and tall.

"Being with you guys," Rosie said at last. "It's like being with Amanda again. You are all so much like her. It's like each one of you is carrying around a piece of her. Because those things you're good at? Your abilities, or powers, or whatever you want to call them? Those are Amanda's powers too. Zoe, Amanda could blend in just like you—people wouldn't even seem to see her when she didn't want them to. She's got Callie's strength, Nia's intuitive connection to the past, Hal's ability to see what is coming—all of you, what you have, that's part of her too."

I put my camera down. "Wow," I said. "That's intense."

"Yes," Callie agreed. "I know exactly what you mean."

When we got off the train just outside the gates that led into Arlington National Cemetery, I thought again of my dad.

Every time I pass a cemetery I do. Even a military cemetery where dead presidents lie next to American soldiers.

In the distance, I saw a hearse followed by a line of cars, leaving the cemetery. A funeral. The good-bye my dad couldn't have.

"Come on," Hal said, and I realized everyone was ahead of me. I'd stopped at the gates as if I wasn't actually going to be able to enter. But I was. This was important. It was something I had to do.

I squared my shoulders and held the last existing part of my dad tightly. I followed my friends into the cemetery.

"I think this place is bigger than the entire town of Orion," Callie said.

Nia sighed, slightly exasperated. "I sort of thought, with the Arlington National Cemetery quote, we'd get here and we'd just be . . . well . . . here. And somehow it would be obvious what it was we needed to find."

"I know what you mean," said Hal. "And frankly, I don't have a lot of brain power left to apply to another mental puzzle. My ability to concentrate is blown to pieces. I don't even know where to start."

"Let's be rational about this," said Nia. She pulled out the by now quite rumpled scavenger hunt. "It says here we're supposed to find the Tomb of the Unknown Soldier. We might as well at least get a picture of it for credit. And maybe there'll be something there to help us know where to go next. After all, Amanda must know we're using the hunt—she's been laying clues along our path all day."

The Tomb of the Unknown Soldier wasn't hard to find. In fact, it would have been hard to miss. It sits at the top of a long run of steps, carved into the mountainside, about the size of the stage in our auditorium at Endeavor. Behind the platform we could see the columns surrounding the Memorial Amphitheater, which sits directly behind the tomb.

"Okay," I said, looking at it. "Now what?"

"Now," Nia said, elbowing me frantically in the ribs and gesturing toward the tomb. "That's what."

Because standing on the steps right in front of the tomb, looking out at us and across all the graves of people who had given their lives in service of their country, was Amanda. Arabella. Ariel. She smiled wide in welcome, as if she'd been waiting here for us all this time.

All through the course of the long weeks that we'd been looking for her, I'd tried to carry an image of her face in my head. And it was there now, but so much more vivid than in my memory. Her gray-green eyes, her wide, high forehead, her mouth that even without one outrageous shade of lipstick or another was shaped like a kiss—it was all her.

Amanda—the master of disguise—for once looked only like herself. Her hair was pulled back into a low pony-tail, she was wearing a black turtleneck sweater, jeans, a pea coat, and low-top sneakers. She was looking down at all of us and for a minute, I thought of the kind of paint-ing you see in a church, of an angel looking down from heaven.

After running through the subway, after the conversa-tion on the train, I was tired. But now, seeing Amanda, I suddenly felt my energy return. Just seeing her alive was such a relief. I remembered how *good* I always felt when Amanda was around. She made everything she touched seem cool. I felt like I'd just had a heavy burden taken out of my hands. My arms fell limp and relaxed at my sides. The air felt deeper and cleaner than anything I'd breathed in a long time.

Amanda took a few steps, down and around the back of the tomb. She had her hands pushed deep into her front pockets. Locking gazes with me, she raised her eyebrows and for a second, I felt like I could hear her counting inside her head, like she was giving me the upbeat on a song I was about to come in on, that she was deciding how fast it was going to go and when it would begin.

I know this is totally insane, but from that moment on, I knew that Amanda was in control. No matter what anyone else did or said, Amanda was going to get the better of this. She jumped down from the tomb's platform and began walking in our direction.

After a long, deep look into her sister's eyes, which turned into a long, deep grin, Amanda turned to us, and we all ran and collapsed into a huge group hug. "I can't believe you're here!" Callie cried. Nia said, "I know!" Hal just squeezed everyone really hard, and Amanda, standing in the middle, smiled warmly at each of us, touching a shoulder, a cheek as she went.

Amanda smelled the same, felt the same. "I am so glad to see you guys," she said, and I said, "Right back at you."

Of course, as soon as we all were touching, I felt the same kind of electric connection come to life with a tingling explosion—it had never been this strong before. I had this plastic puzzle when I was a little kid and I remember loving the way it felt when the pieces clicked into place. I felt that way now.

"*The joy of meeting pays the pangs of absence; else who could bear it?*" Amanda said, her voice soft and moving unexpectedly, like a barely suppressed laugh. As always, she'd found a quote that put what we were all feeling into words.

Nia's face lit up—I could see that Amanda's presence gave her the same energy and sense of possibility I felt also. "Nicholas Rowe," she said. "Totally obscure. How did you know I'd just come across it?"

Amanda raised her eyebrows again and smiled.

"Amanda," Callie said. "Are you okay? You're in danger."

"We all are," she said, her voice sounding anything but rushed and afraid. "But can you feel it?"

I nodded.

"You feel stronger when we're all together," she said. "Because we are stronger together than we are apart."

"That's what you've been trying to tell us, isn't it?"

"Exactly," she said.

"I have so many questions," Nia said.

"I'm sure you do," said Amanda. "I'm sure you all do."

"Yeah, but suddenly they don't feel important," said Hal.

"I feel—" Callie began. "I feel amazing right now."

I nodded, because it was true. Colors were brighter, sound was clearer. The smell of the freshly cut grass somewhere nearby was carried on a breeze to my nose. The feel of my fingers rubbing the fabric of my shirt was heavenly.

Amanda turned to me. "I want to talk to you. I want to be your friend. But your listening is important right now," she said. "Pay attention. To everything that I have said and that you've heard today."

To Callie, she said, "You're learning that strength is not just in your muscles but in your heart. You will not bend."

To Nia: "You can see the past but you must think only of the future."

And to Hal: "There is no such thing as destiny."

Her last comment made me think of an entry I'd seen recently on the Amanda Project website. A girl from Nevada, Rebecca Laewima, wrote in to say that Amanda had once helped her pick out her own totem—the horse, which usually means leader, but which Rebecca said can also mean "destined." Did Amanda really not believe in destiny?

Amanda picked up the scavenger hunt sheet. "Was this horrible?" she said. She smiled and I could see in her eyes that she understood how hard all this had been, how in the dark we'd felt, how scared.

"It's going to get even worse," she said. "But I know we can beat this. I have a plan."

"My mom wanted me to give this to you," Callie said, handing Amanda the enhancement eraser. "Don't drink it now, but if you ever want to go back . . . to the person you would have been without all the changes Dr. Joy made, she thinks this will do it."

Amanda raised her eyebrows. "If I drink this, the Official will no longer want me."

"So drink it," said Rosie. "What are you waiting for?"

"I don't just want to save myself," Amanda said. "I want to save us all."

"Ariel," Rosie said, calling Amanda by her real name. "Are you sure you understand him as well as you think you do? Do you know what he wants?"

"He wants me," she said. "He'll take all of you too, but it's me he really wants. And if he can't have me, then he wants my blood. I think he wants to use our blood to re-create us—like cloning, but less direct." She lifted her head suddenly, like a deer who has heard something. "I have to go," she said. She crossed her fingers, held them out to us in a little wave, as if waving and wishing good luck were the same thing. Then she disappeared behind the tomb.

Suddenly, Hal was pulling at my elbow, just as I heard the rhythm of running feet. We all ducked behind a series of grave markers in time to see the guards who had been chasing us all afternoon take off, running after Amanda, wherever she had gone.

"I guess they're not interested in us anymore," Callie said watching them go.

Hal nodded. "What should we do now?" he asked.

"You should go back to the group," Rosie said. "You're safer there."

"We do have a check-in soon—in less than an hour," Nia said. "And I want to make sure that Cisco is safe."

"Come on, then," said Rosie. "We can walk over the Arlington Memorial Bridge back to the Mall. We'll have to hurry."

Callie sighed. As we started to cross the bridge, I took some shots of the waves, just starting to get choppy in the brisk spring wind. The cherry trees lining the bank formed a cloud of pink. I captured the image of our shadows cast forward on the sidewalk. The five of us walking side by side.

"There's something I think we should do," Rosie said. "Anything we have, any physical evidence of what's going on here, could put us in danger. You want to be careful not to have any of it with you. It could be used against you. Or it could get into the wrong hands."

"What do you mean?" I said. "Whose hands?"

"I don't know," she said. "I just know that my father was very clear about that before they took him, and he told me to be sure to tell you too."

Nia pulled the envelopes out of her pocket. "How about these?" she said.

"Rip them up," said Rosie. "Toss them into the water."

Nia did as Rosie told her to and the flakes of ripped paper were picked up by the wind and swirled high up into the air before they drifted, randomly, gracefully, down to the gray water, like snow.

"Anything else?" she said.

Nia held up the red and blue key cards. "We still don't know what these are," she said. "We forgot to ask."

"Keep them," Rosie suggested. "But somewhere safe." Nia stuffed them down into her boot.

I rubbed the pendant in my pocket.

Was I imagining it, or was Rosie looking at me? Did she know?

I started to put parts of my dad's stories—the ones he and Amanda's mom would go over in our kitchen back in

Pinkerton—together with what we'd seen in the lab. In one of my dad's stories he talked about how kids got woken up in the mornings with classical music blaring, so that the first thought of their day would be light-filled harmony, but it only left them all feeling sick. In contrast, as a kid I got woken up in the mornings with a cream cheese–bacon omelet—my favorite.

Amanda's mom had laughed about the use of stopwatches timing what they ate.

My dad had reminded her about how, for one whole year, they'd never eaten the same food twice—one week it was all curry, another all pancakes, working their way through every culture's foods. My dad was so scarred by this he used to let us eat mac and cheese from the box every single night if we asked for it.

Suddenly, I felt a pang of understanding, for what my happy, goofy dad had gone through. Flash cards instead of family, the rows of beds instead of rooms where you could close a door, weekly check-ins with the nurse instead of spontaneous conversations with a parent who actually cared about you.

It wasn't fair. Any of it.

And this was my chance to help to make it stop.

I pulled the pendant from my pocket, removed the vial, and held it up to the light. The sun shone through it, turning the almost black color of the blood a vibrant scarlet with lights of orange. "This is my father," I said. I turned to the others. "He loved me." I squeezed my eyes shut, but the tears poured down anyway. "And this is all that's left of him."

The others nodded, and it wasn't a fake kind of "we feel your pain" nod. Because I could see in each of their faces that they were experiencing the feelings I was having, that they had managed to absorb what I knew.

The story of my dad was part of them now. . . . I was not alone in my pain. That knowledge gave me the strength to extend the vial over the side of the bridge, remove the seal, and peel my fingers away one by one to let the vial fall into the surf, where it hit and bobbed for a second before the water enveloped it. I watched it sink below the surface.

I didn't say good-bye out loud. But I squeezed my eyes shut and thought it. I pictured his face in my mind, smiling at me, knowing that I was carrying him inside me.

Callie, Hal, and Nia reached out for me, wrapping their arms around me. I felt the current pass from each of them, through me and back out again. But instead of jumping away from it as I had the first few times, I relaxed into it.

This was what we had now. Each other.

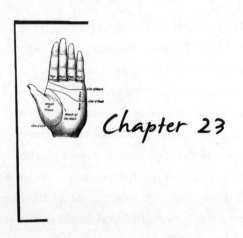

Chapter 23

We walked across the rest of the bridge in silence. On the other side, we saw a kiosk selling drinks and Washington, D.C., T-shirts, maps, and postcards, and Callie moved toward it.

She stopped in front of the rack of postcards as if she were thinking very carefully about which one she wanted to buy. She pulled her phone out of her jacket pocket, and lined it up in front of a postcard of the Museum of American History. She pressed a few buttons on her phone, then held it up to show Hal, Nia, and then me.

"Brilliant," said Nia, getting Callie's idea right away.

The photograph in the phone made it look like Callie herself had taken a picture of the Museum of American History.

Nia picked up a postcard packet—twelve postcards

bound together in an accordion fold: *Monuments in Bloom: 12 Must-See Attractions in Cherry Blossom Season.* "This should do it," she said. I lined up my camera and started to take pictures.

Callie and Hal continued to scan the racks of post-cards for more shots taken while the cherry trees were in bloom. The spinner racks were set up in a row in front of the kiosk, and we worked our way around to the back. Which is lucky, because it gave us somewhere to hide when Hal grabbed my arm, pulling me back. He glared at Nia and then Callie and they froze as well. Rosie, seeing our near-instantaneous stillness, shifted so she couldn't be seen.

Through a space in the racks, I saw what Hal must have known was coming—one of the guards, heading right for us. Between two rows of postcards, I caught the glint of the metal snaps on his shiny jacket, the pleats on his black pants. He was walking purposefully, like he already knew where to find us. In just a few seconds he would have us.

Except that, when he was only five steps away, Rosie dashed out from behind the postcard kiosks. Before we could do anything to stop her, she took off at a sprint. The guard recognized her and took off after her.

It all happened so fast, it was over before we could do anything to stop her. Rosie must have known that we wouldn't have let her sacrifice herself to save us.

Nia's face had gone from olive to gray. Hal pushed his

hair off his forehead and rubbed the bridge of his nose. Callie put a hand on his shoulder and he kind of leaned into her for strength.

We made our way along the mall, passing the Lincoln Memorial, the Jefferson Memorial, the World War II Memorial. As we were getting ready to cross 17th Street, we heard police sirens in the distance, in the direction that Rosie had sprinted. A shudder passed through my body, thinking that those sirens might be connected to her, or to Amanda, or to both. I thought about how their mother had died. An accident that was the result of being chased. Nowhere felt safe anymore.

By the time we reconnected with the group, we were late. The buses were already loaded and Mr. Fowler was standing at the open doorway, checking his watch and looking panicked. We took the last few dozen yards at a jog.

"Well, thank you very much," he said to us in a huff. "I almost had a heart attack here. We will not be able to even *go* on History Club field trips any longer if students behave as inconsiderately as you four have. You have my number—you did not think to call? If not for Heidi Bragg letting me know how routinely irresponsible you four are, I would have alerted the police. *And* you've almost made us miss our tour of the Capitol. Mr. Thornhill worked very hard to secure tickets to a viewing of the Senate chamber, and I would hate for your carelessness to ruin that for the rest of the group."

I barely heard him. I didn't even care that we were getting yelled at, it was so good to be safe inside the bus reunited with Cisco and our group.

"Let's go," he shouted to the driver as soon as we had boarded the bus. It smelled like old lunches and air freshener.

"Sorry, Mr. Fowler," Callie said, hanging her head. I could see that she was smiling. But her smile turned to a thin-lipped look of resolution. Yes, we were safe here on the bus. But what about Rosie? And what about Amanda?

At the Capitol, there was a security check-in just inside the doors. There were a number of students ahead of us—and Heidi had a lot of jewelry to unload—but after waiting for a while we got to the front of the line. I laid my camera carefully in the plastic tray to slide it through the X-ray machine and got in line behind Callie. Hal had a guitar pick, house keys, and his duct tape wallet and duct tape phone. Nia tossed in a giant green plastic ring, a pocket-size edition of *The Death of Ivan Ilych*, a lipstick, a much-chewed pencil stub, an expensive-looking green leather wallet, and a hair clip. Callie had almost nothing in her pockets, but the security guy emptied her backpack of a water bottle, lip gloss, a copy of *Lucky* magazine, some loose change and dollar bilis, a pen shaped like a candy cane, and a pack of bubble gum. The guard picked up my camera, rotated it in his hands, and asked me to take a picture to prove it wasn't some kind of explosive.

"Smile," I said, framing his pimply face—his hair was so light you couldn't even describe the stuff on his upper lip as peach fuzz.

But for a second, as I was focusing in, the foreground of my picture went blurry and I could see only what lay deeper in the shot. And that's when I noticed a kindly-looking man watching from a few steps away, his hands folded together as if he was struggling to stay still. He was staring straight at my camera lens, which was weird—was he watching us? But what was even weirder was that I recognized him, though it took me a second to remember from where. All I could remember was that I'd had a good feeling about him. It was an association with my dad, with grown-ups I liked.

As soon as I pressed down on the shutter—he must have heard the noise—he flinched slightly, like someone who is so modest he doesn't like to think his picture is being taken.

I'd seen him recently.

And then it hit me. He was the kindly businessman who'd picked up the scavenger hunt sheet when we'd dropped it on the way to the Vietnam Memorial. Where we'd come as close to getting caught by the Official's guards as we had all day. How did this man get here, to the Capitol? Was it a coincidence? He wasn't some kind of a senator or something, was he?

I felt like maybe his being here was a good thing. A sign that things were about to turn around for us. He wasn't my dad, but he sure looked like a dad. That had to be good news, right?

Callie must have noticed him at the same time I did. When I lowered the camera, I saw that she'd already taken a few steps in his direction, addressing him with a casual, happy grin. "Hey," she said. "Remember us?"

The man smiled, the same slightly skeptical but intrigued smile he'd given us on the sidewalk. I remembered how likable this man was. He nodded. "You were working on the scavenger hunt, right?"

Callie nodded brightly. I glanced at Hal and Nia. They were both watching intently, and I could see the same kind of hope in them that I was feeling. I remembered Rosie saying we were safe with the school group. Maybe this man had something to do with our safety. He seemed so comfortable and relaxed, and in control of everything.

"Do you work here?" Callie asked, her smile trusting. All of us were ready to believe. I look back and wonder at this—how this man had made us feel we could trust him.

The man laughed, and for the first time, I felt a shudder of doubt. I think a door opened inside my brain, a tiny crack of an opening. I didn't want to change my mind about someone just because he had a laugh that wasn't very nice. But then again, the way people laugh says a lot about them. There are people out there who laugh at things that aren't funny. It doesn't make them evil, it just means they might not have much of a sense of humor.

"I don't work in this building," he said. "I'm just visiting it, like I assume you are. But I do work for the government."

I was starting to trust him again, to forget the suspicious way he'd laughed.

Callie relaxed as well. "You work for the government?" she said. "That's cool. What do you do?"

And then the man seemed to almost wink as he said, "Oh, me? I'm just another of many officials." Or maybe it wasn't a wink. Maybe it was a blink. Maybe he was narrowing his eyes. I don't know exactly what happened to his face, except it changed. Dramatically. And suddenly, he wasn't nice anymore. He wasn't an amused businessman helping a group of kids.

I knew then. We all knew. He wasn't just one of many government officials.

He was *the* government official. The Official.

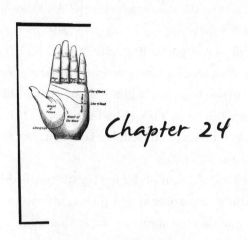

Chapter 24

Again, I remembered what Amanda had taught me. Be cool. Stay still.

I started collecting my things from the bin that had passed through the scanner, moving as slowly as if I had just stood up from sunbathing on the beach. Forcing myself to yawn, which is contagious, I hoped my deliberate calm would travel Hal, Callie, and Nia's way as well. It did. It was as if the deep breaths I was taking were slowing them also.

Callie glanced nervously toward our class, as if she were making sure they wouldn't leave without us, but then, after she sensed me staring at her, she sighed.

"Uh . . ." said Hal to the Official. "We have to get back to our group."

How was it possible for someone to seem so trustworthy

and then transform into someone totally awful? How had it happened just in the course of a laugh? And how had I missed it? I'd believed him. I was generally so good at reading people—too good. But with him, I had failed. Utterly. Like Amanda, he was someone I could not read.

When I turned back to the group, I saw Heidi. She was staring at the Official in a way I had never seen her stare before. Her eyebrows were angled, her jaw tight, her mouth pulled back in expectation.

"Look at Heidi," I said under my breath to the others. I hid behind my camera, taking a picture to capture her expression. "See the way she's looking at that man."

"She knows him," said Callie.

I swung the camera back toward the Official in time to see him returning Heidi's gaze. Right as I pressed the shutter, he winked at her.

Just then, Mr. Fowler introduced a woman named Jackie, who was going to serve as a tour guide. She led us away from the security check-in and to the starting point of the tour, which was a spot directly under the Capitol's rotunda. The man who we now believed to be the Official watched us go.

There are a lot of interesting facts to be learned about the U.S. Capitol, and Jackie mentioned many of them. For example, the dome we were standing under? In the center of it, your voice was trapped, but if you stood anywhere under its perimeter, your voice would travel across it, such that even a whisper at the northern tip of it would be audible to someone standing at the edge that was due south.

Jackie mentioned that the Capitol contains 16.5 acres of floor space. There are 540 rooms, 658 windows, and 850 doorways. The chambers where the House and the Senate originally met are like little museums now. One is filled with statues, and the other is filled with the desks senators used to sit in. You can see the ink wells the senators used to dip their pens in.

There are trains underground linking congressmen's office buildings and the Capitol so that when it's time to vote, they can rush over. There are special elevators and conference rooms as well. There was so much to learn about which laws were made, and when and how all of it was done—right under this roof.

Impressive stuff, and I forced myself to pay attention. It was the only way to keep from screaming or running away. The Official! Here in the Capitol Building! I started snapping pictures with my camera, shots of people's sneakers looking dusty and worn on the shining marble floors, eagles carved into the tops of pillars, their talons vicious and menacing, light pouring through a window that was taller than me, the shadows cast by crenellated cornice work that always reminded me of baby teeth.

What got my attention at the end of the tour was when Jackie led us up a flight of stairs into a hallway on the third floor and then stopped at a set of double doors. "You all are very lucky today," she said. "Not every school group gets to see our government in action, but today the Senate is in session and you all will have the opportunity to take a peek."

I thought we'd see congressmen and -women banging their fists on their desks, shouting to be heard. Or maybe it would be more like the Republican Senate in the *Star Wars* movies, where space-dwelling creatures of all stripes board a little speedboat-like mini-spaceship to be transported to the middle of the Senate orb to speak. I thought at least there would be people in the room, even if it wasn't totally packed the way it is for the State of the Union, when they set the justices of the Supreme Court up on folding chairs in the front row, like they were moms and dads crammed into a classroom on the day of the first-grade class play.

I wasn't prepared for the fact that the only senator in the entire room was giving a speech to no one but a television camera set up a few feet from his face. He was talking as if the room were full, but as we filed through the double doors and into seats in the viewing gallery that stretched around the top of the chamber, I realized that no one was listening, not even the pages holding his briefcase nor the guy dusting the carvings in the back of the room.

"That's C-SPAN," Jackie whispered to us, sotto voce. "You all know the C-SPAN channel?"

Yeah, I thought. Like the shopping channel, it was one to flip past.

It took a lot of concentration to figure out what the

senator was actually speaking about, but finally I worked it out. There was an amendment that had been proposed to a bill that was up for consideration. In the amendment there was a paragraph. In that paragraph there was a sentence. And in that sentence there was a phrase . . . a phrase this guy didn't like. Because it used the word "it" instead of saying "the programs now and continuing."

As soon as I figured that out, I slunk down in my seat and let my mind wander. The Senate looks like an old-fashioned school room. There's an antique wooden desk set up for every senator, but where the teacher would sit there is an elevated dais that looks like the spot a judge might sit in if this were a courtroom. No one was there, of course, except a young woman in a suit who looked like a secretary, stacking papers. Occasionally someone would walk through the room and push in the chairs that were randomly pushed back from the senators' last departure.

"I think there might be a vote coming up, so hold on," Jackie said. "You'll see all the senators rush into the room for that."

But something even more "exciting" happened first. The Official entered the viewing gallery and strode purposefully toward us. He had the same "Who me?" innocent, happy-go-lucky expression on his face, but he clearly wasn't happy, as I'd originally thought. He was gloating. I had the sudden intuition that if things stopped going his way at any point, we'd see an entirely different kind of expression cross his face, and it wouldn't remind me in any way of anything I'd known with my dad.

I exchanged panicked glances with Nia, who had spotted the Official as well. He leaned over to whisper something in Jackie's ear and she clapped her hands together like a child on Christmas in one of those movies where it always snows and Santa is real.

"Students," Jackie said, looking to Mr. Fowler, beaming at him, beaming back at the Official. "I have some really remarkable news. This gentleman here has arranged for four lucky students to have a personal look at the Senate floor."

"I'll escort them down myself and vouch for their, uh"—did anyone but me notice the Official pause?—"safety."

"Would you like me to select the students for you?" Mr. Fowler suggested. "There are some real civics buffs in our midst like Allie K. over there, and it would be an honor—"

The Official cut him off. He pointed—where else?—at Callie, Hal, Nia, and me. "How about those four," he said. "They look like impressive scholars of American history." Was he laughing? I couldn't help but notice that he was looking at us like we should be laughing along with him, enjoying this process, like this was all some kind of great inside joke. I also noticed the tattoo-faced guard had entered the viewing gallery, blocking the door that was our only way out.

I don't know what we would have done if the Official

hadn't bent down to whisper, "If you care about Amanda's safety you'll come with me without a struggle." Maybe we would have tried to run? Maybe we would have asked Mr. Fowler for help? Turned to Cisco? Maybe we just could have screamed?

But we believed the Official that we were saving Amanda by doing what he said, so we stood without protest and followed him out of the viewing gallery. Nia didn't even so much as glance in Cisco's direction as she left.

Following the Official out into the hall and down a flight of stairs, I couldn't help but notice the neat corners of the shoulders of his suit jacket, the trim hair at the back of his neck. He looked like someone who never missed a detail. The shabby briefcase he'd carried when we'd first seen him was gone, and I wondered if that had been part of a disguise—I knew from Amanda that sometimes all it takes is one detail to make yourself come across as entirely different from who you really are.

I also couldn't help but notice the guards. Tattoo-Face followed about ten paces behind, and Falls-Asleep-at-Desk was ten paces ahead.

The Official didn't threaten us, or even check that we were following. He seemed brisk and busy, smiling at strangers we passed, as if he was accepting their congratulations for participating in Take Your Lame and Surly Teenage Appendage to Work Day.

Sometimes he even smiled at us.

We didn't smile back.

I don't think I could have smiled if someone was holding a gun to my head. I felt like I had sandbags tied to my ankles. With every step I felt the dread sink lower into my gut. Was this the end? Was this when we all got tied to a hospital bed in a basement prison, like Thornhill?

I was sure we would never see our class again. I was sure I wouldn't see my family. I looked at the other guides. Did they understand how bad this was?

They must have. Hal and Callie were holding hands. Nia gave me a strained look that showed a lot more fear than she's usually willing to reveal. We had to think of a way to escape. If only we could talk without the Official hearing. If only we knew what was coming—I remembered the van Hal said he'd seen when we almost got caught at the Vietnam Memorial. Was that waiting for us now? Mr. Fowler wasn't the brightest bulb in the firmament, but wouldn't he at least recognize that we were missing?

I remembered with dismay all the tunnels Jackie had told us about, linking the congressional office buildings. We could travel quite a ways before anyone even knew we were missing.

Then the Official opened a door and we followed him into the floor of the Senate chamber. Just as he had promised, we were standing on the dark blue carpeting, facing the dark paneled walls, looking down over the curved rows of polished wooden desks, up to the dais. We could see kids in gray pants and skirts placing a red carnation on every senator's seat. When I looked up, there in the gallery was my class, with Mr. Fowler waving down at us madly and everyone else looking bored. The senator who had been speaking into the C-SPAN camera was leaving as we came in.

But then he turned to face us and all the joviality in his expression was gone. "Don't move or say a word," he said to us.

The woman stacking papers up on the dais turned to look at him sharply and I wondered for a second if we were saved. Maybe he'd forgotten she was there? Maybe she'd rescue us? Then I saw who she was. Blond, beautiful. I remembered her from the Riveras' porch. Nia, Callie, and Hal had been inside and I'd been watching from afar. Cisco had opened the door and the woman had introduced herself as Waverly Valentino, Amanda's aunt. Cisco hadn't believed her, and it turned out that he was right.

Now, I could see the woman was watching the four of us, an I-told-you-so smile spreading on her lips. The Official gave one glance in her direction, then he turned and I had a feeling he was about to deliver some bad news, when the befuddled senator reentered and passed within a few feet of us.

Like watching someone draw a curtain across a lit window at night, the Official changed his expression by muting certain features and turning others on. I once read that psychologists in the 1950s analyzed the thousands of micro movements humans are capable of making with their faces, coming up with a catalog of the combinations that we use to communicate to the world. We cannot consciously control those movements, but it seemed that the Official could. He was so dexterous he could turn his face into a mask. Gone was the evil android, gone was the gloating bad guy, gone was the kindly grown-up. Instead, we were faced with someone who did indeed seem like a government official—officious, impersonal, bland.

"Forget something?" he called out to the senator.

The man held up a hand in a kind of salute and kept shuffling along. "Glasses," he finally said, seeing what he'd been missing on a desk.

I had a flash of a thought. Maybe there was something we could do to get his attention without the Official realizing we were signaling for help. Every idea I had felt impossible—like writing a note and sticking it into his pocket. There wasn't enough time.

The Official seemed to have read my mind. Under his breath, he said, "He's completely useless to you. It's stunning that in our age of television someone that old still appears on top of things in a reelection campaign."

Then he gestured for us to move forward to a row of chairs that had been set up right behind where the television camera had been taping before. The chairs were squeezed up close to each other, and because I was still so scared, I was grateful to be pressed right up against Nia and Hal.

I was getting used to the electric tingle that criss-crossed my body whenever the four of us were touching, and now it felt kind of comforting. It reminded me that we were stronger when we were together. Maybe we still had the power to resist?

"I want to explain things to you," the Official said once we were seated. He spoke with a bored equanimity. That could have been part of his disguise—no one could hear us from the gallery but if he seemed to be berating or threatening us, Mr. Fowler might have noticed. (Well, he might have if he were anyone but Mr. Fowler.) In any case, this was an altogether new iteration of the Official's many faces, and it would have been calming if we weren't all aware of the sinister intentions his bored *pro forma* speech was meant to disguise.

"The bottom line is that you have no more outs," he said. "I know you're thinking that if you've been able to keep from getting caught this long, you have a chance of escape now. So let me tell you now: I haven't *wanted* to bring you in until just this moment. I've been watching you. I saw you kids cleaning Amanda's graffiti off the vice principal's car, and I watched you, Zoe, as you watched them."

"We're not afraid of you," Nia spat out.

"Well, good for you, Miss Rivera," said the Official, and it sounded like he was talking to a three-year-old who'd just learned how to use the potty. "Though you probably should be," he said, chuckling at his own joke. And then he was back to being a kind, disinterested grown-up concerned only about our safety. "The problem with teenagers today is they think they're immortal. They think nothing bad can ever happen to them. That's why they end up in gruesome car accidents, or jumping off trestle bridges where they're not supposed to swim."

"We're not doing any of those things," Nia said. "We're not the ones making the danger. You are."

The Official shrugged. "It's up to you," he said. "If you want to keep running, I'll keep chasing, but you won't ever be out of my sights. Don't think there are things I will do and things I won't do. Your parents can't help you. By involving yourselves in all of this, you've already put your brothers and sisters in danger. Surely, you don't want to put them at any greater risk?"

Hal could not mask the spasm of regret and fear that crossed his face. I could tell that he was thinking of Cornelia—wishing that he'd never gotten her involved. He'd told her about their dad, about the stuff we'd found at the college, about the C33 program as far as we'd understood it. Why hadn't he anticipated the danger though, told her to go underground? To stick close by their dad? Anything.

I felt the electricity intensify as all of us considered the risk we'd exposed our families to—I was thinking of Iris and Pen, how both my parents had sacrificed so much to keep us safe, and how I'd thrown it all away.

"Though frankly," the Official went on, speaking almost to himself now, "the closer you get to Amanda, the closer I get to Amanda, so I'd almost just as soon have you on the run as have you in my control."

"You said you already had her," I said.

"Did I?" the Official mused. "Well, the important thing is that I'll have her soon. She'll come running after you. I want you only because having you in custody will lure Amanda." The Official yawned. "But I promised Joy I'd deliver you all to him in one piece. He wants you to participate in his research. And frankly, once we bring in Amanda, locking you all away for the rest of your lives as human lab rats is fine with me."

"It won't work," Hal said. "There are too many good people fighting against it."

The Official fixed Hal with a stony stare. I could feel Hal shrink back down to a nub of fear.

I felt the fear too, creeping into my body like some sort of fast-moving frost. I was trying not to panic, to not beg. But I didn't know how long I could hold out.

Just then, I started to hear a shrill ringing noise. For a second I thought it was coming from inside my head. My mind was so filled with fear and adrenaline, and questions—it made sense that it would just start ringing. What was going on?

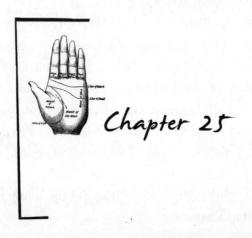

Chapter 25

The noise wasn't my imagination. The kids distributing carnations looked up, laid down their flowers, and filed quickly out of the room. Above us, I could see that our class was standing. As Jackie intoned in her nasal voice about "orderly lines" and "no talking" and "proceeding to the nearest marked exit," Mr. Fowler was counting heads, making sure that everyone was where he could see them.

I can't believe it took my brain that long to process the idea that this was a fire drill. A fire drill? In Congress? Who knew?

Before Mr. Fowler had a chance to finish his count and then remember that we four were downstairs, the Official called up to him. "Mr. Fowler," he said, projecting his voice with the confidence of someone running for president. He had to talk in between bleats of the alarm.

"I have your students here, and in the interest of safety, I will personally escort them to the school group's rendez-vous position on the Capitol lawn."

Looking simultaneously scared, distracted, and grateful, Mr. Fowler nodded, and began to wave his arms in front of his body, as if he could speed the pace at which the rest of our class was filing out of the gallery and through the double doors into the hall. Mr. Fowler looked back down one more time, as if wondering if it was really a good idea to leave four of his students alone with a strange man whose name he didn't even know. At that point, the Official laid a heavy hand on Callie's shoulder, and smiled his safest, most "Hey, I *love* kids" smile. By the time Callie had shrugged his hand off her body, Mr. Fowler had turned around and was gone.

"Oh, don't," the Official said in response to Callie's gesture, his voice languid and draw out as if he were deeply bored.

"Aren't you afraid there might be an actual fire?" Callie said.

The Official just smiled, confirming for me that this alarm was no coincidence. Just then, the woman who I still thought of as Waverly Valentino had come down from the podium and was standing at the Official's side. "Maude Cooper," he said, by way of introduction. "A former C33. Did you read about her?"

"No," Hal said.

"While so many C33s were given enhanced empathetic

capability, Maude was given less. She would make an excellent prison guard or executioner. Joy had intended her as a mole—she would infiltrate secret organizations without ever being swayed by the relationships she formed while there. As you can see, some of the C33s have proved quite useful instead of being troublesome. She'll escort you to your next destination."

"Right this way," Maude said, gesturing for us to move ahead of her.

The hallways of the Capitol building were filled with people leaving it: secretaries in sneakers and pantyhose, important-looking women in bright red suits and enormous pearls, young men reading blue-backed memos as they walked, their wing-tip shoes treading the paths they knew so well they didn't have to look up, a cafeteria worker in black-and-white-checked pants and a chef's jacket.

We turned a corner into a corridor where the river of people slowed to just a trickle, and then we passed through a door and down a staircase where we were alone. It went down several levels into what must have been a basement. There were lockers running the length of the hallway, break rooms, utility rooms, an enormous kitchen—I could smell food cooking—the same steamy smell you get in the hallway outside the cafeteria at school. The alarm was still ringing as Maude opened yet another door, which led through a dining room where tables were set with white tablecloths and fancy napkins. Lunch was long over and the tables looked like they were set up for the next day.

"Is this the senators' dining room?" Callie asked. Nia could not help but look interested. Even with her life in danger, any opportunity to learn could engage her mind and distract her.

"It is," Maude said, no trace of kindness in her voice. Not too far from the dining room's front doors was the train that led through tunnels under the Capitol, connecting congressmen and -women to their offices, the dining rooms, and the floors of both chambers whenever a vote was called.

The trains didn't look like trains. They were more like the kind of trolleys you ride around in at amusement parks—open on the sides with an awning over the top, benches that sit three across.

I wondered if the trains were even running, given that a fire drill was in progress, a question that was quickly answered when Maude beckoned for us to walk down onto the tracks in front of the train and head into the tunnel.

"What if the fire drill ends and the trains start running again?" Nia asked. "What happens then?"

"You'd better hurry," Maude said, "or else we're going to find out."

"Fire drills don't last forever," I told her. "Mr. Fowler's going to notice when we're not there. He'll call the police."

"We fully expect him to," Maude said. "And when the police come, our team will give them all the evidence they need to determine that you four used the cover of the fire drill to run away. Heidi will assure them—and I'm sure she won't be the only one—about how strange you've been acting recently. The police will be sure to discover evidence of how each of you were secretly a friend of Amanda Valentino, how her disappearance stunt inspired you all to try the same thing. You four show all the trouble signs. You're malcontents and you've been using your friendship to concoct this running-away plan."

"My parents will hire a private detective," Nia said. "They'll be all over this. My mom will camp out at the Washington police headquarters, making sure the cops are doing everything in their power to find me."

We were getting to the end of the tunnel where we could see a pinpoint of light.

"And the Washington police will come up empty every time," Maude said. "Because you won't be here."

"Where are we going?" I asked. Since my dad died, I've lived in a lot of places. It seemed that every time I'd get used to one, I'd be forced to leave it. So the feeling of being dragged somewhere against my will is something I was used to. What I wasn't used to was the feeling that this might be the last time I ever went anywhere new. The way Maude's tone had changed as she told us we were leaving Washington, I wondered if that feeling meant we were going to have to get ready to die.

Eventually we picked our way down the tracks to the end of the tunnel. We were in the basement of the Senate office building now, and because this building was not in the midst of a fire drill, Maude rushed us past janitors and men and women in suits. We turned down a few more hallways and up another set of stairs. One flight up, a hallway, then another flight down. I wondered if she was deliberately trying to confuse us, disorient any sense of direction so that if we did try to escape we wouldn't know how to get back.

It didn't matter. With one guard walking in front of our little quartet and another behind it, we weren't trying to run.

We ended up in a parking garage, walking to an unmarked van. The license plate read 2Q2Q10. Hal took a sharp breath in. I knew what he was seeing—the inside. We all saw it, too, when they opened the back doors and unceremoniously shoved us inside. It was there that we were handcuffed with the kind of plastic straps my mom uses to anchor bookshelves to wall mounts. There were benches along the sides of the stripped-out van and we were pushed down onto them. Each of us had an ankle strap attached to bolts in the floor, but we otherwise weren't secured to the bench in any way.

"My mother will be outraged when she finds out about this. You'll be locked up forever when she's done with you," Nia hissed at Maude. Maude smiled.

"For once in your life you'll find yourself in a place where you are outside your mother's control. I would think you'd be happy about that."

Nia glared at her. "Nothing about the current situation makes me happy." And then Maude shut the door.

And it was dark. Very, very dark.

The thing about riding in a van sitting on benches with your hands tied together and an ankle strapped to the floor is that you get very uncomfortable very fast. And then you stay uncomfortable. Every time the van went over a bump, I tried to brace myself on the seat, but still, we all were sliding, careening, and smashing into each other and the walls of the van.

Within minutes of being cuffed, I could feel the sharp edge of the plastic tie on my skin. I couldn't imagine how intense it felt for Callie and Hal. Nia and I, at least, were wearing boots.

Eventually the van must have moved onto a highway because the ride got smoother. I wasn't jerking around as much and the pain in my wrists, arms, and ankle subsided. A bit.

"So I guess we failed the scavenger hunt," Hal said. He and I were sharing a bench with Callie and Nia across from us.

I couldn't help it. The laughter came bubbling up. At least laughing was the only thing that I'd done in the last forty-five minutes that didn't hurt. "I guess so," I snorted.

"But we tried," Callie said, laughing as well. The whole situation—it was absurd.

Nia was laughing too. She tried to talk anyway. "And

no one else had to work on their scavenger hunt while being chased—" It took her three tries to get the rest of her thought out. "Being chased—" she repeated, but still she couldn't do it. "Being chased by—the Official's goons."

I was laughing so hard at this point that I think a few tears rolled down my cheeks. I tried wiping them away with the backs of my tied-up hands. It was too tricky an angle, so I had to let the tears just flow.

When we'd all laughed ourselves out and were ready again to pay attention to the throbbing parts of our bodies, Callie said "What do you think is going to happen to us?"

Even though they couldn't see me in the dark, I shook my head.

"Wish I knew," said Hal.

We were quiet then for a little while. I don't think anyone had the heart to say anything more.

Until suddenly, out of the darkness, I heard Nia's voice: "Train up a child."

It took me a second to remember what she was quoting from. Then I did—it was the line from JFK's inaugural address that we'd excerpted on our scavenger hunt sheet.

"The torch has been passed," Hal said.

"Bear any burden—meet any hardship—support any friend," I added.

"We here shall have a new birth of freedom," Nia remembered.

"The names were inscribed," Callie said.

"They were taken from us," I added.

"The eyes of the world are upon you," said Hal.

And, as with all of Amanda's clues, I didn't know if it was about something real, if it was a secret code, if it was a message sent directly into our souls, or if it was all three at one time. I did know one thing for sure—she had been the one to paint those letters with the highlighting that could only be seen through a camera's lens. These words were her message to us.

And strangely, what those words told me was that whatever the Official was doing, whatever had happened to our parents, we were going to put an end to it. We were going to destroy the Official's plans.

The crazy thing? Even tied up in a van, slipping around on a bench, my arms aching, my back seizing up, my face streaked with tears—I still believed in Amanda. I believed that if Amanda said we were going to take the Official down, we were.

I believed in Amanda because she believed in me. And I believed in her. I knew that what made Amanda who she was wasn't the result of any genetic tampering inflicted on her parents by Dr. Joy. It wasn't special powers, or secret skills. It was her essence, her personality, the look in her eyes. It was the way she transformed everything she touched into a work of art. Her notebooks, her clothing, even her years living on the run had been stamped by her as her own. Her metaphors could not be flattened. Her voice could not be silenced. She could take a city of stone monuments to great leaders and wartime loss and transform them into a poem that brought a little part of her personality into this horrible van. I recited her poem now, in my head, over and over. It was all I had to hold on to, but it was just enough.

> *Train up a child.*
> *The torch has been passed.*
> *Bear any burden—meet any hardship—support any friend.*
> *The names are inscribed. They were taken from us.*
> *We here shall have a new birth of freedom.*
> *The eyes of the world are upon you.*

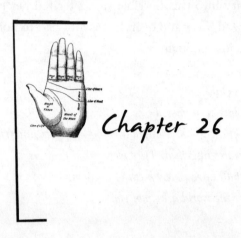

Chapter 26

It was dark out by the time the van stopped and the guards opened the doors. By then, my leg was screaming in pain. As soon as the guard snapped the cord bolting it to the floor, the pain got worse. It was like waking up a part of your body that's fallen asleep. My shoulders were aching, my wrists were on fire.

In the fifteen steps between the van and the building we were being dragged toward, I struggled to make out some sign of where we were. We were in a parking lot. I saw oak trees. The building was brick. We could have been anywhere.

Except that just as the guard was pushing me over a curb, I saw a sign: STAFF PARKING. And under that: ORION PHARMACEUTICAL COLLEGE.

Of course, I thought. The Official would haul us back

to where it all began. Dr. Joy's abandoned C33 human experimentation facility, and in the basement below, his recently constructed, fully operational, state-of-the-art lab.

"Hurry up," I heard. It was Maude, emerging from the passenger door of the van, finishing a call on her cell phone.

"What exactly is the Official going to do with us?" Nia demanded.

"Nothing, probably," Maude said. "It's Dr. Joy you need to worry about. But first, you better hope Amanda really comes for you. That's your main purpose. If she isn't forthcoming, I don't know what the Official will have to do to you to get her attention."

"She won't come," Callie said. "She's too good for that. She knows we can handle ourselves."

Maude smiled, passing us in the hallway, waving a hand behind her.

Of course, Maude was right.

But we didn't know that yet when the guards practically threw us into a room that was empty except for four beds like the ones we'd seen in the C33 dormitory. There was a plate of sandwiches, four cartons of chocolate milk, and a note on a table:

Children:
Enjoy this food. We will talk soon. All will be well.
                                          Uncle Joy.

271

Children? Did he think we were nine?

It occurred to me that the food might be poisoned or drugged, but we ate it anyway because we were starving. And we weren't sure anything worse could really happen to us at this point. After eating, Callie rubbed the red marks on her wrists, Nia limped around the room in a circle, as if waiting for feeling to return to her leg, and Hal sat on the edge of one of the beds, his hands gripping the edge of the mattress, his head tilted back, his eyes closed.

Even though I didn't need to hide from anyone here, I felt myself giving into the temptation of making myself invisible. I stood in the shadow of a cabinet. I slipped my hands inside the cuffs of my jacket. I closed down my face by breathing gently into a memory of watching my dad making Christmas cookies and humming "We Are the World"—my dad had always been ridiculously attached to '80s culture, which I was only realizing just now was owed to his sudden introduction to pop culture in 1984. This memory of him singing, his back to me, stepping from one end of the counter to another was my earliest of him, and now, it was enough to make me strong. Inside my head, I started humming along with the song he'd been humming tunelessly, connecting to the music's vibe.

When I heard Hal say, "Where's Zoe?" I stepped out from the cabinet's shadow, letting them see me. Nia looked up also, as if Hal's voice had taken her out of whatever trancelike state she'd slipped into.

"I just had this weird vision of the Official in his office,"

Hal said. "Come on, maybe if we're holding hands, I can see it better."

We joined hands and Hal was able to share his vision—it didn't even faze us that now, we could see both what Hal and what Nia saw. Our powers had just upgraded again. We were too focused on the vision itself to care.

Unlike Nia's fragmented, film-footage-like visions, Hal's were hyper clear. They had the sharpness and the reflected light of something seen through glass and water—the rocks in a fish tank, plants glowing under a UV light.

And there the Official was, tipped back in his desk chair, cracking his knuckles.

"He's scared," I said, because to me, that was obvious.

"What's he scared of?" Nia asked.

"He's scared of Amanda," I said. "He's waiting for her and the longer she makes him wait, the more scared he becomes."

"Wow," said Hal. "That's amazing."

"It means we can't give up," said Callie. I felt myself growing calmer and more resolute just hearing her voice. "That's what the Official expects us to do. It's what he wants. But we can't let it happen."

"You're right," said Nia, clearly strengthened by Callie's conviction, too. "First things first. Callie, is there any way out of this room?"

The windows in the room were so high up we couldn't reach them. Callie tried the door but it was solid metal and wouldn't budge. Nia laid her hand on it. "It's enclosed by a steel frame. There are steel bars that extend two feet into the walls on each side."

"Wait," said Hal. "How did you see that? I thought you could only see things about people."

"Well, it is actually about people," Nia explained. "I saw the men installing the bars. One of them says to the other, 'That's some strong bolt,' and the other replies, 'What are they trying to do, rebuild Fort Knox?'"

"But you also knew the bars extended two feet into the wall."

"True," Nia agreed. "That is strange. How did I know that?" She thought for a moment. Then her face lit up. "They were holding the building's plans!" she said. "I saw the plans, in the vision—they were holding them out in front of them, studying them. Maybe that's how I knew the measurement? Maybe my brain was reading them without my consciously knowing it?"

"Maybe," said Hal, uncertainly.

"Can you see any more?" Callie asked. "Like, is there a secret door to this room or something?"

Nia squeezed her eyes shut, then shook her head. "I can almost see them. I get close to them and then they blur in my mind. I can see the hands holding the pages. I can see the white of the pages, the lines, the writing, but I can't get it to stick inside my brain all at once, you know?"

"Then I'm not seeing an obvious way for us to get out

of here." Callie pursed her lips.

"Sorry," said Nia.

"You don't need to be sorry," Hal said. "It's crazy you can see those blueprints at all."

"Our powers are getting stronger," Callie said. "But I keep being surprised by the direction they're taking."

"I think the stronger part is coming from you, Callie," I offered.

"From me?" Callie said. "No way. My power is the lamest. I can't see the past or the future or into people's minds the way you guys can. All I can do is break down doors and lift stuff."

"Oh, no," Nia said. "Your power goes way beyond that. It's like what your mom was saying—you can stand up to other people. And I think when we're all touching, we are getting our strength from you. I think you're the one who is making all the rest of our powers grow."

"Wow," said Callie. I noticed a tiny hint of a smile attach itself to her lips.

"Rosie said each of our powers is something Amanda already has," Hal said. "Like together, we make up a whole, and the whole is Amanda."

"All that stuff about *come together* and her drawing us into a team," said Callie. "That was about more than just our giving each other moral support. It was because she knew we would make each other stronger. So now, we need to take these gifts and figure out how to help Amanda."

"Hal, have you seen anything in the last few minutes?" Nia asked.

"Nope. Fresh out of visuals," said Hal.

"Maybe if we all hold hands again?" Callie suggested. "That helped with Nia's visions before."

We all agreed and, standing in a circle in the space between two of the beds, we took each other's hands. I felt the familiar electric connection jump to life. And then something happened. With a hissing sound and a pop, the lights in the room went out.

"Was that us?" I looked around in the dark.

"Actually"—Nia's voice was contrite, as if she were confessing to a burp—"it was me."

"You turned out the lights in the building?" Callie said. "How—?"

"I was able to see the blueprints again," Nia explained. "I don't know why, but they suddenly snapped into focus when we took hands. And when I was analyzing at them, I did this thing. I found the drawing of an electrical diagram, and then I isolated the circuit breaker for the building, and then when I looked at it, I focused really hard on the main switch and suddenly, it just, well, exploded. My brain became some kind of corporeal soldering iron."

"Whoa," said Hal, capturing our collective reaction.

In our silence we began to notice that the building had become silent also—I guess machines had been thrumming away in the basement. In their place we heard running in the hall—footsteps and voices calling out, "Over here! Sector nine!"

Emergency lighting came on in the room, a dim, red glow shining down at us from over the door and some strips along the walls. In awe at what had just happened, we dropped hands.

Then Hal's eyes began to shine. He'd gotten another vision. I could tell.

"What did you see?" Nia whispered. "What's going on?"

"It's Amanda," Hal said. "She's here."

That's when the guards opened our door and shouted, "Get up! Move! Now!"

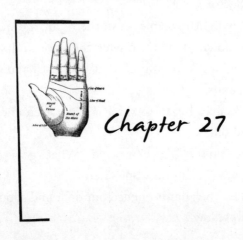

Chapter 27

The guards entered the room at a jog, pushed Hal by the shoulder and took Nia roughly at her elbow. Callie and I were herded forward and we ran with the guards down the hall, past the entrance to the old dormitory, down a set of stairs, through another set of double doors and into the newly refurbished basement lab we'd found before.

Once inside, the guards delivered us to the Official, who was standing in the center of the room on a raised platform that looked like it was a piece of the command module set from the *Starship Enterprise*. Maude was one step behind him. Even in the dim emergency lighting coming from bulbs over the doors and faint beading along the main paths of the floor, I could see that her lab coat was immaculate and her blond hair perfectly coiffed, as if she herself was made of some synthetic rubbery material.

All the workers we'd seen buzzing around when we'd been here before were gone, and it looked like they'd left in a hurry. Papers and test tubes and other mad-scientist-type equipment were out on counters. I also noted ventilation hoods, gas jets, beakers and decanters of all sizes, centrifuges, refrigerators.

It wasn't until the Official said, "There's only three kids here. What happened to the other one?" that I realized I must have hidden myself without realizing it. I was standing behind a pillar now, my whole body thrumming to the sound of the lab equipment, turning myself into something anyone looking would assume belonged in this room.

"Camo-girl. Right," the Official muttered, as if to himself. Then his eyes met Maude's. "Look for her—the Costas kid. She'll be where you least expect her." I guess he'd attributed me with the brains to have hidden myself somewhere along the way—which, duh, would probably have been the smart thing to do. "She cannot have gone far. And in any case, the three here are enough to draw Amanda out of hiding."

Maude beckoned to the guards and together they all stepped out into the hall, the doors swinging closed with a mechanical clicking and grinding that told me the lock—like the one upstairs—would not be easy to break.

"Amanda!" the Official called out. "I know you're here. I have your friends."

Was Amanda here? Turning to look, I caught a glimpse.

She was inside the room where Hal, Callie, Nia, and I had hidden when we'd snuck into the pharmaceutical college before—the room labeled GENETIC SAMPLE STORAGE, i.e. blood. Amanda's face was in shadow but the emergency lighting caught the edge of her cheek, the slant of her nose.

"You're too smart not to comprehend that you need me more than I need you," the Official went on. "You see, it is possible for you to advance only so far on your own."

At that, the door to the Genetic Sample Storage room opened, and Amanda called out, "Oh, I need you, do I?" The Official jerked his head, his gaze landing on the shadowy version of Amanda. She stepped out of the room and was now walking down the center laboratory aisle.

"Remember," Hal said in a low voice as she passed us. "He's afraid of you."

"I'm not afraid of her," the Official scoffed.

Amanda stepped into the light at the center of the room now and I could see the ironic, half-cocked smile. "*The only thing we have to fear is fear itself*," she said.

She furrowed her brows and looked into the Official's eyes, almost as if she were seeking something on a distant horizon—a bird someone had told her was in flight, a landmark barely visible in the distance.

"You know," she said, and her voice was strong and reassuring, mysterious, soft, deep, and impossibly clear. "You're not going to get away with what you're trying to do."

Callie, Hal, and Nia had gathered around her, letting her know that they were there to support her. The Official tried to stare back into her eyes, but he couldn't quite do it. He looked away, then straightened up and looked at the guides, registering that he was alone in the room with us, as the guards and Maude were still outside. He laughed that soulless, android laugh, and then Amanda's mouth curved up into the approximation of a smile. She was ready to fight. "You see," the Official said, "you are enjoying this, aren't you?"

Amanda's trace of a smile faded, and I could see that his comment had hit its mark. The Official must have seen this too, because he kept after it. "It must have been hard all those years, feeling yourself growing in ways no one else was, being told by your mother not to think about it, to ignore what you knew you could do. Is that why you turned to these soul-searching teenage pursuits—the enigmatic loner routine, the costuming, the cataloging, the acquiring of arcane knowledge?"

Amanda grimaced, as if she were being made to eat a food she didn't like.

"Why don't you let go of the charade and become who you were meant to be?" he said. "Imagine the feeling of accomplishment you would have when you finally unleash your potential? Just imagine how much more powerful you will be when you accept my help, when you let me direct you?"

"I don't want you to direct me," Amanda said calmly.

"If you remain out on your own, what will you become? An artist? A healer? You're strangely artistic, Joy tells me.

Perhaps you will grow famous writing books? Making films? Perhaps you'll be a painter and have work shown in museums?

"None of that can compare with what I can offer you. You know this. You know I can give you the chance to be truly great."

"Great at what?" Amanda said. "Great at being your minion, doing whatever you tell me to?"

"There are countries where people are starving," the Official said. "Their leaders do nothing to help them. In six months there, you could reform their governments. With your vision, your understanding of past, present, and future, your strength, you could change the fate of millions."

Amanda stood stock-still, seeming to listen.

"International crime is on the rise," the Official continued. "Illegal arms dealers, drug traffickers, smugglers work outside the jurisdiction of all major governments and the United Nations. Their money protects them. With your knowledge of languages, your facility with disguise, your ability to read people's minds, to see into the future—you could infiltrate the high-security worlds in which these criminals manage to thrive.

"You would be important, a friend of world leaders, royalty, the people who build the businesses that change the way we think. Imagine the life you would have— yachts and parties, jets, everything at your fingertips.

"At the end of your life—and trust me, if you join me, there will be teams of scientists looking into every possible way of extending it—you will be able to say you have made a mark in shifting the history of our planet, of the human race. Surely you understand the logic of what I propose?"

I saw a rush of images flash before my eyes. There was something about these visions that didn't look like what I saw with Nia and Hal's. They were more muddy, almost sepia-toned, like an old photograph. I knew without knowing how I knew that I was now seeing what Amanda saw. Her future.

There she was in a backless, sequined dress the color of the tropical ocean on a white sand beach, her hair long behind her, a glass of champagne in one hand, laughing as a gray-haired man in a soldier's uniform decorated with many stripes and medals bowed down to her, lifting his glass to her in admiration.

I saw her in khaki fatigues, heavy boots, her hair pulled up into a soldier's cap. She was standing on a rise in the desert, looking through field glasses into the shimmering heat, a missile launcher balanced on one shoulder.

Then there Amanda was again on a crowded sidewalk in Paris—I could see the Eiffel Tower behind her. She was dressed in a business suit, pencil skirt, and high heels, carrying a briefcase, her large gray-green eyes made even larger by heavy black glasses. She stepped into a glass office building with a modern lobby, through a revolving door. She swiped an ID card through a security turnstile, then headed for a door marked NO EXIT. AUTHORIZED PERSONNEL ONLY.

It wasn't the fancy clothes or the cool disguises. It was the power that I could feel her being tempted by. I knew why, too. Amanda and I had both lost parents. We lived on the run. We never felt safe. Sometimes it felt like the only way to be truly safe was to be the strongest person in the room. Amanda could have that.

But Amanda didn't want it. "I will not work for you," she stated flatly.

"You know, sweetheart," the Official said, almost sadly. "I don't know what your warped little vision of the universe is, but the world is about power. And either you have it or you don't."

"You're not proposing to give me power." Amanda tossed her chin defiantly. "*There is no subjugation so perfect as that which keeps the appearance of freedom for in that way one captures volition itself.*"

"Ah, Rousseau, of course," the Official scoffed. "Volition, self-expression, free will—they're overrated. Either you pull yourself up and over the edge of the mountaintop or you spend your life looking up at the bottoms of the shoes of the people who've managed to claw their way up." The Official pushed a button on a control console and one of the medical bays suddenly glowed with light. I guess there

284

was a reserve power source beyond what Nia had found when she tapped into the building's electrical grid.

I had to shield my eye against the glare at first, but as they adjusted, I saw what was inside the bay. Two exam chairs like you might see at the dentist's office were set up side by side, like twin beds. There was an old man standing between the two chairs, adjusting a machine that sent tubes and wires into position on both—he looked vaguely familiar but I couldn't see his face.

One of the chairs was empty, but the other was occupied. By none other than Heidi Bragg. She was reclining, and though her hair was pulled back into a neat ponytail, and her hands folded in her lap, I could see she was scared. Her hands were clasped because they were trembling. Her shoulders were hunched up to her ears.

I could see why she would be scared, too. There were an awful lot of wires and tubes attached to her body, she was wearing an oxygen mask, there was an IV in her arm and electrodes on her wrists and temples. Brittney Bragg was standing right behind her, a hand on her shoulder as if to steady her before some standard medical procedure.

What was Heidi doing here? What were the tubes and wires for? Why was her mother part of this—wouldn't she want to fight to get Heidi away?

Then the old man controlling the machine turned and I realized I had seen him before. At the airstrip where Thornhill had been kept prisoner—I'd been hiding, following Hal, Callie, and Nia, but I had seen him, a passenger in a Jeep.

I knew this man. I knew what he had done to all of our parents. I knew his name. This was Dr. Joy.

Despite being in his seventies, Dr. Joy looked vibrant and strong. His hair was thick and shockingly white, and his back was ramrod straight.

"Ah," he said, opening his hands like he was welcoming us into his home. This man: I thought of all the terrible things he had done to my dad. I thought of the little boy getting his blood drawn on the exam table—the one we'd seen in Nia's vision. "The children," Dr. Joy said now. "At last I have you with me."

"I see you have recognized Dr. Joy," the Official went on. "And I'm sure knowing that he has developed a new technology to assist in our project will not surprise you."

With Hal and Nia, Callie was still standing at the edge of the Official's command center. She gently rubbed the railing, but left a soft dent in the metal. I felt the gesture as clearly as if she had rubbed my back. It sent a signal of strength coursing through all of us. Amanda squared her shoulders. I felt stronger too. But maybe not strong enough to face this man.

Dr. Joy took a step forward. "Children," he said. "I am not a monster. I had only the best intentions for your parents. I was a loving Uncle Joy."

"Uncle *Joe* was what they called you," Amanda interrupted him. "As in Uncle Joe Stalin. You destroyed many lives," Amanda said.

"*I* didn't destroy them," Dr. Joy objected, his teeth flashing, his eyes bright. "The government did—when they terminated my program. Your parents were my babies, my chicks in the incubator, and I hated—oh, how I hated— to be compelled to release them into the cold unknown when they were still only half-formed."

"If you cared about us, you would destroy this lab." Amanda stood firm, her back straight, her hands relaxed at her side. "You would trust us to be who we are."

"Oh, I trust you," Dr. Joy practically purred. "I trust what is inside you. Amanda, your blood, your DNA, what you have grown into being—it is too beautiful to let it go to waste. You are my gift to the world. So please come nicely. If you don't, you see, that machine—we are prepared to salvage our work."

"What do you mean, salvage?" Amanda's eyes began to scan the equipment, as if noticing it for the first time.

"I mean this," the Official interrupted, his voice growing growly with anger at being challenged. I could see that he was not accustomed to it. "If you took the blood flowing through your veins and examined it under a microscope, more than half of what you see came out of a test tube. You do not belong to yourself. You are a product of this lab. You are government property. You are not a person, but a collection of enhancements that we have spent far too much money and time and energy bringing into the world to abandon now.

"You are blood," Dr. Joy went on. "We all are. But you my dear, are made up of blood that is mine. I made it. With the machine there, I am prepared to distill that blood, extract the enhancements and translate them into a new host," Dr. Joy explained.

Amanda turned again to Heidi. "This is what you want? You want to be me?"

Heidi removed her oxygen mask. "I would never settle for being you," she corrected. "I'm going to be better than you. I am going to be me, but with your powers."

"Or you might come out of all of this a mess," Amanda said. "You might not be able to think and see straight. You might be a scientific experiment gone horribly wrong, a Frankenstein of a human being."

"What if something happens to her?" Amanda said, speaking to Mrs. Bragg now.

But before Mrs. Bragg could answer, I noticed the Official's attention suddenly veer away from Amanda for the first time. Sensing that he'd lost his patron, Dr. Joy followed the Official's gaze. We all did.

The Official was looking at something orange. And red. And flickering. In the window of the Genetic Sample Storage Room, where Amanda had been hiding minutes before.

"Why is the room glowing?" Dr. Joy barked, his voice

short and sharp as if he were upbraiding a careless lab assistant.

"Is it—" the Official started to ask, but stopped when he realized he didn't want the answer to the question.

"It is," Amanda assured him, her smile now returned. "It's on fire."

"What!" Dr. Joy shouted. "How did that happen?"

"You're a scientist," she said, pretending to casually examine her nails. "You understand how fires start. A combination of fuel, oxygen, and heat."

"But—" Dr. Joy sputtered.

"Or, more specifically, I doused the room in lighter fluid and dragged in some of those old dry mattresses that for some insane reason you kept on the beds in the old dorm where our parents spent their childhoods—you should be more careful. Stuff like that can really become a hazard."

The Official and Dr. Joy were giving her looks that clearly said, "How did we miss that?"

"You see," Amanda explained, "while you were busy kidnapping my friends in an attempt to lure me to the lab, I was here already, ahead of you, preparing for this little party we are having."

"You set—" the Official began. "You set the blood storage room *on fire*?"

"And know what's crazy?" Amanda continued, "I did it without the help of any of the superpowers Dr. Joy spent so much of his life trying to instill in my mom and dad. You see, sometimes you don't even need powers. Or *power*. Sometimes all you need is a match." She held up a matchbook from Play It Again Sam's, her favorite vintage store run by former C33 Louise Potts, who was crazy about little touches like matchbooks, a detail Amanda appreciated. "Sorry," she added, seeing Dr. Joy's face, which had gone white. He'd aged ten years in a minute. "Was there something in there you *didn't* want barbecued?"

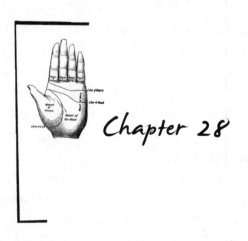

Chapter 28

Dr. Joy ran for the blood room door, opened it and was immediately engulfed in flames.

Or at least I thought I saw that happen. When I blinked I realized he hadn't moved an inch, but was standing, mesmerized by the fire. I glanced at the rest of the guides. They all had their eyes wide open in awe, as if they had seen the same thing—the same *vision* that I had. We had *shared* a vision.

So now our brains were connected even when we weren't touching? Was there no limit to what we could do?

"Zoe," Amanda hissed, breaking me away from my thoughts. "Go!" And I knew what I was supposed to do.

I ran toward the fire. Dr. Joy, the Official, Heidi and Brittney Bragg, and even Callie, Hal, and Nia were watching the light. They were hypnotized by it. No one saw me move.

And then, just as he had done in our vision, Dr. Joy started to run to the room.

As Dr. Joy was making his dash, I quickly pushed a wheeled tray of empty beakers in front of him. He ran right into the cart, and it was enough to knock him off balance, to keep him from throwing his body into the door that was hot as an oven.

Then, I watched in horrible slow motion as Dr. Joy stumbled to his feet. And despite my new powers, I couldn't stop him. He tried the doorknob, but it was too hot, and he burned his hand. Wrapping his hand in the bottom of his lab coat, he tried again. But before he could so much as turn the handle, the knob burned his coat. When he released his hand and coat, I could see brown holes the size of tennis balls scorched into the fabric.

He scrambled suddenly for something on the counter: a glove that looked like a cross between an oven mitt and something an astronaut would wear into space. But by then, Callie had joined us, and with the strength of one hand she was able to hold Dr. Joy off. She, Amanda, and I had saved his life.

But he didn't seem to care. He backed away from the door, staring at it in disbelief before collapsing on the floor. "All my work," he cried, his arms open toward the door as if he expected the blood samples to turn into people, and come running for him. "My life. My legacy. The future of the human race."

"Rendered inert," Amanda said with a matter-of-fact tone. "Cooked beyond recognition."

Hal said, "Amanda, the guards are coming. They're on their way."

"Nia," Amanda said. Was she speaking out loud? Or was she using our newfound power to communicate telepathically? "Nia, it's time to lock the doors."

I had no idea what Amanda was talking about. I could feel Nia's confusion echoing mine.

But then, within an instant, Nia was sharing an image with us—something bold and clean and factual. Something that was a relief to my clouded, terrified brain. It was the drawings Nia remembered from her vision of the workers installing the locks on the door.

But the workers weren't part of the vision anymore. All I saw were blueprints propped up in front of me. Clear lines, clean proportions, grids and graphs. Schematics. A drawing of rooms, bays, hallways, doors, and on top of it all, smaller, lighter lines. Looking at them I was able to discern that they were the electrical wiring plans, data cabling, power, remote control activation of the system that controlled the alarms, the locks, the window closures, venting. It should have taken a computer to understand and break this information down, but Nia was reading it like it was a bumper sticker—something to be understood in a flash.

I heard a clicking, sliding, thudding sound. Followed by the sound of the doors being rattled by the guards.

The Official pressed a button on a handheld radio. "Get in here," he called.

A voice buzzed back through: "Sir, we're locked out." It was Maude speaking in a flat voice.

"You did this," the Official said, glaring at Amanda.

Amanda shrugged and shook her head. "Actually," she said, "it was Nia. She's figured out how to tap into the building's systems. You're completely at her mercy."

The Official's head swiveled around and his gaze now landed on Nia. "But that's not your power," he said to her. "I thought you were confined to visions attached to objects. Visions of the past."

"I thought so too," Nia said, pleased, despite the situation, to acquire new knowledge.

"But that's—" the Official began. I think he was going to say "impossible," except by the time he'd got to that part of his statement, his brain registered the fact that he was looking at the spot where Amanda had been standing, and she was no longer there.

"They're evolving," Dr. Joy said, rousing himself from where he was still sitting on the floor. His words were nearly inaudible, as if he were speaking more to himself than anyone else. "Just as I believed they would. They're growing even before our very eyes. I knew they had this power. Like Amanda, they have the capacity to adapt and become more powerful when their powers become necessary."

And then we all became aware of Amanda's presence again. She was standing on a countertop in the middle of the room. She was kicking things off the counter—lab equipment shattering as it hit the floor, stacks of papers drifting.

"Guys, help me," Amanda said. "We've got to trash this place."

And this part, at least, was fun. We emptied out drawers, dumped files, smashed beakers, overturned neat lines of tubes in racks. I glanced over at Heidi and Mrs. Bragg. They were staring at Amanda impassively, resolved and confident in their ability to wait out the storm, to not get in anyone's way.

For a few seconds, Dr. Joy just stared too. Then he rushed toward us, starting to pick up what we'd scattered. "You . . . ," Dr. Joy said. He looked up at Amanda. He took a step toward her.

"Zoe!" Amanda said—and, thanks to a vision Hal shared, I saw what was about to happen, what I was meant to prevent from happening. It wasn't hard to keep Dr. Joy from seeing me as I cut him off as he moved toward Amanda.

"You had no right," Dr. Joy was saying, taking one step after another toward Amanda. "Those samples. Those mutations. They were my life's work. I created you but you are too strong now. You are like your father—determined to thwart me. You are spoiled. I have to stop you."

Dr. Joy pulled a syringe out of his pocket, raising his arm up as if he were going to use it to stab Amanda in the chest. But I was more than ready for him. As he plowed by me to lunge for the counter, I reached out and plucked the syringe away. "What?" he said, turning to me, his lab coat flying out to the sides as he moved.

"Zoe?" he said, looking into my eyes, darting down to take in the syringe I was holding, then looking back up at me. "Give it to me," he said.

Amanda hopped down from the countertop, held out a hand so that I could give her the syringe. The Official chose this moment of distraction to lunge at Amanda himself. But just as the Official pounced on her, Amanda jerked out of his grasp and turned herself around and into a crouch behind him. He crouched to match hers and swung out a leg.

Amanda jumped backwards, with amazing strength. The Official leapt for her again and she stepped away from his grasp, hopping into the air to lunge across him before he could get to her. He stepped back with a laugh. "You realize of course that in training to use your powers against me you developed the very strengths I am going to need. You take a large risk in doing so—for if you delivered yourself to me defenseless you would also be—for the most part—useless to me."

Amanda said, "I will always be useless to you."

But this time, she wasn't fast enough. The Official reached out his hand and got it wrapped around her wrist. He tugged on her wrist, pulling her toward him even though she was struggling to resist. Nia, Callie, Hal, and I rushed toward them—we outnumbered him five to one, but before we got there, Amanda swung her arm over to his, and stuck him with the needle at a spot just above the elbow. "Don't move," she said.

"What's—?" the Official started. He looked down at the needle as if for the life of him he could not imagine how it had come to be stuck in his arm. "You stabbed me?" he said. Then, after thinking for a few beats: "What exactly is in there? Joy?"

Dr. Joy was back to muttering. It was as if he hadn't even heard the Official speak.

"Do you know what it is?" the Official said, looking up at Amanda now.

"I don't but I've got my thumb on the plunger," Amanda said. "So unless you want to find out, I'd suggest you do whatever I say. Even now, drops of this solution may be leaking into your bloodstream."

The Official didn't move.

"I'm sure Dr. Joy would never have wanted to inject me with anything but some harmless saline, right? Dr. Joy loves me. He promised that just now, didn't you hear him? So he'd never inject me with say, promazine, that stuff he used on my dad when he tried to break out that time? Or phenobarbital, the stuff he used on my mom to keep her docile after they made those bogus tests of her powers out in the real world?"

"Uh," the Official said. "Joy? What's. In. The. Syringe?" the Official said, but Dr. Joy was busy trying to reassemble papers that had cascaded to the floor. I was starting to wonder exactly how sane Dr. Joy could really be.

"Come with me," Amanda coaxed the Official, leading him by the elbow to the computer station in the center of the lab. He winced as the needle dug into his arm.

"Sit," Amanda said. The Official sat in a chair at one of the stations. You could see he was terrified from the spasms that kept crossing his face.

"Start typing," Amanda commanded.

"What do you want me to type?"

"Whatever sequence wipes the data," Amanda said. "Nia, come watch him. I think if you put a hand on the computer, you'll be able to follow what he's doing."

The Official hesitated.

"Don't you see?" Amanda spoke softly, her voice calm and clear, as if this were all in a day's work for her. "As heavyweight champion Joe Louis once said, you can run, but you cannot hide."

The Official started to type. Nia put her hand on the computer and nodded occasionally to show Amanda that he was doing as he was told.

"Are we done?" he said.

"Not quite yet," she said. "I want you to access all the

accounts where you are storing the money to fund any further research, investigation of former C33s, data collection, blood storage, lab creation, everything. I want you to donate the funds inside those accounts to these charities." She pulled a list from her pocket. "You'll be happy to know your gift will support programs to help children without parents, like the ones Dr. Joy originally collected for the C33 program."

Amanda looked over in Brittney's direction. "This might be a good time," she said, "to unhook Heidi from the machine. I don't know what the adjustments we're making to the computer might do to it."

Brittney backed off toward Heidi, but didn't start to unhook her. She looked conflicted, her selfish little eyes getting small with the strain of her decision. I guess she was holding out hope that the Official would regain power.

"I can't destroy the system in the way you want me to," the Official announced at last. "The system is set to repel any attempts to delete this information. I would need an override card and I don't have one."

"An override card?" Amanda squinted suspiciously.

"I keep them in a lockbox in Washington D.C. There's no way you could get to them. Especially now. So I'm sorry. You can kill me. But you can't destroy the operation completely. Without those key cards, it will live." He could not keep the smug smile off his face.

"Oh," Nia said. "Do you by any chance means *these* key cards?" She leaned down and pulled the red and blue

299

cards out of her boot. It says something about Nia's innate elegance that she managed to make that gesture look cool.

Looking at the Official's face, waiting for the squirm, Callie added, in her sweetest, most innocent voice, "Just think, guys, how Nia almost threw them into the Potomac! That would have been a shame."

Amanda smiled ruefully, then slid the cards into two slots located under the counter on the Official's left-hand side. "Let's go," she said, giving the needle a tiny wiggle.

Again, the Official started to type, but now something started to happen to the machine attached to Heidi. The lights on the sides faded out and you could hear the low whine as the machine powered down. At the same moment, Heidi lost consciousness.

"No!" Dr. Joy shouted, sounding very much like the Wicked Witch of the West when she is melting at the end of *The Wizard of Oz*. He was directing his gaze at the Official. "Morton," he said. "If you activate the system malfunction, you'll kill the subject in the chair."

"Heidi!" Mrs. Bragg cried out. "Help me, someone please help me!"

I guess caring about whether Heidi lived or died was what did Amanda in. Because she turned to look at the Braggs just then, and in that momentary break in her concentration, the Official took a short sharp breath, grabbed Amanda's wrist and threw her off so she stumbled, catching herself on the railing near Hal. Nia started toward him, but with one shove, he carelessly tossed her small form to the ground.

He pulled the syringe out of his arm and threw it across the room.

Mrs. Bragg was standing now, keeping one hand on Heidi's arm, but stretching the rest of her body as much as she could toward the rest of us. "Something happened to Heidi!" she called out. "Dr. Joy, help me!"

The Official was fumbling for something in his pocket, and as Amanda got closer to him, the Official pulled out something in the shape of a coin, small and silver. Palming it, he slapped it onto a wall where it stuck and began to emit vibrations. It wasn't loud, but it made noise, uneven and high-pitched. Within seconds, I was in tremendous pain.

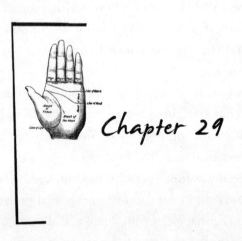

Chapter 29

Amanda, Callie, Hal, Nia—they felt the pain coming from the Official's metal disc also. It was emitting a sound that was causing us agony. Like dogs, we were attuned to the machine's whistling. It wasn't that it was loud. It was that it was perfectly calibrated to hurt us.

Amanda let go of the Official's arm and bent her head down to her knees. Callie covered her ears. Hal squeezed his eyes closed. Nia blocked her face with outstretched palms.

A smile crept across the Official's face. His eyes were reenergized, hands shaking with excitement, his hair—which had been combed back before—was standing on end. He grabbed his two-way radio, "Maude," he spoke into it as he was busily typing into the keyboard. "I'm bypassing the internal locking system now. Activate intruder protocol."

"What about Heidi?" Mrs. Bragg shouted across the room to him. "Get some help for Heidi!"

"Joy, what's happening over there?" the Official barked. He gestured toward Mrs. Bragg with his chin. "Can you fix it?"

But Dr. Joy had stopped working on Heidi and the blood-exchange machine. He pointed to the little silver disc on the wall and looked at the Official curiously. "What is this device?" he asked. "You were keeping a secret from me?"

"It's immunity," the Official boasted. "It's like kryptonite. It prevents these kids from using their powers."

"You made it?" Dr. Joy said.

"I had it made."

"And I had no idea."

Gray-faced and ashen from fighting the noise coming from the disc on the wall, Amanda lunged at the Official, stumbling. She actually was able to get his elbow into her hand, but her grip was weak. The Official tossed off her one-handed grasp.

At that moment, the doors burst open and Maude came running in, followed by both guards we'd been seeing plus the third guard—the one we'd last seen at the Metro station in Washington.

The guard with the tattoo and his sleepy sidekick ran

straight for Amanda, but she ducked behind a lab desk and ran for the back of the room. They followed her, knocking over a tray of metal instruments, holding onto the edges of counters as they took corners going too fast.

Maude took Callie roughly by the arm. She tried to free herself. Ten minutes before, she would have been able to shake off Maude like she was nothing more than a cardigan sweater. But now, no matter how much she struggled, Maude was holding her too tightly. The Official was right—this woman had no empathy.

The third guard came for me and I ducked behind a pillar. I'd be out of his line of sight for only a few seconds, but it would be enough. I saw a tall, draped, boothlike structure a few feet behind me, and I knew I could slip inside there. Or turn to one of the desks and assume the identity of a lab worker. All I needed was a white coat, and there one was. The name badge read Kelly Black. I slipped my arms into it and stared down at the table, moving my hands as if I were decanting liquids into tubes. I concentrated on elevator music—an orchestrated version of "Windy," by the Associations. I hummed in a way that was so calm and peaceful no one hearing it, thinking it, inhabiting it could not help but feel a cold, numbing gel descending between their eyes and their brain.

But it didn't work. I felt the guard's hand on my shoulder. He grabbed me at the waist, too, and yanked me over to the side of the lab where he shoved me unceremoniously into a rolling desk chair, gathered my hands together behind the chair's back, and attached a new plastic strap around my wrists. Callie and Hal were already similarly tied. Nia was being subdued as I got my bearings.

Two guards had Amanda by her arms. In her struggle, her hair had fallen into her face so I couldn't see her eyes. Was that why I couldn't read how she felt?

This wasn't supposed to happen, was all I could think. I longed for the comfort that might come just from sharing that thought with Amanda, Nia, Callie, and Hal, but it was not there. I could still hear my own thoughts, of course, but theirs were gone. I felt not only like I'd gone deaf, but like I'd lost my friends. I hadn't realized how used to our connection I'd become.

"Heidi?" Mrs. Bragg said. "Heidi, darling!" I looked over to see that Dr. Joy's efforts at reviving the blood exchange machine had paid off. The lights were on again, and Heidi's eyes were open.

The lights on the machine were blinking again. Mrs. Bragg seemed to have calmed down.

"Is the machine prepped, Joy?" the Official asked. "Let's get Heidi activated. Once she's powered up and on the team we'll be able to work on repairing whatever damage *she*"—he gestured to Amanda—"caused." He looked at the guards holding Amanda and gestured toward the empty seat near Heidi's. "Put her in the chair," he ordered. Heidi was holding her temples also, clearly in the same kind of pain we were.

Dr. Joy turned to the Official slowly. He looked at him

a few good minutes before he nodded. I wouldn't say he was moving like a spring chicken. And that wasn't just because he was nearing eighty years old. There was something about the way he was moving that was—

Actually, I wasn't sure I could say.

I had the feeling like a word was on the tip of my tongue.

"You're still letting him have Heidi?" Amanda called to Mrs. Bragg. In spite of the fact that the guards had her by the arms and were dragging her across the room, she spoke calmly and appeared to be completely poised, as if the guards holding her arms were simply members of the modern dance troupe of which she was the star. But when she looked at me penetratingly, I wondered what her look meant. Was there something she wanted? Did she want us to do something? Amanda looked back to Mrs. Bragg. "You're giving Heidi over to the people who didn't bother to try to save her life?"

Again, I couldn't complete the thought. I couldn't come up with the word to describe what I was seeing— I could read Amanda right now no better than I'd been able to read Dr. Joy.

And that's when I knew. I hadn't just lost my ability to hide. I'd lost my ability to read people. And where before I'd felt like I'd gone deaf, now I felt like I'd gone blind.

Amanda was tied securely in the chair now next to the weakened Heidi. Amanda had no hope of escaping the chair's straps, but she had enough freedom of movement to prevent Dr. Joy from sticking her with the needle. "Be still!" Dr. Joy was harsh-whispering to Amanda. "If you aren't still, I'm going to stick you somewhere else."

"Stick away, old man," Amanda growled. "I'd rather bleed out onto the floor than let you suck my blood up into your precious little invention there."

"Wait," said Heidi, weakly, looking directly at her mom. "I don't want to do this. I don't want this anymore."

"Heidi—" Mrs. Bragg said. She looked at Dr. Joy. She looked at the Official. She smiled her perplexed anchorwoman smile at Heidi.

"I said I don't want to!" Heidi roared.

Mrs. Bragg started to undo Heidi's arm straps, her hands shaking. She looked over at the Official. "I'm sorry," she said to him. "But you promised none of this would happen against Heidi's will."

"Sit down," the Official said to Mrs. Bragg.

"But . . ." Mrs. Bragg hovered, her hands still touching the straps.

"I said, *sit*," the Official said. Mrs. Bragg sat. Maude was back at the chair in a flash, her hands tightening Heidi's restraints where Mrs. Bragg had loosened them.

Heidi's eyes opened wide. How many times had she faked the feelings she was having now in an effort to get her way? Tears formed. "Mom?" she said in disbelief.

Mrs. Bragg looked at her, clearly in pain. "I can't fight these people," she said. "They're more powerful than we are . . . that's always been the point."

Amanda was struggling so furiously now that she managed to dislodge one of her arms from the restraints.

"Can't you sedate her?" the Official asked Joy.

"You promised she'd come willingly," Dr. Joy grumbled as he shuffled toward a different part of the lab.

While they were waiting for Dr. Joy to return, the Official walked over to Amanda, and said, "In your last moments of consciousness, I might as well tell you," he said, "that you will live." Even without my powers, I could see that the Official was still a little leery of Amanda. He was talking to her confidently, but he was careful to remain out of reach. If only I could read what he was thinking, to get into his head, to figure out more about his fear—to see what he was really worried about—maybe I could shout out some kind of warning to Amanda.

But I had nothing to offer her. I was useless.

"In a few minutes, you will begin a new life," he explained. "You will be just another regular high school student at Endeavor High. You won't have any actual memories of what has happened to you today. You won't remember your new friends here, the loyalty you inspired in them, the powers you used to possess. With the exception of some persistent nightmares, you will have no sense of the destruction you have caused. It will all be wiped clean."

I thought about the antidote to all Dr. Joy's work—the bottle of liquid Mrs. Leary had been working on since Callie was born, the one bottle we'd given to Amanda to drink when the time was right. Was this what it would do to her? Render her incurious, powerless, haunted, and in pain? All Mrs. Leary had told us was that she didn't want us to drink it while the Official was after her—that without our powers, we could not save Amanda.

But she hadn't known about the little silver disc that even now was emitting a sound so piercing it was hard for me to think. I felt like it was smashing my thoughts. Interrupting them. Unraveling them.

And that's when I figured out how the disc worked. Just as Dr. Joy was approaching Amanda with the sedative, just as the guards were holding her down so he could inject her with it, just as her body slumped into a pose that looked like she was sleeping in the most uncomfortable airplane seat ever invented, just as Dr. Joy easily slipped the IV line into the raised vein on the inside of her elbow, I realized how the machine that looked no bigger than a silver coin was preventing us from using our powers.

It was doing the opposite of what I do. I could turn invisible because I could slip into the rhythms I could read in other people. I could move in a pattern that matched the pattern of their blinking. I could slip into a song that harmonized with the music of their own minds, such that they couldn't hear the new voice in the room—mine.

And this machine, this random, painful, noise-erupting machine was throwing off everything that came naturally to me, every logical conclusion to every song or thought that entered my head—and it must be doing that to each of us. The machine followed no pattern. It made no sense and so it was impossible for our brains to assimilate, to get mastery of, to understand.

What the Official had invented was something that did not take away our powers. It simply stunted them, like white blood cells attacking virus cells and rendering them inert.

What we needed to do—I could see this now—was pound out our own rhythm, sing our own song, overwhelm the hasty cycling of the machine on and off at irregular intervals. We needed to prove to it who we were.

Which would be easy because, thanks to Amanda, we knew who we were.

What Nia, Hal, Callie, and I had in common was that after becoming friends with Amanda, everything in our lives had changed. But maybe change wasn't the right word. Maybe it would be more accurate to say that she revealed us to ourselves. She'd helped us escape our fears. She'd helped us come out of hiding.

And now it was our turn to help her escape. Already I could see Amanda's blood flowing into the IV from the needle in her arm. It was collecting in a reservoir on the side of Dr. Joy's machine, rushing into it. The machine was starting to whir and make gurgling noises, beeps, electronic hums.

"We can still reach her," I murmured to the others, trying to talk between the irregular beating of the crushing sound. "But we need to stop listening to this place.

Together, we can be more powerful than this machine. We can work together to make Amanda hear *us* more than she can hear *it*."

Nia, Callie, and Hal looked at me like I was crazy, their eyes full of fear and pain.

"What should she hear us saying?" Hal finally gasped.

"I don't know," I said. I had vague thoughts of saying her name over and over. Or all her names. Or her totem name. Or all our totems. None of these ideas felt right.

"The poem!" Nia said.

"What poem?" Callie asked.

By way of answering her, Nia began to recite, and as soon as we knew what she was saying, we all joined in:

Train up a child.
The torch has been passed.
Bear any burden—meet any hardship—support any friend.
The names are inscribed. They were taken from us.
We here shall have a new birth of freedom.
The eyes of the world are upon you.

Then Callie said, "Amanda, I know you were there that night on Crab Apple Hill. I don't need to see you to believe anymore."

I heard Hal's voice next. "Amanda, one day I will paint you the way I saw you in the woods that morning, a daisy chain in your hair."

Nia quoted from a poem I later learned she and

311

Amanda both loved, "Ariel" by Sylvia Plath. "*Stasis in darkness. / Then the substanceless blue / Pour of tor and distances.* Amanda," she said. "You are God's lioness to me."

I said, "Amanda, I love you like apple pie loves cheddar cheese." I don't know if she could have heard the word *cheese* as my voice broke. It was getting impossible not to cry.

Hal didn't let us stop calling out to her though. "Sunflowers," he said.

"Stars," said Callie.

"Words," Nia answered.

"My dad," I said.

And then we repeated those words: *Sunflowers, stars, words, my dad*, over and over, letting the magic of their importance, the love connected to them flow. I felt them raining down over me, softening, blocking the noise of the Official's machine. They blanketed the noise like snow, light as a feather pillow. I closed my eyes, my entire body relaxed and suddenly peaceful, like I was lying down in a field to watch clouds drift across a late-summer sky. I felt as if I'd fallen into a tank of extra-heavy water. Lifting my arm was an effort I could not summon the strength for. Not that I wanted to. I just wanted to live inside the warmth of the way the four of us felt about Amanda forever.

And then I opened my eyes, sleepily, lazily, as if I were waking up from a long nap, not even sure right away where I was. I saw something. It was the Official. And suddenly I could read him again. He was afraid. His fear was a cloud gathering into a storm. He was scared because he was starting to think his plan *wasn't* going to work.

Wait, no. He *knew* his plan wasn't going to work. I saw that information in the way his pupils were small, his breath coming fast, his shoulders raised a few inches higher than they had been before.

And he was right. His plan wasn't going to work. Because the fact that I could read him so easily meant my power had come back. And if my power had come back, then maybe everyone's had too. Had they?

I didn't even get a chance to ask that question aloud, because Callie suddenly burst through the straps on her chair. Our minds opened up to one another again, and I felt the resurgence of Callie's strength, of her beautiful courage, and realized how much I'd missed it. There Hal was, shouting, "On your left!" to her before the guards came at her from that direction. There was Nia, freed by Callie from her seat, running over to the disc, putting her hand on it until she knew what it was and how it worked. Then she squeezed her eyes shut, concentrated really hard, lifted her hand away and the disc shot off the wall and landed with a few short complaining bursts of sound on the floor. It vibrated a minute and then died.

Callie ran to Amanda, pushing the Official out of her path. She pushed over the machine between Amanda and Heidi, and it fell with a crash. That didn't stop it whirring and humming though—the sucking sounds were still there.

"She has to wake up," Hal said. "She'll lose more blood than she can afford to if she doesn't disconnect from it immediately."

I could see Callie didn't quite know what to do. Did she shake Amanda? Go back to attacking the machine? Was it dangerous to pull Amanda off the machine before it was turned off?

In the end, it wasn't Callie who acted. It was all of us. It was all of our thoughts, all of us focusing our desire into one keen blade of need.

Wake up, we all wished as hard as we could. Hal and I were still tied to our chairs, but it didn't matter. As Amanda had shown us, our spirit transcended physical strength. *Come back, Amanda, please.*

I don't believe there has ever been anything I wanted more than to see Amanda open her eyes at that moment. I had lost so much: I'd lost my dad, I'd lost Amanda. My dad was never coming back. But Amanda was still here. Separated from us only by the thin skin of her eyelids. *Open your eyes*, I whispered. *Please, please come back.*

Amanda did open her eyes. She rose in her seat. She took a great, deep breath in, her eyes growing wider, her forehead impassive, her jaw soft. Her face was as calm as someone sitting for a portrait—all her focus was in her eyes as she summoned up what seemed to be a great deal of strength. She pulled the IV needle out of her arm and stood, facing the Official, ready for a fight they both knew he would lose.

But then suddenly the Official had the syringe Amanda had used on him clutched in his hand. And before we could move, he had grabbed Heidi, and held the syringe to her neck. He looked at us wildly, eyes flashing.

"Joy told me we could not bring you in without appealing to your sense of right and wrong," the Official said. "So I'm betting I can bargain for Heidi's life. You let me go, and she lives."

Amanda's mouth twitched slightly. She blinked, the calm of her resolve shaken.

Because the Official was right. She couldn't let him hurt Heidi.

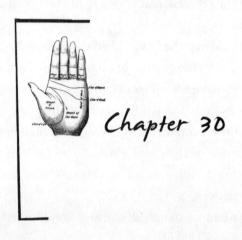

Chapter 30

Just then, the doors to the lab burst open and we all turned to see our parents running toward us frantically. Mr. Thornhill was at the front of the group, with Rosie, Mr. Bennett, Mrs. Leary, and my mom. Mrs. Rivera and Cisco came in next, and then there was a crowd of adults—Louise Potts, the woman with the cornrows who'd sold us the sunflower purse, and then, shockingly, Chief Bragg among those I recognized.

Taking advantage of the momentary distraction, Callie brought the Official to his knees with two swift kicks, the syringe flying out of his reach and skittering away on the ground. The guards charged at Amanda, but before they could reach her, Thornhill had jumped into the fray.

It was amazing, watching Amanda and Thornhill fight

side by side. I wasn't sure I had the chronology right, but I think they'd only ever had a few minutes together to spend as father and daughter—Thornhill had kept his identity secret from Amanda until the night she confronted him, just before he was attacked. They seemed so in sync with each other; they seemed to relish fighting the guards off. It was almost like they were dancing, their legs were flying in patterns, their arms reaching out in self-defense, their heads down, occasionally sharing a look that meant, "I've got this one," or "Nice move."

It was a blur while the C33s—Amanda, Thornhill, Mr. Bennett, and people I could not see—subdued Maude and the guards. A C33 I didn't recognize used a pair of clippers to release Hal and me from our chairs. We stood, just in time to see that Amanda and Thornhill were left alone fighting the Official. Nia, Callie, Hal, and I made a circle around them, together with the other C33s, and we watched the Official fight. We could have helped, I guess, but it really seemed like their fight to finish. He held out a long time, but eventually, Thornhill pinned him on the ground.

"Who are you? What's your name?" Thornhill growled. "I've looked everywhere and I can never find your name."

"I'm air," the Official said. "You can't name me. You can't know who I am. I don't belong to you."

"No," a voice spoke from behind the group and we all turned to see Brittney Bragg standing tall, seemingly frozen with one hand on Heidi's wrist. She looked directly into the Official's eyes. "Your name is Morton Clavermacle," she told him. "Otherwise known as C33-2138."

A collective gasp went up among the C33 adults present. "*Little* Morton?" Mrs. Rivera gasped.

"I was *nice* to you," Mrs. Leary breathed. "I held your hand when you had nightmares."

I saw a flash of an image—the little boy, begging not to get a shot from the nurse.

"That was *him*," Callie said, looking at all of us, and pointing at him. Well, I guess we were a bit less sympathetic now.

Just then, Chief Bragg stepped in and pulled the Official up by his shoulder. "You're right about one thing, buddy," he said. "You don't belong to Vice Principal Thornhill, or whoever this man really is. You belong to me now. You're under arrest." An officer, just arrived and looking around in confusion, pulled the Official's hands behind his back and cuffed him.

Then our parents finally took a good hard look at us, too, and I realized how crazy all of this must appear. We had a lot of explaining to do.

Our hair and clothes loose and disheveled, lab equipment smashed to pieces on the floor, papers blown onto every surface. Heidi was sobbing, her head in her hands. Mrs. Bragg was trying to comfort her, but her lipstick was smeared on her cheek and Heidi wouldn't meet her eye. She seemed to really want her dad. Amanda's hair was tangled and her face was flushed. Where she'd pulled out her IV, a thin trickle of blood had drawn a line from the inside of her elbow down to her wrist.

I couldn't stop shaking. My teeth. My hands. My shoulders. "Kids," Thornhill said, putting a hand on my shoulder, touching Nia next, then working his way down to Callie, Hal. "You did it. It's over."

"It's over?" Nia said, like someone had just told her the whole thing had been a practical joke. Hal kicked at some broken glass on the floor. Callie pinched her nose at the bridge. I noticed for the first time that my legs were aching, that I hadn't eaten since that tuna sandwich Dr. Joy left us.

Then my mom swallowed me up into the biggest embrace ever invented. I could feel her wet tears on my cheeks when she kissed me and I could smell her perfume that reminded me of our old life together, back before everything changed and then changed again.

Over my mom's shoulder I could see that Mr. Bennett had an arm around Hal. Callie and her mom were hugging like they would never stop. Mrs. Rivera was holding Nia's face between her palms while Cisco hung off her like for once he was the adoring cheerleader and she was the star. Which, of course, she was.

I saw Amanda standing between Thornhill and Rosie. Thornhill was looking at Amanda, shaking his head and kind of half-choking, half-laughing. Rosie had a smile across her face that could have powered the lights of Times Square. Amanda was smiling, too, that so-Amanda smile: her lips curved up into a bow, her gray-green eyes calm and knowing. And then she shook her head in disbelief, and, looking at her dad and her sister like she never wanted to take her eyes off of them, she drew them both in and buried her head in their chests.

As soon as the hugging sessions had ended—and they went on for quite a while—the grown-ups began telling us how they found us and we told them what had just happened in the lab.

Apparently, the Official's cover-up of our disappearance had nearly gone as planned. Heidi started planting the story about how Nia, Callie, Hal, and I had run away from the field trip in a copycat version of Amanda's disappearance, and everyone on the trip had believed it, with others coming forward to corroborate her story. Cisco had almost fallen under Heidi's control himself. Listening to her story in conference with Mr. Fowler, he'd felt strangely unsettled, but attributed the feeling to concern for his sister. It was only when Rosie called his cell and she'd heard him repeating Heidi's story that she was able to break Heidi's hold. "Cisco," Rosie had shouted into his ear. "Get to the train station, pronto."

Once he was two blocks from the Capitol, he came to his senses. Just as he and Rosie were hopping onto the next train back to Orion, he called his mom and told her everything he knew. Rosie and Cisco reached Orion just in time for the emergency meeting of the C33 Underground Rescue.

(Claiming to be upset by the disappearance of her "friends," Heidi announced that her mother had arranged for a private car to bring her back to Orion also—Mrs. Bragg got on the phone with Mr. Fowler to set it up, and that was when the Official whisked her away to the pharmaceutical college.)

But back to the meeting of the C33 Underground Rescue: This was a group founded by Thornhill when he first came back to Orion, realizing that he could not rejoin his family until he was sure that Dr. Joy and the Official had been stopped. Working with Hal's dad, they had located and spoken with as many of the former C33s as they could find, building a network through which they could share information about what the Official and Dr. Joy were up to and protect themselves and their families.

Oh, and the boyfriend I was sure my mom had started seeing even though I didn't think she was ready? He didn't exist. My mom had been spending her nights working with Thornhill's group, which had gone into overdrive after his abduction. After our trip to the airstrip, which the former C33s had been aware of, the group had liberated Thornhill, and now he was back to lead the group. She'd been taking care of him at our house when I'd called earlier that day—it was his voice I'd heard in our kitchen.

The last person to be invited to the C33 Underground Rescue meeting was Cornelia. She almost fainted when her doorbell rang and it was Cisco Rivera on her porch, asking her to go for a ride in his car. Hal was teasing her now about how her social status at school on Monday would shoot through the roof as soon as pictures of it went up onto Facebook. Pictures Cornelia herself probably leaked.

It had been a good thing she was there, though: using theamandaproject.com, she had collected reports of an unmarked black van careening off the Orion highway exit about an hour after we'd disappeared from the capital. It had been spotted heading in the direction of the pharmaceutical college.

Cornelia's updates had also clued in Mrs. Leary, who'd become a frequent theamandaproject.com contributor. She'd rushed up from Washington, bringing a fresh batch of her formula for eradicating genetic tampering.

They had been in the midst of planning how to get to the pharmaceutical college—suggestions from the floor ranging from contacting the military to using poison gas—when Chief Bragg had walked into the room, accompanied by Louise Potts. "We've been infiltrated!" a nervous C33 shouted in the deafening silence that greeted his presence. For a second, a collective shudder passed through the room, as everyone pondered the thought that Louise had been spying for the Braggs, Dr. Joy, and the Official all along.

But as it turned out, despite appearances to the contrary, Chief Bragg had not been working with the Official. Also, as he explained, he had never known the full story of what was going on with C33. Brittney had never explained it to him in detail. And now, his wife and daughter were in danger, and he was there to help.

All he'd known about Brittney's childhood, he'd explained, was that it had been very painful and that she was determined to make things better for Heidi and Evan, Heidi's younger brother. So Heidi and Evan were given every possible luxury and never told "no." As Chief Bragg valued peace in the home above all else, he'd shrugged off Brittney's plans for a secret office inside their house and the strange boxes she stored there. He'd suspected that something was off after Brittney arranged a cover-up for Heidi's hit-and-run. He'd even told Officer Marciano to give Hal a hard time after Thornhill's disappearance, based on school rumors Heidi had fed him about Hal painting Thornhill's car and being seen many times in detention.

But when Brittney then arranged—and paid for—Bea Rossiter's plastic surgery and rehabilitation, he'd begun to quietly look into things and make some notes.

But he hadn't been willing to act until one of his deputies flew into his office with the news that four Orion ninth graders had disappeared during a class trip to Washington, D.C., and his daughter was insisting they had run away. And then he hadn't been able to reach Heidi on her cell. And Brittney was not picking hers up either. Suddenly, he feared for their safety.

Checking to make sure his gun was in his holster and his radio was fully charged, he rushed out to his car and drove straight to Play It Again Sam's. He recalled spotting Brittney coming out of Louise Potts's store one afternoon, and though Chief Bragg was not up on fashion, he was pretty good at detective work. He knew that name had come up in the Amanda disappearance so he looked up Louise. When he saw her Social Security number and realized it was a few digits off from his wife's—he knew there must be a connection, so he went right to the store. And when he demanded some sort of explanation from Louise, she brought him to the meeting so he could learn firsthand what was what.

And that was how, with the assistance of all the C33s they could gather at short notice, Chief Bragg, some undercover members of Orion's finest, and our parents stormed the door of the lab.

"So now," said Mrs. Leary, as Chief Bragg's men carted the Official, Dr. Joy and the guards off to jail, "it's time to end this." She turned to Amanda. "There's one more thing we still need to do to put this nightmare to bed." She pulled a bottle of the liquid solution she'd created and started pouring it out into little paper cups she'd found by the water cooler.

"You too," said Chief Bragg, beckoning Heidi over. She was fully unattached from the machine now, smoothing down the front of her sweater, trying to regain her dignity.

"But Mom—" I heard her say under her breath.

Mrs. Bragg looked at her husband, saw that he was done making exceptions on their daughter's behalf and said to Heidi in a low voice, "I think you'd better drink it like the rest of them." Her husband looked at her pointedly. "I will too," she added.

And you know how medicine usually has a flavor, like cherry or bubblegum or grape, and you sometimes wonder why they even try to make it taste good, when, no matter how hard they try, it's still disgusting?

After having tasted Mrs. Leary's concoction, I can now truly, one hundred percent appreciate the importance of adding cherry, bubblegum, and grape flavors to medicine, no matter how disgusting it tastes in combination with whatever grossness lies beneath.

Drinking Mrs. Leary's concoction tasted like drinking the slimy water at the bottom of a flower vase that has been left out too long. Mixed with coffee grounds. Mixed with dirt. Mixed with the stinkiest stinky cheese. And smelling it was almost as bad as drinking it. Something

325

about that smell made you wonder—really wonder—if you would still be alive after putting whatever it was into your system.

Did I mention that it was sludge green?

And that it was foaming?

And that Mrs. Leary casually mentioned that we should drink it fast before it *ate through the cup*?

Even the adults were groaning and holding their noses, closing their eyes against the nasty green color, but after the noise had died down, Mrs. Leary explained how it worked.

She had a look of excitement and discovery on her face as if it were the latest miracle cleaning product that was going to change the way people lived. In direct contrast to everyone else, who was simply struggling not to puke.

"Dr. Joy's breakthrough," she explained, "was his discovery of an agent that could bind new genetic material to old. He would withdraw spinal fluid, introduce new genes, introduce the agent, and the new material would attach itself and begin to direct the growth of new cells in the body.

"What the stuff you're drinking does is attack the binding agent. It breaks it down such that any genetic material that's been added to the body is flushed away.

"Of course, we are all the products of much more than simple genetic product specifications. Our life experience determines to a great extent who we are and what we can do. It will be interesting to see what stays with us versus what goes. I can't imagine I won't be able to work as an astrophysicist anymore, or that Edmund Bennett will lose his crackerjack handle of numbers. But Callie—" She couldn't resist the impulse to smooth Callie's hair off her forehead. "Callie, I don't think you're going to be quite so strong."

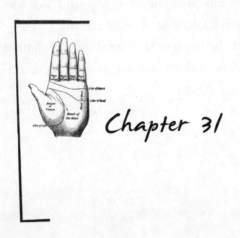

Chapter 31

When Amanda first brought me together with Nia, Callie, and Hal, we had almost nothing in common, except for the fact that we were in danger. What linked us was only that we all divided our existence at Endeavor High into two parts. Before Amanda. And After.

When Amanda had come to our school, she'd made me feel like I could tell her anything, that she saw the good, the bad, and the ugly inside me. Sure, Amanda called me on the lies I tell myself, but she also made me feel honest and strong.

Amanda did all of this for me. She did it for Nia, Callie, and Hal too. Our search for her had forced us to learn about ourselves—and what we could do. We'd become as close as four people possibly could be through our powers. But now Amanda was back. The parts of us that were linked were being erased. The danger was gone. What would be left behind?

After we drank the medicine and left the lab, we all returned to our houses and slept. Not for the night. More like for three straight days—our parents told the school we had the flu. And it *felt* like the flu—you'd wake up, feel like you never were going to be able to get back to sleep and then check the clock six hours later and realize you'd been out cold.

My mom kept me home from school until Friday. Alone in the house, I picked up the sax and practiced until I noticed I was hungry—looking at the clock, I saw it had been three hours.

I texted Callie, Hal, and Nia and heard they were staying home Thursday as well. Callie had been up late stargazing with her mom—she did all the calculations most people used a computer for in her head. Nia was reading Dickens—she said it helped her unwind. Hal was drawing—none of us, I guess, had lost the abilities that we'd always felt defined us. Mrs. Leary's Funky Juice had left that part of us alone.

I guess I could have texted Amanda too, but I was so used to her being gone . . . I was so freaked out by the idea of what she'd be like without her powers. Was she going to live with Thornhill now? Was she going to go back to using her original first name?

But when Friday morning rolled around and I went back to school for the first time, Amanda was still Amanda. I was walking up from the faculty parking lot—I'd gotten a ride with my mom—and Amanda was waiting for me just outside the front doors of the building. She was dressed in a navy blue Chinese-style velvet jacket buttoned up to her throat, black jeggings, and purple high-top Chucks that looked like she'd had them forever.

As if nothing had changed, she didn't bother with the formality of saying hi. She looked, if anything, a little bored. "It's so weird to see you here," I said. "Back in school."

"Plus ça change, plus c'est la même chose," she said.

"I—" I started. "I don't even know what name to call you."

"I've had a lot of them, haven't I?" she said. "But Amanda is the first one I chose myself, so I think it's the one that I will keep."

"Nia told me it means, 'She who must be loved.'"

"I like that," she said. She didn't say a word about the "must" in that phrase—but it was important, I thought. I'd never had a choice with Amanda. We'd been instant friends since the first time I met her. That night, my mom made lasagna and Amanda's made a salad; the grown-ups talked over cheese and crackers on the back deck my dad built himself; and Amanda and I swung upside down

330

from the monkey bars on my ancient swing set.

Now she smiled, as if she knew I was thinking about that night. Did she? "Have you been sleeping a lot?" she said.

"For days."

"Me too," she answered. "And when I wake up and go downstairs, my dad's sleeping on the couch. He keeps jumping up and offering to make pancakes."

"Can you still—?" I started. "Do you still have powers?"

She looked at me mysteriously. "Do you?"

Later that day, I had a free period and was heading to the band room to practice—I could not get enough music around me, it seemed—when I saw Nia at her locker. "Come to the library with me," she said. We sat for the full period pretending to read magazines.

"Is your power totally . . . gone?" I asked her.

Nia looked down. "I've been putting my hands on all these super-significant family things. My grandma's wedding portrait, my brother's first soccer trophy—"

"And—?" I said.

"And nothing at all," she said. She shrugged. "What about you?"

At the table next to us, Kevin Hwang threw a crumpled-up paper at Elizabeth Mop. "You loser!" he said. They were both laughing. And I realized something. I didn't know if they were flirting because they liked each other or flirting because they were bored. Four days before I would have known the whole story. My ability to read people so well that I knew more about what they were thinking than they did? That was gone.

"Have you tried to hide?" Nia asked me now.

"I saw Mr. Fowler this morning on my way to French. I kind of ducked away from him. After everything that happened in Washington, I just couldn't deal."

"Oh, my," Nia said. "I wouldn't have wanted to run into him either. So you hid?"

"Well, I don't know if you could really call it hiding," I said. "All I know is I looked away, I imagined myself playing the most un-Mr. Fowler-ish music I could think of."

"What would that be?"

"Joni Mitchell. Cerebral, female, deep."

"Okay, I can see that."

"And he didn't see me. Or at least he didn't say anything if he did."

"Coincidence?" Nia said.

I shrugged.

At lunchtime, I stood for a few seconds at the cafeteria door, surveying the scene. How was it possible that so much had changed and yet the lunchroom looked exactly the same? The band kids still sat together, the newspaper kids, the basketball guys, the lacrosse team, the I-Girls. Cisco was holding court at the cool juniors' table, Bea

Rossiter was laughing with a group of friends.

But wait. The I-Girls table. Heidi, Lexi, Kelli, and Traci were sitting the way they always sat, grouped around their queen, leaning toward her, trying to get her attention, to share a comment, a laugh, a stick of gum.

Except Heidi wasn't the queen. It was Lexi sitting in the middle now. Heidi was sitting at her side. Heidi was the one leaning in, the one looking to get Lexi's attention.

"Um, what is Heidi wearing?" I heard someone say behind me. I turned around to find Hal and Callie. When I met their gaze they both looked down and blushed. They were holding hands.

I smiled, but quickly brought the focus back on Heidi. She was dressed as she always dressed—leggings that showed off her shapely legs, chunky boots that said "I just rolled out of bed and into $500 worth of leather," a long sweater that looked like it was made out of something expensive like cashmere, and then on top of all of that, a man's tie.

I couldn't see the tie's details from here, but I could tell the colors didn't match the sweater—it was stained as well. And the tie looked all wrong against the sweater's graceful neckline. "What *is* that?" said Nia, joining us in the doorway.

"It's a tie," we all heard, and turned to see Amanda, standing behind us, her hands on her hips, the light behind her so we couldn't see her expression, only make out from her tone of voice that she was one part amused, three parts intrigued.

"Shall we go in?" Amanda said. I walked in first, Callie after me, then Nia, Hal, and Amanda. Kids were staring, it couldn't be denied. After all, Amanda had disappeared, then Thornhill had been attacked, then Callie, Hal, Nia, and I had supposedly bolted during a fire drill in the U.S. Capitol during a field trip the week before. And now here we all were, the five of us back in school with no disciplinary action being taken. Thornhill was back in his office, giving out detentions as if he'd never been gone. Except, oh, yeah, Thornhill and Amanda were letting everyone know they were father and daughter, and living together. Oh, and Amanda was back in school. Needless to say, we were going to be attracting attention for a little while.

But it could have been worse. We all could have started accessorizing with vintage neckties.

"Did she get that vintage thing from you?" Nia asked, once we were all sitting down at a table.

"You think the partial exchange of blood left her a little bit more of an outsider than she was?" Hal asked.

"But look," said Callie. "She's not choosing to be an outsider. She never would. Lexi's muscling her out. Heidi's lost her edge—her power was to get people to do whatever she wanted, remember?"

"So what's with the tie?" I said.

Amanda raised her eyebrows. "Maybe she did get a little bit of me."

"You mean she got the whole vintage look, but didn't get the sense to wear it right? " Hal asked.

Amanda smiled. She stirred her chocolate milk with a straw. Pointedly ignoring the question, she turned to Callie. "Nice having your mom back?" she asked.

Callie blushed. "My parents are so happy to be back together, it's actually embarrassing. Last night I came down to get a glass of water and they were slow-dancing in the kitchen."

"Empanada?" Nia said, offering them around.

"Baklava?" I said, because this week, with no secret meetings to attend, my mom had filled the house with food.

"Maybe my mom will pack me something I can share too," Callie said, biting off the corner of her empanada.

"Yeah, about that," said Hal. Callie looked up, uncomprehending. "I don't know if any of us are up to eating—or drinking—any of your mom's 'concoctions' any time soon."

Callie threw a carrot stick in Hal's direction and he laughed. We all did. Including Amanda.

It was great to see her laughing. She didn't have to be guarded. She didn't have to wonder who was watching her, how long it would be before she had to skip town and start living under a new name. She had a dad now, a house, and her sister was back at college in D.C. but just a phone call away. And, oh yeah, Amanda had us too.

You see, Callie, Hal, Nia, and I, we still divided our lives into two parts—before Amanda and after. We had all made sacrifices: Amanda's mom, my dad, and other C33s had given up their lives. But now the secrets were over. Our lives made sense again. We were with Amanda like we'd always wanted to be. We weren't her guides anymore. We were her friends.

MANY THANKS

As you all know by now, when Amanda disappeared, I was determined to find her on my own. But I couldn't. If there's anything you can learn from my journey, it's this: Sometimes you need a little help from your friends.

So now I want to send a shout-out of thanks to all my friends at theamandaproject.com. You might not have known I was reading, but trust me, I pored over every word you wrote. Before I hooked up with Nia, Callie, and Hal, you guys were my lifeline.

I wish I could thank every person who made a comment that gave me an insight, or wrote a poem that made me feel like I wasn't alone in my search. Here's a super-short list representing some of the many, many people without whom this book—and search—could not have been concluded.

—ZOE

SPECIAL KUDOS*

Kenzi (page 7)

Habbinson (page 25)

AriannaAdore (page 41)

Astoriamiller (page 86)

MariaH (page 102)

Bubblesnsky (page 111)

Stef Stone (page 118)

HannahRox (page 128)

BlueBerries (page 135)

Bellaronda (page 166)

Primaplus (page 221)

S.he.b.lie.vd (page 226)

Mille#32 (page 235)

Loicamar (page 238)

AllieK (page 252)

2Q2Q1 (page 265)

KellyBlack (page 304)

Jester (page 330)

ElizabethMop (page 331)

* And to those of you who know *kudos* is a Greek word, even more kudos. My yiayia would be very proud!

FASCINATING STORIES AND ARTWORK
ABOUT AMANDA CONTINUE TO FLOOD
IN FROM ALL OVER. TURN THE PAGE FOR
ANOTHER TOTALLY AMAZING PIECE!

—HAL, CALLIE, NIA, AND ZOE

AMANDA VALENTINO

Amanda and I were polar opposites. She preferred change and I preferred constant routine. She always said, with a large smile on her face, "Change is the only permanent thing, so you should be willing to change!"

I, being such a social leper, was drab and quite hesitant.

Amanda and I were not intentionally friends. It just happened because it happened. I could list all the things I was indifferent to that Amanda was not, but then we would be here all day.

If you loved Amanda, you would certainly hate me—that's just how I felt. In my high school in New York, I wouldn't ever expect so much as a slight wave toward me from my classmates. I was an outcast and a loser.

Maybe if I hadn't met Amanda, I would still be dreading the weekdays. I never thought I would ever change. I never thought change was necessary. I just never put thought into it, but Amanda injected the subject into the conversation every time.

Once when we were just hanging out on some swings, Amanda said, "You know what? I love parks. They're peaceful and beautiful." She was gazing out onto the green fields. I figured that Amanda loved anything that was peaceful. I figured that, as her guide, I would have to be there whenever she needed help, which she didn't need most of the time.

"Yeah? You think so?" I asked. The words just fell out of my mouth as my eyes focused on the dirty pile of trash next to one of the park benches.

"I do," Amanda said softly. Then she locked eyes with me before speaking again. "Don't you?"

I felt that the answer had to be yes.

"I believe that a park is just a place. You can make any place a peaceful and beautiful place," I said.

She cocked her head to the side. "That may be true, but parks in general are beautiful. No?" she questioned. Where was she heading with this? What did she want me to say?

"Sometimes . . ." I trailed off.

"If you can make any place peaceful and beautiful, what do you need to do if it's the opposite?" she asked. She was staring at me, although my face turned away from her, facing the field.

If something is the opposite of peaceful and beautiful, what do you do to make it peaceful and beautiful?

She knew that I wasn't going to think parks were beautiful. She knew that I was going to lecture her that everything was not rainbows and sunshine.

"You have to change it," I stated. There it was. As clear as day.

"Right. So change is good," said Amanda, with a slight questioning inflection. She wanted me to agree.

"Correct, change is good. In that case. But I'm not willing to change, Amanda," I almost whined. Amanda's head tilted back as she laughed. Her blonde wig flowed in the breeze.

"Change is good for everyone, Lauren. Change is good for everyone." Amanda ended the conversation right then. How was I supposed to argue when I secretly knew it was true?

Maybe if Amanda had not gotten it into my head that change is good, I would still be skulking through the halls of the school, trying to go unnoticed.

Now, thanks to Amanda, I'm no longer the social leper I used to be.

Amanda's probably helped us all in ways we never imagined. But she has. And she's the best thing that's ever happened to me—my savior, Amanda Valentino.

—JUMPINGBEAN

Jumpingbean is fifteen years old.
Member Since: December 6, 2010
She always believed that Amanda was telling the truth.